TRUTH & PAIN

starring the

GANGSTERS & RETARDS

in...

The Mystique-cal Person-a of MC Cripple Crip

or

How Carlos Ramirez Villagomez Gutierrez Valenzuela Hacienda Cruz Rancheros Dos Grandes Huevos del Toro almost learns how not to let his Hispanic heritage derail his musical ability, and Moonaaauuuh learns to slow down time, and Learoy learns to (once again) not trust boys, and Janice learns that getting your heart broken really does suck, and Bryan stays honest, and Dutch probably gets even more stupid, and Mad Girl seems to learn nothing, and Pho proves that someone does care about him, and you learn who all these teenagers are and decide that you cannot wait to read the next book in this series so you create your own blog extolling the virtues of Gangsters & Retards and tell all of your friends and even convince your grandparents (yes, your *grandparents*) that they like it too, and you wonder why nobody ever wrote about this kind of thing before because it sure seems like somebody should have. But that's not a very good title which is why it goes under the "*or*" category.

by

DC Curtis & Bones Kendall

Chapter The Dark

Valley City: An outrageously buzzing bowl where the sun shines sweetly on the privileged hilltop fringes as puffy white clouds float across a pure blue sky.

The lucky people rich enough to live up there swim in custom lap pools, cruise in cherry red convertibles, and never dust because it just never gets dirty. But way down below in the bowl's center, the place the residents know is the butt crack of the world, the place where God would stick the giant rubber hose were he giving the planet an enema, the sun beats starkly on the dustily depressed inner city. Down there, under thumping ghetto bird cop-choppers, sided by glaringly graffitied buildings, where crack whores and drug dealers meet police sirens, Truth Avenue crosses Pain Street. Right there, on the north-ish west-ish corner, sits the Green Rainbow Acres State School.

Across the street (but don't forget about the school, call it G.R.A.S.S. for short) is an ugly, really ugly, black, four-story parking garage. When they built it a while back they made it black to discourage tagging. Silly them. Everybody just bombed it with light colored spray paint so it got all done up anyway. The building itself wouldn't matter except the lot there used to be the local park. In fact the residents, the ones who recognize they live in the butt crack of the world, nicknamed it "The Park," and it held the only bit of beauty in the area.

But, as perhaps you've witnessed yourself, the ruling authorities, who always know best, judged that "urban congestion" had caused the need for "upgraded enhancements," which required that "outdated elements" be "disposed of properly." Using their vast wisdom, Valley City's local government, the same genius decision makers who kept using asbestos and lead paint for new construction even *after* scientists decided those materials were bad, "reconstructed the lot in question for the betterment of the whole."

Mr. Biggs, the developer awarded the parking structure construction project, who yes indeed is one of the privileged hilltop fringe dwellers up there in the blue sky place, was a friend of "ex"-crack-addict Mayor De La Gente. It's an interesting story because the city contract inconveniently called for the developer, in this case Mr.

Biggs, to provide space to keep The Park "preserved." But Mr. Biggs had an attorney friend, his hilltop fringe dwelling neighbor, who found this fantastic loophole in the deal that allowed Mr. Biggs to "creatively alter" The Park (while secretly pocketing a ton of dough, of course). And everybody thought a slight creative alteration would be just fine because they loved The Park, and isn't that Mr. Biggs the most thoughtful hilltop-fringe-dweller-developer ever to want to keep us butt crack folks happy?

Until, of course, those butt crackers woke up one morning and saw that the parking structure had been placed right on top of The Park. True to his word and the contract, Mr. Biggs "preserved" the playground by fully walling it in and capping it off with an eight-foot ceiling. The solution was especially clever because he hadn't even needed to put in new stuff.

Park goers did have to make some *minor* adjustments.

Up for "Shootin' some hoops?" Sorry. Too tall for the ceiling, the backboard and net were ground off. Fortunately, a resourceful construction worker wired an abandoned shopping cart to the pole about six feet off the ground and said to start calling it "Fillin' some carts."

Traveling upwards on the teeter-totter too fast led to several concussions caused by the cement ceiling (*Tell them to duck their heads.*); the slide's ladder terminated abruptly into the cement ceiling, so they made do by just running up the end (*Don't kids love doing that anyway?*); you could use the monkey bars if you were willing to cut your fingers by forcing them between the rungs and the cement ceiling (*So keep your fat fingers out of there already!*); when on the swings your toes got smashed---smashed by what? By the CEMENT CEILING!---(*Quit your whining would you please!!!*).

The trees stood a *little* shorter.

And sure, you had to adjust your eyes because there was no lighting (the contract called for "preserving" The Park, not "enhancing" it, don't you know), which left the natural illumination quite diffused.

In honor of its new condition the residents had re-nicknamed it "The Dark."

There was one small source of light in The Dark, a natural source. The generous Mr. Biggs, at great expense but don't worry he didn't go over budget, installed a four-foot by four-foot skylight in the building's roof. Under the skylight a corridor of the same dimension ran from the roof straight down the building's center, exiting through the ceiling of The Dark. This caused a small square of feeble sunlight to fall right onto the center of the ground. Mr. Biggs felt quite bighearted for providing this, and "ex"-crack-addict Mayor De La Gente, along with the ever-present-at-public-events-that-attract-the-press African-American Congresswoman Charlene Rivers, shook his hand at the parking structure's ceremonial opening. They thanked their lucky stars that forward thinking "life shapers" like Mr. Biggs always kept the "vertically eco-challenged" in mind when they created "new progress opportunities" in "urban units in need of recovery."

Whenever they heard words like those, the butt crackers knew they were screwed.

Mr. Biggs went back to his hilltop mansion after making a large deposit at the bank; "ex"-crack-addict Mayor De La Gente's day ended happily with a massage and a beer; African-American Congresswoman Charlene Rivers had a very nice donation placed in her re-election slush fund; and someone in the 'hood spruced up that bit of sunlight, the only light one could find in The Dark, by placing a small, dirt-filled pot right in the middle of it.

The pot? Set in the small square of weak sunlight, it grew a defiant, five-foot tall plant that commands the surrounding darkness. Basking in that dismal glow, the plant's stance communicates a quite visual "F you" to its place in the world.

It is, of course, a Sunflower.

Chapter the Kids

Inside out at The Dark, at what used to be their sunlit corner bordering an alley off of Truth Avenue, under what used to be their favorite tree but is now a bark covered pillar, eight very differently shaped teenagers hide themselves behind a small-scale theatre stage whose curtains currently hang closed.

The empty gloom sitting before the stage holds no audience, which means it's rehearsal time, and the backstage voices sound tense.

"Okay," Carlos says impatiently, "let's do it ag---"

Mad Girl interrupts sharply, "Who made you head wheelman here---"

"Lissen up, Fat Girl," Learoy bluntly interrupts the interruption, "just do it! I'm already late openin' up the salon!"

"Cooler heads shall prevail, friends," Janice's culturedly dictioned voice trills in. "By all means someone say action and let us commence."

Laughing, Bryan says, “Action!”

A length of tan twine running out the side of the stage ends in a loose loop around a firm ankle. It's given three short tugs, signaling Moonaaauuuh's dim form to begin engineering the production from her laptop. She hits the enter key then clips cables to an old car battery to power the stage. The performance rolls forward with her fingers deftly keystroking, smoothly trackpadding, and softly tracing over the laptop's screen.

The lush velvet curtains slide open sideways. High definition mini-speakers sprinkle soft piano music and whistle bird chirping sound effects while cool little spotlights emote warm, colorful feelings. An impressionistically foggy, beautifully spray can crafted, rolling green countryside peacefully backdrops the scene. A one-foot tall string-puppet takes the stage.

Wow! It's a marionette show! I hope it doesn't suck.

Dressed for the barrio, the puppet on stage looks to be a fourteen-year-old, slightly built Latina with an enormously pregnant belly. She throws her hands in the air and shouts, "Oh! No! Some villain has sur...sur...sur-ep-ti-tious-ly rustled my cow!" Mad Girl, the unseen person mastering this puppet and who, by the way, is fourteen, a Latina from the barrio, and enormously pregnant herself, struggles with the dialogue. "Without my be-lov-ed cow's milk for sus...suste...sus-te-nance, however shall I nourish my baby, now, with the blessed event drawing ever so close! My ges...my ges-ta-tion-al period has almost fully e...elapsed. The baby cometh! Post! Haste!"

"Hey, yo, didst thou say thou required a bo...bo-vine, yo?" A second puppet enters, handled by the hidden Dutch. It looks just like him being that it resembles a fifteen-year-old, lanky, pasty skinned white boy, inner city "urbanized" with false bling, wife beater, and trainers. Dutch Puppet tugs a little black cow puppet, with an even blacker heart-shaped spot on its side, on a short rope behind him. Like Mad Girl, he stumbles on his lines. "Perhaps, yo, I can ass...ass...ass-ist you, fair damsel in dis...dis-tress, yo. I happen to have this chat...chattle?---Janice, shouldn't it say cattle, yo?---ready for purchase, yo."

"Alas," Mad Girl Puppet laments, her hands hanging hopelessly, "money have I none. All I possess lies under our feet. It is mere...mere-ly the cool spring water of the valley flowing through-out the verdant fields."

Dutch Puppet talks matter of factly, "Then thou shan't have this milk pro-vi-ding farm beast. Cer-tain-ly your baby, yo, will come to know the truth and pain of hunger, yo."

A third puppet jerks on stage, addressing Dutch Puppet with dramatically passionate motions: "Hold there, var-mint! That 'tisnot thou's chatter to sell!" This puppet replicates the unseen manipulator Bryan, so it looks like a fourteen-year-old, slightly dumpy, red freckled white boy with awful looking, thick framed eyeglasses. Bryan Puppet, suffering through his own dialogue issues, takes a knee in front of the pregnant Mad Girl Puppet. "Fair-iest dam-sell! That evil man tows your very selfish-same bo-vine, dish-guised to hide its eye-den-titty from you!"

Rising, he walks stiffly to the cow as he arcs a hand through the air. Pre-stringed for the special effect, the animal's black fur magically whisks up and away, revealing it's not really black, but brown, with a golden heart spot on the side. "Dear valley maiden, I here-by return your cow to you! Your new child shall not face hunger!" Bryan Puppet, obviously the hero, faces what will be his future audience's adoring cheers. He bellows, "Evil lies are re-buff-ered by the ul-ti-mate virtue, Honesty!!!"

Wow. It's a marionette show with a nice message. Looks like it does suck.

The soft music and twittering birds cut out, replaced by drum 'n bass beats that want to jam hardcore but only pop bubble gum.

A new backdrop falls: a happily yellowing sun bursts through pinkly billowing cotton candy clouds. The mini-spotlights exaggerate the glow with inanely frosted goody goodness.

Another puppet strings on stage. It's a Carlos clone, so it copies a Mexican-American boy of fifteen, wiry and rectangular. Because the real Carlos has no arms and only one leg, his puppet likeness rolls in a wheelchair, but not just any wheelchair. Carlos Puppet sits tight in his custom tricked out, bicycle-tube framed, lowrider-esque wheelchair with cool chrome pieces and long shiny spokes, just like homeboy Carlos's chair. Carlos Puppet rocks it the best he can, rapping the preachishly mind-numbing words to the silly music.

Honesty, Honesty!
It is the numero uno virtue!
You must maintain your scruples!
Honesty, Honesty!
It never can be disguised!
Choosing it makes us all wise!
Make it your best choice today!
Make it Honesty all the way!

Four more teenager puppets enter the stage as backup dancers: a small Asian girl whose eyes are noticeably shut (Moonaaauuuh, but controlled by Carlos since she's busy engineering the production), an emaciatedly skinny white girl with crutches and leg braces (Janice), a monstrously gigantic Vietnamese boy (Pho), and a totally sexy, voluptuously curvy, awesomely gorgeous, African-American female (the exquisite Learoy; now that's one hot puppet).

The first three puppets, and the cow, join in the disjointed dancing.

Wow. This thing is *rated* Suck.

In the middle of it all, Carlos Puppet stops moving and Carlos person stops singing. Moonaaauuuh Puppet's movements still as well. One by one the other marionettes stall out, until only Janice Puppet continues with graceful ballerina crutch 'n brace pirouettes and spins.

Off to the side, Moon senses disharmony. She cuts the music and all the lighting except a single lamp shining down harshly from above.

"Don't desist!" Janice Puppet's proud voice resounds. "Keep it alive people! The show must go on!"

"Janice," Carlos Puppet says to Janice Puppet, "this is lame."

Mad Girl Puppet joins in. "You said it, cholo. Janice, I wou-int never say these words. You put 'em in just to make us sound duuu-mb."

"Words?" Dutch Puppet scratches its head. "I don't even know all these letters, yo."

Janice Puppet finally concludes her ballet solo's *Grand Pas*. She tries hiding the hurt. "You...you don't like my show?"

Bryan, always the honest one, makes his puppet say, "Yes. It really sucks."

Janice Puppet gets snide, "And you could do better, Bryan?"

Learoy Puppet doesn't dig that. She closes on Janice Puppet. "Watch your mouth, Skinny Shins! Don't you dis' Bryan like that."

Janice Puppet shifts to pointed politeness. "Well, none of you helped compose the show this week, so someone had to step up to the stage, as it were. Ungrateful lot you are."

Seven cell phones set on vibrate go off. From behind the stage come the scrambled sounds of fingers fiddling, handsets flipping, and buttons clicking. The dolls droop from their strings during the distraction.

"Here's a blind taste test opinion, Janice." Carlos sounds vindicated, "Moon's text reads 'Why'd we stop? It sucked, didn't it.'"

"Yes, Carlos," Janice answers, "I am literate, thank you."

Moonaaauuuh doesn't always text when they're all together, but right now she does for speed and convenience sake.

Why not speak instead of text?

Moon can't. She's deaf-blind, which means she's deaf and blind and unable to verbalize (some still say dumb or mute, but those are old school terms). Like that chick Helen Keller in that book---what was it...*Miracle Mockingbird*? Could have been *To Kill A Mouse of Men*. Or *Catcher In The Mouse*. *The Miracle Killer Maker Of Mouse Catching Mockingbird Men*? No, *The Miracle Maker*, that's it---but not at all like her either.

Moon, a half-Japanese, half-Korean, all-American teenager, is seventeen but looks fourteen, at least partly because she's a diminutive five-foot-one. Neither thin nor large, she carries a toned gymnast look escorted by a stance that's ready for anything. Brush her face with mystical and mysterious timelessness, top her head with bobbed green hair edged down to her jawline and yes, you see her clearly.

When Moon finished her Braille edition of that Helen Keller chick book, assigned in one of their G.R.A.S.S. classes (Green Rainbow Acres State School---we'll get there eventually), she chucked it across the room and texted everyone that they had better not label or pity her in the same way.

Carlos texted back: "Pity you? Deaf, dumb and blind hotties got soul fo' sho'!"

In response to Moon's current text, Mad Girl hangs her puppet's cradle on a hook and emerges from the performers' backstage area. She waddles her big, pregnant belly over to catch Moon up on things, saying, "I'll fill her in."

Under the stage's single spotlight, Carlos Puppet resumes the discourse. "Janice, you made a big deal about wanting to write the show yourself this time!"

"What choice had I?" Janice Puppet reaches for her holier than thou voice, "Miss Petunia specifically said the G.R.A.S.S. kids needed a lesson on honesty this week. This is the best I can do without any help!" Janice puts up her puppet and moves to stand in front of the stage. Like her smaller, stringed form she's skinnier than thin. A sort of pretty, Jewish-white girl, Janice Kaplan-Rosen has a spinal muscular atrophy disorder, the type known as Spinal Muscular Atrophy Type II (or SMA II for short---has quite a ring, don't it?).

SMA II hits everyone differently, but generally its victims' muscles waste away, leaving those afflicted unable to support their own bodies. That's why Janice is dangerously thin and needs the leg braces and crutches. She's very intelligent and strong-willed, but with her slender body stooped forward she always looks like a feather desperately fighting to keep from getting blown away in the wind.

"I am, after all, the production's manager." Janice jabs a crutch end into Carlos Puppet's chest to make her points. "You, Carlos, are supposed to be the writer! I would not have dared attempt the task had you been attending to your own duties in the first place."

Mad Girl calls over to stir the pot, "Yeah Carlos, you lazy beaner. You the writer! Do your own job."

"Thank you, Mad Girl," Janice smiles at her. "I appreciate your support, if not your candor."

"Ain't supporting you or your condor," Mad Girl snaps. "What's a bird got to do with this? Your show sucks."

Carlos Puppet looks up at Janice. "In case you forgot,

Janice, we were all busy this week hunting down Bryan with that megaphone. Or don't you remember the cult? The almost blood sacrifice? The parade?"

Bryan Puppet looks sheepish. "Sorry. Thanks again for saving me from those FBI guys."

"No problem," Learoy Puppet says.

"Right!" Carlos Puppet points its big toe up at Janice. "So there, Janice! It's not my fault that your show sucks."

Pho hangs up his puppet and grows, like a mountain, from behind the stage. He's a solidly thick, 400-pound, six-foot-seven (six-eleven someday), seventeen-year-old, Vietnamese-American. He looks at Janice and sighs. The thinnishly thin girl recently dumped him (she swore it wasn't a dumping...they just needed space), and he's still got it bad for her.

He lives up the street with his two grandmas, his Ba's, who do their best to baby him; he does his best to play that down. After prying himself from the local hardcore gang scene, Pho started hanging with these kids because they: A. didn't see him as a freak, and B. didn't want him to kill anyone. This giant brutally ripgrindshreds on his skateboard, then expresses his soft, artistic side by creating spray-can murals, such as the puppet show backdrops, but usually better than those. These two talents flow together within him, communicating an exterior aura of easygoing lightness centered by deep power.

Right now, Pho just wants to make his lost love feel better. He searches for the right words. "It's not that it sucks so bad, Janice. It just sort of..."

"Blows!" Carlos Puppet finishes. The other kids cannot stifle the giggles. "It blows, Janice. Big time! And if we march those sweet little G.R.A.S.S. kid underlings over here to The Dark with their blankets and teddy bears to see what us head counselors came up with for the puppet show this week they will riot and laugh us off the stage. Off---The---Stage!"

"Ho'd up ho'd up ho'd up." Oh crap, Learoy's hanging up her puppet and stepping out to stand near Janice.

The "Oh crap" is stated with utmost respect: she's sweet sixteen, African-American, and a total brick house. This girl's figure joggles three steps past perfect *ummmpphhhness* plus one jaggle more. Mercilessly made up and robustly dressed hot (her finely featured face surrounded by coiled ringlets, her full, gravity-defying torpedo tip bosoms and heartishly shaped rear tripping up oglers by the dozens), she puts rap video hoochies to shame. But she ain't no ho', unh-uh, snap snap. Never been touched, but she totally uses her looks to advantage. And personality to spare, if she spares you.

You do not want that all up in your grill, yo.

"Carlos," Learoy faces Carlos Puppet, "you be braggin' all the time 'bout this and that. So no matter what, you gotta get that and this done."

"Yeah, Carlos," Dutch Puppet shuffles up to Carlos Puppet, "this is your job, yo, and you definitely don't have our backs. You gotta fix up this mess Janice made---sorry Janice, yo---and get us back in action."

"I can't fix Janice's crap," Carlos Puppet spins to face Dutch Puppet, "it's just too stoooopid."

"Nah, man," says Dutch Puppet, "I'm stupid." Dutch hangs up his puppet and joins Janice and Learoy in front of the stage, busting some moves and rapping on the way: "*Carlos, you can play, but you can't stay if you can't save the day, so make yo' play, playa'. Yo!*"

Dutch Obama (he's named himself, several times over the years) believes he's the only talented white rapper in existence because deep inside he knows he's just gotta be part black. His puppet depicts him appropriately; actually, not enough: in real life he's an even more wiggarized caricature of his puppet than his puppet is of him. In fact, having crossed so far over the line in his wannabe quest for hip hop blackness, he's somewhat cool, in an odd, semi-unique kind of way. It's hard to know for sure, maybe.

"If you can't write the show this week," Dutch continues, "then let someone else do it who can, yo."

"Like who?" Carlos Puppet spits.

Dutch waves his hands at himself. "Like *moi*, yo. You know, someone who can bring out the real black issues that need to be spoken to!"

Janice asks, "By black I take it you do not refer to the inclusion of *noir* elements?"

Mad Girl's caught brainy Janice this time. "Janice, 'course he won't put in *no R*-rated stuff! It's for kids. Wha'sup with you?"

Janice looks puzzled, then gets it. "No, Mad Girl, not '*no R*,' but '*noir*.' It's French for black."

"Yeah," Carlos says, "like dark genre detective films from the '50's. She was making a joke---ah forget it."

"You write the show, Dutch? You?" Bryan Puppet laughs and laughs. Then Bryan hangs it up so he can walk out front and laugh at Dutch in person. Similar to his miniature stringed twin with the red freckles, Bryan is near pudgy but not fat, topped with those awful looking, thick framed eyeglasses. His puppet does not, however, completely capture the rounded facial features that show he has Down syndrome (or Down's syndrome if you prefer, or you can also call it trisomy 21 or trisomy G, but Bryan actually has what's known as Mosaic Down Syndrome, or MDS, which is a little different than straight trisomy 21, so don't call it that after all).

Knowing the world moves a second or three faster than he does made Bryan grow up streetwise and tough. This self-awareness works because it keeps him honest with himself, and in this part of town that keeps him alive. Dude's also an awesome basketball player.

Bryan finally stops laughing to say, "Dutch, you scored a thirty-three on your G.R.A.S.S. IQ test! They made *me* your tutor, and *I'm* retarded!"

"Hey," Dutch defends himself, "I didn't even know that IQ thing was a test! I don't have to be at G.R.A.S.S. I stick around and help out 'cause I wanna. I'm a dense thinker, yo, an interdependent agent, free as a fish. I can leave anytime, yo. Not like you, Bryan."

"Dutch, man, give it up," Bryan says. "You're like all of us. You got no where else to go, man."

"You write this show?" Learoy spouts off. "White boy, please! You a cracker that can't even read!"

Dutch is hurt now. "Don't need to read to come up with a stupid puppet show."

Carlos Puppet rolls his lowrider chair to front center stage directly under the solitary spotlight, getting as up in Dutch's face as possible. "Stupid puppet show! Oh how soon they forget." Carlos Puppet puts his big toe under his chin in a thinking manner. "Have you forgotten how much those little kids learn from these 'stupid' puppet shows every week? You think *Don't Blow Away The Tooth Fairy* wrote itself? And there wasn't a dry eye in the house when we finished *Cheer Up Child, Mamma's Comin' On Visitin' Day*!"

Remembering, Bryan sings, "*Don't be sad, Mamma ain't mad, You ain't been bad, Visitin' Day's a comin.* Bimp-bop, bo-do-bee, do-bop, bop. That was awesome!"

"See, Bryan knows!" Carlos Puppet goes on. "Then there was *Po-lice Man's A Good Man...Sometimes*. And what about *Bedtime Is Quiet Time 'cept For The Gunshots*? No one can say that wasn't great."

"Carlos," Janice says, "one admits your past credits

speak for themselves. But the curtain for this week's show will rise in the future, not fall on the past. With so many successes behind you, perhaps it is time to take on writing partners to help. Dutch and I have kindly volunteered. You should consider our assistance a boon, not a detraction."

"Whoa, whoa, whoa." Carlos Puppet's sole foot waves side to side, warding off the invitation. "No way. I don't need nobody telling me how to do things. I'm a tough Mexican hombre, a lone wolf running on big sky dreams. I work alone."

Learoy laughs in Carlos Puppet's face. "Alone! You! Mr. Four Wheeler! Hah! What, we're all standin' 'round here doin' nothin' all the time?"

Carlos Puppet squares his armless shoulders, gathers his dignity, and says in a proud voice, "Well, I am, after all, the world's foremost, preeminent, one-footed puppeteer. I can perform any puppet, anytime. I already do two puppets at once, mine and Moon's."

Learoy takes the bait. "Go ahead then, String Boy, show us. Do my puppet if you so good."

"Sure, Learoy," Carlos Puppet shivers with double meaning, "I'll be happy to *do* you, baby!"

Learoy Puppet comes to life, street walking like Super Hooker, shaking out the booty and thrusting out the boobies, bouncing it all bad.

Carlos mimics her with a sexy voice. "Oh, Carlos, big daddy! I wants you! I neee-eeeds you." Learoy Puppet, down on all fours, crawls to Carlos Puppet, panting all the way.

"You stop that right now, you Perverted Pinocchio!" Learoy shouts.

"Tha's right," Carlos Puppet nods his head, "and you just watch what grows longer on me!"

Once again the other kids can't stop their giggles. Moon, who's being kept apprised by Mad Girl of the goings on via trace-talking, a hand communication system they all use with her, lowers a perky stripper pole onto the stage. A sparkling mirror ball sneaks down above it. Quick on their heels, sexy hoochie mama music cavorts in to join them.

Carlos Puppet holds a little dollar bill between its toes. "C'mon, baby, take it all off," he croons. "Let's call this money the *un*-cover charge."

Learoy Puppet stands and whirls around the stripper pole, then grasps it with both hands. "You've got the only pole I need, Carlos," she purrs. "I'll give you everything baby, everything you want, oooh, oooh, yeah, baby. Pull my strings like you mean it, you real man you."

Learoy reaches on stage and snatches her puppet away. She stands there, silently inferno-ing.

The music zip-skip-scratches to a stop. The stripper pole and mirror ball caper upward together to escape the wrath. Moon and Mad Girl hi-five, discreetly, then join the others in front of the stage.

Learoy points at her puppet. "No way you ever, never, ever never ever gone get that, Little Toe Boy."

"The hoochie doth protest too much, methinks. Most surely that caught up the conscience of the Learoy." Carlos Puppet aggrandizes, "My performances are so real, so honest, you can't help but jump up! I say again, that's what makes me the world's best, single footed puppeteer."

"You gonna be the world's best no footed dead nothin' if you keep on!" Learoy shouts. "Get out here now and talk for reals, Thin Wheels!"

Carlos Puppet takes a bow then stills its strings. Carlos rolls out from behind the stage to join the group, leaving no doubt that he is, indeed, his puppet's clone.

Carlos is the ultimate bad luck kid. He's a fifteen-year-old Mexican-American butt cracker, the unluckiest thing he could ever be in his opinion. But that's not really it.

When he was five his right arm was severed at the shoulder by a Border Patrol helicopter. You may remember the story: the abandoned mother bringing her son to the land of opportunity, getting stuck on a rock for three days during a flood, television cameras covering the drama while the world prayed for their safety, that stirring song playing behind it all (*Carlos, Carlos, Carlos, Your Madre is your friend. Don't let go or you'll die in the Rio Grend...*), then the helicopter crashing into them, severing his arm, killing his mom. Remember? Of course not. His story was overridden by some other immigrant kid with a dead mom in some other part of the world, or even just down the street, because the media loves bouncing from story to story in search of the next miserable wretch for everyone to eyeball. Consigned to G.R.A.S.S. for rehab, Carlos found himself quickly forgotten. The record company still makes bank on the song.

Then at eight his right leg was crushed by Pho. It was a friendly neighborhood football game, but Pho is so utterly gigantic, Carlos's leg had to be amputated at the hip.

Two years later he lost his left arm. Rolling through a crosswalk he got plowed over by a cop, local peace officer Sergeant Strap, chasing down a drunk driver. The drunk got away. Strap was pissed.

With only his left leg remaining Carlos is a triple amputee, but he's tight in his custom lowrider wheelchair. He perches there now, his slim torso proudly straight, his foot smoothing his thickly pomaded hair back onto his tall, lean head. He does everything with that foot and those toes, like gaming, eating with chopsticks, deejaying and scratching out mad beats at his coffin, or making the cool gadgets he invents, such as Moon's special touchscreen laptop, that help him and the others function in the world.

Carlos boasts that cruising at wheelchair height is cool when you're an ass man. Think about it.

He also knows that if he weren't in a wheelchair he'd be just another hungry kid on the Tijuana bridge peddling chewing gum. Think about that.

"All we're saying," Janice restarts her point, "is that we are all in this together and you could use some help."

"Yeah, yo," Dutch agrees, "I thought we were homies, yo."

"'*I thought we were homies, yo,*'" Carlos whines the Dutchspeak. "Dutch, if we're such homies, YO, than instead of getting in my way on this show right now, why didn't you help me out when I asked for it two weeks ago?"

Dutch looks lost. That whole numbers and time thing is really tough. "What? Yo?"

Carlos makes it clear, "Remember that demo CD of my music I sent off to the record label? I wanted your help with it, but you didn't show up so I did it all myself."

"Let's talk about the puppet show," Mad Girl says. "I don't wanna hear you say 'I'm gonna be the famous MC DJ Five Toes' again!"

Janice agrees, "Yes, Mad Girl is correct. Thank you again Mad Girl. We need our attentions focused to fix the debacle at hand."

Mad Girl already knows she's right. "Sure, Janice, whatever, but I don't need to fix my buckle. I ain't even wearin' a belt."

Dutch ignores them both. "Listen, El Dude," he accuses Carlos, "you send your rap demo CDs off like every week, yo. And it's always something with you, like how come you can't buy just one shoe, why light switches are so high, or something about being black."

"Ho'd up ho'd up ho'd up," Learoy gets back in it. "I'm the only black one here. Carlos, you ain't nuthin' but a greaser in a wheelchair. Get over it. As for you, Dutch, don't you even start."

"Learoy, sister, don't drink the haterade white society forces down your throat, yo. We both got ancestors from the Great Dark Continent. My father was from Nigeria, The Pridelands themselves!"

"Oh man, not again," Carlos mutters.

"Dutch Boy, please!" Learoy says. "You can't possibly be Nigerian. You whiter than Casper the ghost!"

"Can I help that my mom was from Holland? I stand cursed by my white side, chained by its shackles that oppress my true identity!" Dutch hangs his head. "Just another example of the man keepin' a brother down, Learoy. Yo."

"Dutch, you so white that even if *both* your parents were black, you'd still be white!" Learoy says. "But it don't matter. Outside, inside, color, no color, doesn't mean anything."

Janice chimes in with her concise syntax, "Learoy does, in her own inimitable style, make a valid point." Janice speaks so much differently from the rest of them because she keeps a big secret: she resides in the privileged, fringy, hilltoppy, blue sky place noted in the prior chapter. She sneakily joins her friends while her parents think she's at a swanky, rich-cripple-girl school. Only the chauffeur knows about her double life. She finds the ghetto more alive and stimulating, so she grabs it up while she still can. Janice's type of SMA will probably kill her before she's twenty, and she knows it. Plus, her parents travel constantly, fronting for expensive charitable events, only requiring her when they need to publicize their devotion to their sick and almost dead daughter.

All this makes Janice pretty sure that if she weren't already facing death, she'd be suicidal. So luckily for her...

"What you sayin' now, Big Words?" Learoy questions her.

"I'm saying, Learoy," Janice responds, "that you are

correct. A person's skin pigment matters not. Researchers in hard science and social science alike continually find new data prescribing that racial differences measure so minimally as to prove insignificant."

"Insignificant differences," Carlos says. "Insignificant until it comes to MONEY! Janice, if I was black OUTSIDE the record companies would be beatin', I mean beatin' down my door. It's because I'm NOT black that I'm not playin' the big time hip hop game already."

"Sure," Mad Girl's turn, "just like you always say no one's grabbin' up your invention gadgets 'cause you a Mexican. Well, Mez-can's what you are, vato, so accept it!"

Carlos looks stunned. "C'mon, chola, we gotta stick together. You know my inventions don't sell because they can't believe a Mexican is technologically savvy. What technology does Mexico contribute to the world? Nada. So how can I? Least that's what my rejection letters say."

"Then invent something we need," Mad Girl retorts, "like something that makes free money." Mad Girl doesn't just talk tough, she is tough, perilously so. The oldest sibling to five brothers and six sisters (no visible father), until reaching seven she thought the welfare office was where mommy worked. She's grown up a first class scammer, conner, and swindler, but only when it's funny. She's also a dope graffiti artist. When she bombs around town it's all violent images, but in her private book she sketches pictures of little girls loving childhood. Mad Girl never had one, and now pregnant at fourteen she knows she never will. It's hardened her heart just that much more.

Learoy and she were as close as sisters until a falling out over a boy who left Learoy a virgin and Mad Girl pregnant. Patching up their friendship moves at glacier speed or not at all. Trying to be hurtful, Learoy once said to her, "If you weren't pregnant you'd have nothin' to love."

That was when Mad Girl decided to keep her baby.

"S'nomatter 'bout the inventions," Carlos says. "When they finally hear my music, the labels will be showin' up lookin' for me. Y'all be givin' me props, beggin' for my autograph. And Learoy," Carlos flashes her a cool smile that fails to hide his forever crush, "you'll finally realize that my love's the biggest gift ever, waiting for you to unwrap."

"You, unwrapped?" Learoy laughs scathingly. "I'd laugh at your unwrapped skinny butt and give it a slap, Wheel Boy."

Carlos contemplates the scenario. "I might be into that." Then it's back to the hard talk: "But I say it's true that black rappers dominate the music world at the expense of Hispanic ones. You all just don't want to admit it."

Pho finally breaks the silence with his deep, musty voice: "C'mon, we are so outta here." He flips his ultra-heavy-duty skateboard up and rolls away. Grace and balance diminish his size when he rides.

Dutch says, "Yeah, yo, let's ROLL!" He looks at Carlos and laughs. It's his favorite joke, and he never tires of it. Carlos did years ago, by the look he gives him.

"Wait!" It's Bryan, who isn't moving from in front of the stage.

"What is it?" Learoy asks.

"Do I get to rescue Mad Girl's cow from the evil Dutch villain in the puppet show or not?" he asks.

Learoy looks at Carlos. "I'm sure Carlos will keep that in the new version, won't you Carlos?"

Without hesitation Carlos says, "You got it Bryan. You're the hero. Always. No doubt."

Learoy's smile spreads before she can stop Carlos from seeing it. She quickly nods a comforting look at Bryan and takes his hand. "Let's practice your lines as we go."

"Cool, Carlos," Bryan says, "you're a homey!"

They all move away, each in a distinct fashion. Carlos foot-steers the cool lowrider wheelchair, his toes flicking toggles and pushing buttons on his switchbox to make the hydraulics bounce. Dutch busts moves beside him, talking smack. Pho cuts slow, playful patterns through them all. Moon walks lightly, radar sensing the friends around her, hands reaching out to touch now and again for confirmation. Janice crutches along, deporting herself the way Madame at rich-crippled-girl school trained her. Mad Girl holds her belly up and apes Janice's walk, making faces behind her back, then laughs with her. Learoy just can't help but slink sexily and wiggle wonderfully, but her hand on Bryan's shoulder while she whispers to him puts her beyond being objectified. Bryan's motions are slightly uncoordinated as he concentrates, multi-tasking to hear Learoy's soft voice.

And each of them, every one, as he or she passes the Sunflower, without even thinking, reaches out and runs a gentle finger along its leaves, holds a moment, feels the small warmth from the light coming down, then disappears inside The Dark.

Just a slightly irregular bunch of kids being a regular bunch of kids.

The Chapter of the Cripple Crip

Outside in the stark light, beater cars, tagged busses, and dented city trucks cough by over potholed blacktop. Cracked sidewalks crumble to sprouting weeds. Trash in the gutters rots until it disintegrates or gets washed away by the rain. Eternal city grime and dust coat everything. It's the place you drive through on your way home from somewhere else saying, "I'm *really* glad I don't live here."

Pho checks his vibrating phone. "Moon wants to know if we're rollin' to Mario's." He cocks a thumb down the street.

This is funny: Pho is motioning at a taco joint that's an abandoned McDonald's. It still has the golden arches and everything. Now, however, it's painted dayglo green and orange. The arches are checker-boarded black and pink, and the giant M turns into the name "Mario's" and not the other one. The clown statue outside sports a fu-manchu mustache and a sombrero. You see this place and you think, "Not even *McDonald's* wants to live down here, and they live everywhere!"

"Naw, man," Mad Girl says, "Mario's away in Chihuahua."

"Is he getting puppies?" Bryan asks.

"No, dawg," laughs Dutch, "he's getting cousins."

The kids, ignoring the crosswalk at the light, cross the crappy street toward G.R.A.S.S.'s long, tall, dark green wall.

The green wall is ten feet high and topped with another three feet of ornate ironworks. It encloses the entire city block on which G.R.A.S.S. sits. In the front, it runs 150 yards down Truth Avenue, takes a ninety-degree turn, then runs another 150 yards on Pain Street. Each wall turns to continue up alleys bordered by rundown projects with rusty fire escapes dangling from peeling paint.

Where the green walls meet at the street corner stands the gate, consisting of two very solid, very tall, metal-strapped wooden doors. The G.R.A.S.S. moniker arches over them in black wrought iron. The address under the name is 100.

It's a bitch of a place to find because, since it's addressed directly on the corner, people can never tell if the place is meant for Truth or for Pain. The kids think it's funny.

Not too funny though because not many people ever come looking for it.

Outside the tall wall, off to the left of the giant wood doors a bit, is where the kids head now. It's a good place because a thick, leafy tree limb grows from inside out over the G.R.A.S.S. wall running along Truth Avenue. It gives them shade in the heat and cover in the rain. It's one of their spots.

Crazy Billy Butt Cracker is there. He leans against the wall under the tree limb, talking on a discarded, broken cell phone, quite loudly, waving his free hand through the air in wild gesticulations, his wiry gray hair long and loose. His tentbox home sits behind The Dark in Truth Alley. A grungily grubby and gritty old white guy, he's a little off but fairly harmless; just a locally grown rat in the 'hood turned drug-addled bat in the alley with age.

And he's naked, again. This happens once a week when he rinses his clothes then hangs them to dry.

"Ah, geez," Carlos says. "Janice, this is definitely your turn!"

"Yes, I believe it is my go to perform the honors." Janice approaches him while the other kids hang back.

"It's the packing," he's screaming into the phone, "mixed in with the bubble wrap. That's how they're cooking it." He glances at Janice. "May I help you?" he asks condescendingly. "I'm on with the Pope."

"Which one?" Janice has seen this before.

"Deteronomous The Fourth. He's in my Sanctified Seven." Crazy Billy Butt Cracker holds up the phone so the kids can see the screen, but it's blank, scratched, and some of the keypad's missing as well.

"Who are your other Soulful Six?" Janice asks in total seriousness.

"Jesus, MLK, De Niro," Crazy Billy responds, then

screams into the phone, "NO! DO NOT tint the orange toasters! He wants the cat scratch on the banister, not the balcony. Hello! Hellooo!" He shakes the phone under Janice's nose. "You lost my call! *You* did!"

"Billy," Janice uses a soothing voice, "you're naked on the sidewalk again. Remember last time, you said you'd stay home until your clothes dried? Remember the terrified small children, and that nice Sergeant Strap with the mean billy club and handcuffs?"

Bryan adds, "And remember us not needing to see your PEEEE-NUS!"

Squelching a chuckle, Learoy shushes Bryan with a soft touch to his shoulder.

The naked Crazy Billy Butt Cracker starts heading toward his alley, shouting over his shoulder. No, we will abstain from making ass crack jokes.

"Get off my ass! You're all on crack!" He answers his phone suddenly. "Yes, Cairo, that's the place, Africa, under the South Pole, reservations for 200..."

Carlos maneuvers to their spot, stops suddenly, scowls. "Aw...he pissed here again."

"I'm goin' beat that crazy man's bare ass!" Mad Girl shouts. "His pee reeks the worst."

They all creep up slowly to see how bad it is, some of them sniffing quizzically. Moon becomes overwhelmed being that her olfactory skills are bloodhoundishly sensitive.

Bryan sees something down the street.

"Hey," he says, "who's that? Is it...a stranger?"

On the sidewalk, traveling their way, comes a black teenage boy's baby face under dark shades, a crooked baseball cap over his long dreads. He flares a huge smile, and from fifty feet they see three gold teeth right up front. A crisp white T-shirt peeks out of an unbuttoned red and black plaid. Excessive gold necklaces challenge the way-huge, gem studded belt and buckle.

Think 1980's Los Angeles gangsta rapper mixed with 1990's Jamaican dance hall rapper and you are most truly getting the picture. Except this off the hook booghetto pimp is rollin' deep in a wheelchair.

Yep, he's hand pumping a beat up, old school wheelchair, straight up to the group.

Bryan speaks first with one of his always honest observations: "Hey, you're in a wheelchair."

"Yeah," the young stranger responds, "it's cool 'cause I got lucky. The other guy, I capped his ass."

Making a gun with his hand, he jabs the index finger barrel to Janice's forehead.

"BAM! Right between the eyes," he finishes.

Janice absolutely melts.

Learoy, always suspicious and cocksure, gets in his face right off. "Mmm-hmm. Tell me, Too Short, what's your thing?"

"Shoot, I'm on the positive tip, baby." He flashes real charm her way. "Me go back to jail? Not a chance in hail. I'm making me a grip, being MC Cripple Crip."

Pho shadows over him, towering, and rumbles his deep voice, "We don't like violent people hanging out here, Mr. Crip."

"Easy there big guy," Cripple Crip looks contrite. "I killed, I robbed, did my run as the Boss Baller...but then, the accident...," one almost hears the spiritual humming rise in the background, "and I saw the light! It was a wake up call."

Janice composes herself. "Cheating death like that can really change people."

"Cheating death?" Cripple Crip talks sense to her, "Girl, what you mean? I'm talkin' 'bout prison when you got no legs to run and your eggs the ones they lookin' to beat."

Pho and Carlos shudder at the thought; Janice steams

full on for this wheel-bound hunk; Learoy lets her major doubts burn through.

Dutch is totally impressed. "Yo, I'm a rapper too, like you."

Cripple Crip sizes him up and looks to have some fun. "Whoa, hold on now. A white rapper? Now that's original, gangsta, a real first for the ages."

Dutch, not the sharpest marble in the bag, takes it as a compliment and busts a move in deference, then smiles like a total dweeb. Actually, the busting of the move is not bad; the kid does have some talent, and he's not totally a total dweeb. Just a little bit of a total dweeb.

Cripple Crip hesitates, not sure if shooting Dutch down is the right thing to do. "A'ight. Not like me, not quite like MC Cripple Crip. I got no spat with white rappers, unless they rich. You ain't rich, is ya? You ain't no boogie hangin' in the 'hood are ya?"

Janice flinches just a snib, relieved when no one looks her way.

Dutch lets it flow, "*Brother, I'm rich with soul, I'm rich with rhyme, but if we talkin' money, I ain't even got a...a... a...a...*"

Carlos can't help himself. "A DIME! *Pendejo!* A DIME!"

Cripple Crip laughs. "That's good. You okay, cracker rapper."

Pho's phone vibrates from a Moon text. The sharp Cripple Crip picks up that they are communicating.

Nodding at Moon he asks, "S'up with the 411 on her?"

"She said she can't smell where you're from," Pho says. "You from Valley City?"

Cripple Crip looks puzzled and smells his armpit.

"Moon's blind," Mad Girl loves explaining things, "and deaf. She smells real good. I once seen her whiff up Dutch from four blocks away."

Now Dutch smells *his* armpit.

"S'cool," Cripple Crip doesn't slip a beat, "I dig blind Asian chicks too. I'm from CeePeeTee...Compton, LA. Back there, everybody wanna kill me. I'm here for a fresh start on life."

Janice jumps at another chance to gush, "Well you came to the right place! Everyone, no matter what cards the past has dealt them, gets a fresh start at the corner of Truth and Pain."

"A'ight. So, ladies," Cripple Crip makes it smooth, "what's the game in this 'hood?"

Learoy can't bear it, "Nigga, please! You got a ways to go before you can play like that."

"Oh, you one of them," he comes back. "Okay, we won't be talking much, but it was sho' nice meetin' you, Miss Nigga Please!"

The kids crack up. Learoy is uncharacteristically caught off guard.

Cripple Crip leans back over to Janice. "How you like black guys, white girl?"

"We were just discussing how race is meaningless in the world. I mean, except for certain cultural issues, perhaps demographics, environment..." she trails off and bats her eyelashes.

"Yeah, baby, race. I wrote a song about it."

"Really?" Janice asks. "A rap about race? That's so unique!" The girl is way gone.

"Yeah," Cripple Crip draws himself up, "it goes *I'll kill you if you white, yellow, brown, or black. So shut yo' mouth! Quit talkin' that smack!*"

"Yo, man, that flows, yo," Dutch says. "You know, there are other rappers in wheelchairs around here with the wrong attitude." He gives Carlos a BIG look. "But you, yo, you've got the right attitude for a crippled rapper."

"These days, my urbanically oppressed, light hued friend," Cripple Crip becomes the teacher, "the proper term is 'Handi-Rapper.' But 'Non-Typical-Hip-Hop-Artist' will also do."

Carlos, strangely quiet throughout most of this meeting, suddenly starts smiling, then shaking, then rocking in his chair, almost bursting with repressed mirth.

Then he can't help it.

"HAAAAAAAAAAAAAA ha ha ha ha ha ha!" He takes in a big gasp of air. "Ha ha ha ha ha! I showed you! I showed all of you! This proves what I been sayin' all along: If I was black you'd think differently about my rappin'!" Carlos does his version of a victory dance in his chair, which is a bit of bumping up and down on his rump and snapping his toes under Dutch's nose.

"Check this," he goes on, "MC Cripple Crip is a persona, not a person, a PERSONA, I created. This guy's not a real rapper. He's my pal, pretending. His whole story is what I made up and told him to say. Go ahead, tell 'em Reggie. Tell 'em about the persona."

As one, the kids look from Carlos to Cripple Crip, then back, then back again, then sort of sideways. There's doubt, tension, silence.

Cripple Crip cocks his head at an angle, taking in Carlos. "Who's Reggie?" Then he gets beasty on Carlos's ass, "What you talkin' bout, fool? Cripple Crip is a person-uh, you created? The old me, I'd a killed you for saying less. You lucky you din't get shot just now."

"Yeah, Carlos," Dutch is sold, "you sure are one lucky beaner."

Carlos can't believe it. "I'm telling you! This guy's name is Reggie Troupe. I paid him twenty bucks to pretend to be MC Cripple Crip. I got that wheelchair out of G.R.A.S.S.

storage even. It's not his. I did it to prove you guys would flock around a rapper in a wheelchair just because he's black! Those were even my rhymes he busted out. C'mon, Reggie, tell them!"

"Tell them what?" Cripple Crip is hotter now. "Fool, I never did nothin' to you. Why you trippin'? This is like what I tried leaving behind me in LA."

Carlos's phone vibrates from its holder on his switchbox. He snatches it up with his foot, flips it open, and reads a text from Moon: "Dude, I never thought I'd say this about you, but you're a player-hater." He jams the phone back down in disgust.

"Wait, I'm not lying." Carlos grows more and more anxious while his eyes dart about. Then something dawns on him. "Look, this guy's not MC Cripple Crip. Shoot. He's not even a cripple! I'll show you!"

Carlos grasps his wheelchair's joystick with his toes and jets over to Cripple Crip's side. On the way he pushes a button on his switchbox and the footrest down below flips over, converting into a small cattle catcher looking thing, like what used to be on old fashioned train locomotives.

He rams into Cripple Crip's chair, wedging the cattle catcher looking thing under it, then backs up and rams it again, over and over, getting it into a rocking motion, trying to build up enough steam to upset it.

Mad Girl can't help herself, "Yes! Git 'em, Carlos, git 'em! Git 'em good!" She loves a brawl.

"Carlos," Janice uses her everything-will-remain-under-control tone, "this is NOT how we greet attractive young men whom I like at Truth and Pain."

Carlos finally succeeds in tipping Cripple Crip over. He crashes onto the sidewalk.

Janice shrieks!

Mad Girl wobbles over to Cripple Crip and starts up,

"*UNO! DOS! TRES!* GOOOAAAL! GOOOAAAL! GOOOAAAL!" She shoe-slides around him chanting: "He put your smack hand way down, way down, way, way, way down!"

"There now, see!" Carlos's eyes glaze fanatically. "Watch him walk. Go on, Reggie, get off your lyin' butt and walk! WALK I say!!"

Cripple Crip rests on his side, entangled in the wheelchair. He curls his hands up under his chin, so weak, so paralyzed, so pitiful. He doesn't get up.

"Please, hep me," Cripple Crip rasps. "Hep me, please. I can't move. Oh the pain and humility, gettin' dis'd by a fellow cripple, just because I'm black."

Now Carlos shrieks, beyond the point of no return, eyes blazing, face blotching red, lips in a snarl. He rushes Cripple Crip, brandishing his ultimate weapon: The Foot!

He goes for Cripple Crip's throat!

The kids scream at him to stop! Only Mad Girl keeps egging him on, loving that it's going too far.

He does stop! But only because his foot can't reach. He stretches his leg out as far as he can but it falls short. For a brief, silent second his toes hover inches above Cripple Crip's chin, quivering in the air.

"*Ay, chingada! Pinche cabrón* foot!" Carlos flicks switches and the cattle plow retracts while the hydraulics lower the front of his wheelchair, allowing his foot to settle slowly down onto Cripple Crip's Adam's apple. Ahhh, that's more like it.

Carlos strangles Cripple Crip with his foot, thrusting it at his larynx and wrapping his violently homicidal insole around his gullet. He's possessed! Nothing, nothing can stop him!!! Holy fu--------

Twist the Chapter of the

--------dging moly!!!!

Through the strangling and the wailing and the waving of hands a mammoth form sweeps through the fray. Majestically, imposingly, single-mindedly, Pho, in his immense behemonolithic calmness, steps in and lifts Carlos, wheelchair and all, with one hand yet, up over his head.

"Goddammit, Pho," Carlos yells, "put me down and let me finish handling my business."

"No," is Pho's simple response.

"Aw, man, Pho, I wasn't really going to hurt him." Carlos realizes the futility of the situation and hangs his head.

The other kids rush to Cripple Crip's aid and begin righting him, apologizing for Carlos's insensitivity, throwing out speeches about making it all up to him. Janice especially pampers him with looks and kindly worded questions about his well being.

The sound of squealing tires interrupts their doings. Sliding round a corner and slamming onto Truth Avenue, in a blaze of speed and burning rubber, an ultra-decked-out-jet-black-shiny-as-hell-stretched-and-overly-hyphenated limo careens down the street. In its wake of swirling litter, bums and crack whores shake their fists after it.

The limo screeches to a stop at the curb in front of the kids, who become an absurdly frozen picture with Carlos still in the air and Cripple Crip halfway up from the ground. All nine mouths drop open then snap closed as one. Pho gingerly lowers Carlos while the other kids gently finish straightening Cripple Crip. On cue they all strike tough poses, prepared for whatever new trouble steps from the flash ride.

A glossy, white-guy record exec pops from the back door. He's all Hollywood bullshit wrapped in a sharp Italian suit. He must be wearing $6,500 worth of clothing and accessories. Oh, wait, the iced out Rolex must be worth $25K all on its own. My bad.

"Yo, kids," he says smoothly, almost cool, "I rep for Behind Bars Records, and word on da street," okay, maybe not almost cool, "is there's a righteously talented handi-rapper round here."

He draws a homemade CD from a plain brown envelope.

"You gotta hear him hip hop his flows, baby!" Dude is definitely not cool. "This handi-rapper has got it so goin' on that these tracks be shootin' to Number 1 in like five minutes." He wiggles the CD in the air. "This playa's got a mystique that busts so mad he didn't even bother putting in a picture of himself. He let his music speak for him!" He kisses the CD and wiggles it in the air some more.

Carlos's expression exclaims that all his hopes, dreams, and countless demos have finally paid off. He barely contains himself now that his moment of being discovered is at hand. Even Dutch looks at him, surprised and encouraged.

"But I don't need a picture. I know who I'm looking for." Record Exec Guy loves being dramatic. "I know by his soulful words he's in a wheelchair. I know by his hip-hoppin' attitude he's from Compton, LA. I know by his rock-poppin' street beat he's a boss baller who reformed his life after taking a bullet. And I know he's sitting right here, right now."

Realization hits the group.

"I especially know," Record Exec Guy goes on, "because he tagged his handle right on the disk. I know I'm looking for," he flips the CD and reads what's written on it in bold marker, "BLACK HANDI-RAPPER MC CRIPPLE CRIP!"

"Him! Him!" all but Carlos shout and point at Cripple Crip. "It's him!"

Carlos sinks in his chair like he's going to pass out.

"S'bout time you got here," Cripple Crip says. "Been waitin' on you for hours. I'm Black Handi-Rapper MC Cripple Crip, and let's get on with our trip, Mr. Really-Not-Hip."

"Check that!" Record Exec Guy fawns. "That's all just ad-lib, right? And they said I was crazy for coming down here. Eat your doubts now, Executive Vice President Marvin Kibblestein!"

Carlos jets up in between Cripple Crip and Record Exec Guy. "Listen, Record Man, there's been a mix up. Those aren't this faker's songs. I am Carlos Ramirez Villagomez Gutierrez Valenzuela Hacienda Cruz Rancheros Dos Grandes Huevos del Toro, and I sent you that DC! I mean CD. It's me! I'm the mad handi-rapper you're looking for." Carlos is desperate and nervous. "Listen: *I'm the guy you want, I even got my own font, I'm cooler than snow,*" uh-oh, "*I defy what you know, I don't blow,*" this is not going well, is it, "*I just go, don't you know, yo, yo, yo...*" how pathetic, "yo?"

"Oh right, sure." Record Exec Guy searches his audience. "Whoever heard of a talented Mexican rapper? In a wheelchair no less! Am I right?"

The whole group explodes in laughter at Carlos's stupidity.

"Carlos, man," it's Mad Girl, "you're a loser."

They all laugh again!

Carlos shrinks, totally humiliated.

"Now, Mr. MC Cripple Crip---" Record Exec Guy starts.

"You can call me CC, for short, Mr. Wangster," Cripple Crip interrupts.

"Right on, CC, you the step on G! I've got a contract, promo spots, tour dates, all set up here in the limo. What we'll need to do is get moving on this business and get you out there ASAP like now, right now---"

Cripple Crip shushes Record Exec Guy with a raised hand. He turns to Carlos and calls to him, "Hey, Carlos."

Carlos looks up, unsure what's coming.

"There are two kinds of people in this world, my friend," Cripple Crip philosophizes, "those with record deals and those who suck. You suck."

In a bedlam of words and motion and slamming doors Record Exec Guy whisks Cripple Crip, wheelchair and all, into the huge limo. It roars and screeches away just as it came, in a whirl of swirling litter and shaking fists.

The other kids walk through the G.R.A.S.S. gates, buzzing excitedly about their new superstar friend MC Cripple Crip, leaving Carlos behind, utterly dejected.

Chapter What Reveals the Sensation and a Few Important Conversations

Dig it, baby: Record companies, movie companies, computer companies, heck, tampon companies, all sort of do the same thing when they market new products. One day there's "The Shit!" and the next there's "The Real Shit!!" and the next there's "The Really Shitty Shit!!!!" When they reach that point the company people exhaust themselves calculating profit margins until they can say, "Whoa: The Really Shitty Shit looks gooooood."

Check this out, man: So they take their new Really Shitty Shit and all the departments talk and yell and argue about production schedules, packaging, and artwork. Then they shoot commercials and lease billboards and set up ancillary markets and contract cross promotions, and people in offices start phoning and emailing and berrying and messengering and saying we better get our act together because it's dump time. When they get to that point the CEO kicks back to calculate his bonus because, whoa, The Really Shitty Shit looks gooooood.

This is totally awesome, dude: Then they send The Really Shitty Shit up the ladder to the high dive platform, the same place The Shit dove from two days ago, and The Really Shitty Shit emerges, clings, poses, gets ready to drop and have its fantabulistically free-falling moment in the air before hitting the bowl full of consumers waiting for the next big thing to buy and enjoy. When it gets to that point the end users all take out their wallets and say, "Whoa: The Really Shitty Shit *better* be gooooood."

Now, Witness: The MC Cripple Crip sensation.

It's an eruption, an explosion, a cataclysm of sights and sounds and colors. Magically, Valley City blooms with new billboards, lamp posts sprout banners, bus stops look freshly splashed, and yes, the busses themselves appear to drip wetly with new ads. In the shops and malls, the Wal-Gets and Tar-Marts, people grab the T-shirts, the hats, the shoes, the coffee mugs, lunch boxes, bumper stickers, kid toy meals, colognes, and those little personal electronic device covers.

The Really Shitty Shit is all over everything.

Cripple Crip's face flashes across TV screens, gets pasted onto cereal boxes, makes the cover of *Rolling Stone,* is drawn by kindergartners, is contemplated for placement on a new postage stamp, then the dollar bill, but finally makes it to the ultimate status of toilet paper.

Some people even buy the CD; most just grab it off the net.

The album artwork catches everybody's eye: MC Cripple Crip in prison stripes, strapped and wired into a wheelchair converted into an executioner's electric chair, and he's getting zapped!

The pithy slogan:

BLACK HANDI-RAPPER MC CRIPPLE CRIP:
THE SURVIVOR
and his NEW ALBUM
SENTENCED TO LIFE IN THE ELECTRIC CHAIR

It's sick. Dig it, baby.

On the side of the ugly, really ugly, black, four-story parking garage that faces G.R.A.S.S., a gigantic copy of the artwork glows in the early morning light.

Down on the sidewalk, looking tiny when juxtaposed with the image above, two people stare upwards. Janice and Learoy stand dead in their tracks, each for different reasons.

Janice breaks the silence. "You know how I have jungle fever and all..."

"Un-huh," Learoy responds.

"I don't just like him," Janice's voice is sultry.

"Un-huh."

"I loooove him."

Learoy blows up: "That's it!" She whirls, her finger under Janice's chin, "Girl, who's the bigger fool? You? Or MC Too Bad up there?"

"Learoy," Janice is hurt, "you spellbind any man you desire. I am not quite so lucky. A positive body image is a self-confidence I lack. At present I have at last discovered there might be a chance for me to find love, and you refuse to assist. You may have it all 'goin' on' physically, but Cripple Crip, at least he's open minded."

Learoy rolls her eyes.

"Open minded here," Janice puts her hand to her temple, "in his head," then places her palm softly on her chest, "and here, in his heart."

She gives Learoy a puppy dog look.

"Damn, girl," Learoy flinches, "don't give me the big old sad eye!"

Janice gives her even more of the big old sad eye.

"Woo! Okay, okay!" Learoy relents. "Geez, you really are in love."

Janice lays on just a dash more of the sad eye.

"Yes, yes, I'll help you," Learoy absolutely cringes, "I'll help you already. Now stop it!"

Janice does a little spin on one of her crutches, excited.

Learoy gets into it. "Let's get over to the salon. We'll make you such a hottie his next video director will feature you in the front row."

At the same time just outside of Moonaaauuuh's door (which, by the way, is inside G.R.A.S.S.) Mad Girl pushes the doorbell button, impatient as always.

Inside the room Moon is sitting up in bed with the sheets askew. She's frazzled, her short green hair a mess from an uncomfortable night's sleep, or lack thereof.

Moon's place is not large, merely another dorm room containing a bed and desk with the laptop computer Carlos built and customized for her. The computer is cool: its keys are Braillewriter-style, but the flexible screen raises whatever words and graphics appear on it so she can touch-read them. It's plasma with a lift, and Moon always carries it in a sling on her back.

What's truly spectacular here are Moon's puzzles, designed, hand cut, and assembled by her. Framed puzzles of mystical places she hopes to visit someday cover the walls: the Great Pyramids, the Bermuda Triangle, Machu Picchu, the bath house in *Spirited Away*. More scattered pieces litter the floor, and puzzles under construction cover two small card tables.

Truly unique are the three-dimensional puzzles on the shelves behind her bed.

On those shelves, in places of honor, sit statuette replicas of her seven best friends in different stages of their lives. There's a one armed Carlos, then a one armed, one legged Carlos in his first wheelchair, then a one legged Carlos in his lowrider wheelchair scratchin' at his coffin. Learoy fully develops from skinny preteen to VaVaVoom in three steps. Mad Girl goes from young and thin to young and pregnant in only two. Bryan shoots hoops as Pho arcs by on his board. Sporting an afro pick, Dutch b-boys it with all his might. Janice's five statues create a freeze frame montage that captures her in a ballet run, leap, and landing, all her movements executed with the elegant fluidity of a swan gliding over still water.

Moon is there as well, her comforting aura radiating outwards as her puzzle statue exudes the appearance of sensing the friends surrounding her.

And each of them smiles, caught in the act of what they love doing most, living life as they want, showing perfect joy in a moment of bliss; attaining, in a posed glimpse of reality, what each of us ultimately searches for: security.

Mad Girl pushes the doorbell button again. Okay, so it's not a doorbell button, it's more like a door-attention-getter button. The room doesn't contain a bell at all, of course, because she wouldn't hear it. Rather, the button activates a radio transmitter that emits a signal to the small butterfly charm hanging from the necklace around Moon's neck. When the door button is pushed, the butterfly flaps its wings, giving Moon a fluttery tickle on her breastbone. It's another of Carlos's inventions for which he received a patent rejection letter, but Moon loves it.

This time, in her current mental condition, the

flapping wings startle her into jumping from the bed to the door. Even in this early morning, agitated state she nimbly floats across the floor.

Mad Girl bursts in as soon as the door opens. She sees Moon's disheveled appearance and takes her hand, trace-talking by tapping and finger sketching patterns onto her palm as she speaks out loud.

"Girl," she asks, "what's wrong with you? You look like you din't slept."

Moon responds by trace-talking on Mad Girl's palm.

Mad Girl says Moon's words, "I had a nightmare. It was awful."

It's a habit for the kids to speak out loud when they trace-talk with Moon. They do it so that when they're together, and Moon isn't texting, she's not left out of the mix. Moon also picks up their vocal vibrations as indicators of a conversation's emotions.

Mad Girl trace-talks on Moon's palm, "Really? What was it?"

"I dreamed I was a...a..." Mad Girl as Moon hesitates. "Here, I'll spell it. L-E-S-B-I-A-N."

Mad Girl mouths the letters, working hard at it, spelling not being her strongest suit. Then finally, "Oh, A LESBIAN."

Moon raises her fingertips to trace Mad Girl's face, touching the curve of her lips, the firmness of her eyes and brow, the set of her jaw, all as gentle as a cat's whiskers grazing a blade of grass. Confirming that her meaning was conveyed, Moon nods and returns to trace-talking on Mad Girl's palm.

"I dreamed," Mad Girl as Moon goes on, "There was a girl about to take off her top. And I really, really wanted her to do it."

Mad Girl thinks, smiles, then grimaces, then looks

unsure as she trace-talks back, "That could be hot, homegirl, but I don't know fo' sho'."

"I don't know either," is Moon's response, "I'm confused. I've never had feelings or thoughts like that before. What's sticking with me is how much I wanted her to pull that shirt up. I was cheering her on. It's just that it didn't seem sexual...but there was something about it...I can't tell. It's weirding me out."

"Let me be straight wich you---oh, sorry, not straight---I mean clear, let me be clear," Mad Girl says. "You wanted to see this chick's upper floor, but down in your basement the boiler wasn't steamin' up?"

Moon blushes, then replies, "No, the steam wasn't on! I don't think it was...but in my dream I was so excited, what else could it be?"

"Your dreams usually mean stuff, like that time you dreamed about Carlos driving a car, but then the car drove over him instead." Mad Girl both traces and talks slowly and thoughtfully. "Maybe it means you're gonna be a stripper or somethin', like my Aunt Lupiente! She makes a lot of dollars."

"Have you ever heard of a deaf-blind stripper?" Moon wants to know.

"Maybe you'll be the first!" Mad Girl wants to make Moon feel better. "But don't worry. If it's just one dream it ain't nothing. Probably nothing." Then she moves her fingers more excitedly. "I once dreamed I ate a ten-pound burrito, but when I woke up I remembered I'm just pregnant! That's sort of like yours, right?"

Moon doesn't quite know how to respond to that one.

Mad Girl doesn't notice and feels good about consoling her friend. "Let's go get some breakfast," she trace-talks. "Baby needs a meal!"

Across the hall and several doors down from Moon,

Carlos's place is a disaster of electronics rampaging the walls and traffic jamming the corners. Clustered here and there are technical magazines like *Electro-Geek Week* and *Sound Benders Monthly,* mixed in with *Vibester, SourceShield,* and *411*. Odd looking gadgets of all kinds, some completed and some not, cover shelves, desks, and floor space.

Only two places are in perfect, tip-top, immaculate order.

First: Against the far wall in a custom entertainment cabinet a 52-inch flat screen snuggles with the latest video gamer systems, namely, a polished XPLAY Nitrobooster Series VII, a sexy HalonStation BravoExtreme (Raptor Edition, of course), and an ancient, beat up NeoVision (just because). It's a haji's Mecca, a crusader's Grail, an infidel's Hell. Amen.

Second: His ultra-custom DJ Battle Coffin and PA, next to the TV Gamer Shrine area. Amen Amen.

Somewhere in this major chaos and minor order a worn couch grows from the floor. At present Dutch sprawls on said battered furniture flipping through a *Today's Baby Loke Rappers* magazine. You can guess who's on the cover.

Carlos is in his face. Well, more like he's in MC Cripple Crip's face because Dutch won't lower the mag.

"C'mon, that demo disc the record label dude had was mine and you know it," he's boiling. "You're doing this on purpose."

"How can you possibly say that?" Dutch is all innocence. "Yo, you know I got your back. But how can I know for sure those aren't Cripple Crip's songs? I seriously doubt he's a liar, yo. Besides, the guy showed us the CD with his name written right on it."

Carlos rolls back and forth as he talks, "pacing" the carpet. "First off, how can you say he's not a liar! You don't even know him! And second, like I told you a hundred times now, I made it all up! I put that name on the CD. Didn't you recognize my writing?"

"And you going off," magazine still up, "with those wild stories about creating 'this person'..."

Carlos stops and faces him, "That's 'persona'! PERSON-AAAHH! Not person! There's like a HUGE difference."

"...and on and on about you're wanting to be black and everything..."

"I don't want to be black! That's the whole point. I am a Mexican rapper! I only pretended to be black to catch a break. Are you even listening to me?" Carlos is just incredulous.

"...and then jumpin' him like that, like he's some gangsta invading your turf or something..."

"He IS invading my turf!" Carlos the flummoxed and flabbergasted is just about out of his mind. "And he's stealing my songs. And my friends, obviously."

"...and I don't know, man, I just like the dude, yo. He's just for real." Finally, he drops the magazine and looks Carlos in the eye, deadpan. "And besides he's just, you know, cooler than you."

Carlos stares for three long, aching, just-got-stabbed-in-the-heart seconds. Then, "ARRRRRRRRGGG-GGGGHHH!!! I can't believe this!"

Chapter 6

Early morning sunshine caresses the streets of Valley City! The buildings' architectural beauty, the bustle hustle of traffic, people jetting off to their productive days, the hints and smells of activity. The lawyer strides confidently on his way to protect the innocent; the stockbroker BMW's it to move the world's finances; the doctor enters the gleaming white hospital, calmly considering cures for his patients' ailments. A traffic cop smiles at a little old lady while a suited gentleman holds the door open for a heavily laden shopper. Attractive, well dressed men and women sipping lattes chat in front of cafés. Nothing like the big city rush to get one's blood going, one's thoughts percolating, one's feet synched to society's heartbeat and humanity's wonderful achievements.

Life sure is grand when you're on the nice side of town.

Meanwhile, back where even McDonald's doesn't want to live, the kids hang at Learoy's beauty salon, a couple blocks up Pain Street from G.R.A.S.S. The place looks ghetto but nice.

It's actually not Learoy's, yet. Her mother ran it for ages, until she passed a few years back. Her auntie manages it, just until Learoy's old enough to take over. Learoy works almost every day, learning, remembering, hearing the echoes of her mother's scissors snipping through the past. Next to being with her friends, Learoy feels most fulfilled and secure here, practicing her mother's art and developing her own artistry.

Inside, the girls perform in a flurry of motion with MC

Cripple Crip's blaring CD setting an MTV video mood. Janice sits, the center of spinning attention, while Learoy cuts, teases, fluffs, colors, and maniacally attacks her hair. Mad Girl bops her big belly everywhere, at once cheering them all on and tagging miniature graffiti patterns on Janice's nails. Moon braids striped tassels into intricate, flowing designs as she accessorizes Janice's whippishly thin customized crutches. It's a flamboyant dance, a harmony of sisterhood, a celebration of friendship.

On the sidewalk outside, the boys kill time in front of the big window with the WE NAIL YOU! BEAUTY SALON sign over it.

Bryan and Dutch sit at a little iron table playing dominoes while Pho and Carlos shoot Cee-lo against the bricks under the window.

Carlos grips the three dice with his toes, brings his foot to his face and blows on them. "You going to have to cash me out, Pho, big time!"

He shoots. The cubes fall: 1, 2, 3. The lowest possible roll; an instant loss.

"Cool whip," Pho smiles.

At the table Bryan clicks his tongue and says, "Dutch, dude, you owe me a bigface!"

"Don't come at me crooked," Dutch acts tough, "or I'll check you wicked, yo."

Bryan stands, pushes his awful looking, thick framed eyeglasses back, and leans over the table. "Dutch," he says sternly, "you best cut throat right now before I mop you."

"Yo, dawg," Dutch growls, "you on the broccoli! Not only did I win, but I could chunk you any day, yo."

Bryan looks puzzled. "I don't eat broccoli."

Pho rolls his eyes at Carlos before addressing Dutch. "*Yo, dawg,* count the bones again, Dutch. No. Have Bryan count them. You know the cat never lies."

Bryan slowly, painstakingly slowly, counts the dominoes again. Not slow because he has to, but so Dutch understands. "See, Dutch, six and five make eleven..."

Dutch silently shifts his lips, transfixed by the magic that is math. Plus, twenty bucks is on the line.

Carlos looks into the salon window, gawks, then motions Pho over. "Big Man, quick, check this out!"

Pho steps up. Through the window they see Janice, standing now, decked out in a new, tight, slinky, sparkly green outfit. Hair, nails, makeup, crutches, everything matches stunningly. The girl is smokin' hot.

Pho whistles through his teeth.

"...and," Bryan goes on, "three and two make five..."

The boys see Learoy place her hands on Janice's slumped shoulders. Normally Janice hunches forward over her crutches; Learoy wants to change her posture.

"...of course two and two," Bryan points out, "make four..."

Learoy continues talking and trying to move Janice's upper body while Mad Girl flaps her head up and down in approval. Moon massages her shoulder blades, finding key pressure points to relax her. Then, to model what she's talking about, Learoy gradually rolls her shoulders back while pushing her chest out.

"...and one and one is what? C'mon, Dutch," Bryan encourages, "don't be a retard, you can do it..."

Learoy's exquisitely round, firm, enormous, perfect breasts push out even further.

Carlos's eyes pop.

And even further.

His jaw drops.

And further.

His tongue lolls out.

Further.

Carlos's chair falls backward onto the sidewalk.

Okay, done.

"...and seven and seven are fourteen..." Bryan is so patient.

Janice gets the picture and repositions her crutches. Drawing her shoulders back she imitates Learoy.

Pho gets ready to enjoy heaven.

Janice tries and tries.

Pho waits an eon.

She keeps trying; her shoulders roll back, her upper arms relax to the rear.

Pho silently cheers her on, his fists raised over his head.

"...and so, Dutch," Bryan is humble, "you can plainly see..."

Janice is there!

Pho faints.

Bryan looks into the shop and shouts, "Hey! Janice has BOOOBIES! Now gimme my money, Dutch!"

The music inside cuts dead. The four girls saunter out of the salon, delighting in their femininity, exuberantly sharing their victory with Janice. They stop short and look down at the comatose Pho and Carlos.

"Now what, pray tell, is all of this?" Janice asks.

"Aw, ladies," Dutch rises, discreetly flips Bryan a bill, and glows at Learoy and Janice, "you blitzed yourselves out. I see you've finally decided to join my stable of girls. I knew you'd see the light someday, yo."

"Ho'd up, Dutch," Learoy's all scoff, "I know you ain't addressin' me in that manner. And my girl Janice don't need you, uh-unh. Not when there's a big, successful rapper around."

"I heard that," Carlos says, flat on his back, "and it hurts."

Dutch doesn't hesitate, "You mean my boy, Cripple Crip? Yo, he's on his way here right now."

Janice's excited smile expands way big. "Where is he then? I've got to see him!"

Pho sits up on the sidewalk and says with a sad face, "Janice, you look so very beautiful."

The overly-hyphenated limo jets up to the curb. A black tinted rear window glides down.

Janice hisses, "There he is, there he is!"

"Whoa!" Learoy whispers. "Calm down girl."

Cripple Crip pops his head out the window, the sun glinting off one of his gold teeth as he smiles suavely. "Wha'd up my peeps! How'z the ballin'?"

Dutch walks up and they slap some skin when Cripple Crip sticks his hand out.

"Yo, yo, yo. S'up, dawg?" Dutch is all about acting the mister coolness, and this time he pulls it off pretty well.

"Chillin'," Cripple Crip says chill-ly. He spots Learoy and Janice. "Damn, girls! You both lookin' fine as silky smooth Colt 45."

Janice totally blushes. Learoy rolls her eyes and strikes a don't-bullshit-me-bullshitter stance.

Cripple Crip scopes on Janice, "Whoa, girl, you done stepped up your game! Today you're more my style, fly-girl."

Janice turns giddy. "Thank you, CC. Learoy gave me a little makeover."

"Little!" Cripple Crip responds. "Then I ain't never seen big before now." He looks to Learoy again, "You sure know what you doin'! How about you style me up before my next show?"

Learoy looks the other way. She will not be pulled in.

"C'mon, don't be Miss Nigga Please no more," he's charming and sincere. "That's an attitude that does not befit an artist of your caliber, a lady of your grace."

Learoy glances back at him; her dukes are still up, but the thinnest layer of ice melts.

Cripple Crip's eyes twinkle.

"Um...maybe, Two Spokes," Learoy says, "if you start showing the proper respect."

Janice registers that it was supposed to be about her, but now it's somehow about Learoy. She steps in between them. "Perhaps we should be---"

Cripple Crip dodges the girl conflict quick: "Hey, y'all, the label's sending us out on the town. It's pure PR bull, but it means free food and a ride in this limo. Who's in?"

No one wastes a second as the back doors flip open. They all jump into the car shouting, "Me, me, me, me!!"

Everyone except Carlos.

Faces appear in rolled down windows. Pho's head sticks out of the sunroof.

"C'mon, Carlos," Dutch says, "hop in."

Squabbles of "Yeah, Carlos, c'mon, quit holding us up" emit from the limo in different voices. Carlos pops the screen on his vibrating phone and reads Moon's text: "It'll be fun! Let's go!"

Cripple Crip quiets them all with a steady hand. "Hey, man," he says to Carlos, "no hard feelings about you messin' me up. I, for one, know how difficult it is being in a chair, tryin' to get your big break."

Mad Girl quits being patient and gives it to him, "The dude's being cool, Carlos. Get in, vato!"

Carlos relents. He rolls toward the limo.

Cripple Crip slaps his own forehead. "Oh, we can't be bending corners with two chairs in here. There's not enough room, but I got an idea."

He pushes a button for the driver. "Hey whozit, James with the bars, get out here. We need to get this hooptie outfitted for my well wheeled homey."

Moments later, the limo cruises up the street, windows down, radio blasting at full, kids hollering and chatting and whooping it up, waving to people. Dutch sticks his bare ass out of the sunroof. It's outrageous, once in a lifetime fun for all.

Except for Carlos. Blasted by the wind and being jerked by every bump in the road, he's precariously perched in his chair, which has been tied haphazardly to the rear bumper with yellow nylon rope.

There go his sunglasses. Now he's got dust in his eyes to boot. Bummer.

A Day at the City

Fade in on the limo, cruising. Short inter-cuts reveal the scenery shifting gradually from decrepit to nice to awesome the further they get from Truth and Pain.

The radio's knockin' through the open sunroof and boomin' from the trunk, vibrating the heck out of Carlos. He's chillin' as well as he can, making the best of it.

The radio deejay's voice rumbles smoothly through the air. "Here's a brand spankin' new, world premiere, never been heard until this very moment, sure to be another hit from Black Handi-Rapper MC Cripple Crip. It's called *Put Another Bullet In It*."

Carlos's head snaps up. He's got an idea. "Another one of my songs! Hey, Dutch!"

Dutch pops up. "Word."

The song starts. Carlos raps with it perfectly, even matching the singer's voice:

Put another bullet in it,
I said to your----MOM.
Put another bullet in it,
I said to your----DAD.
Put another bullet in it,
I did your date at the----PROM.
Put another bullet in it,
That's right, I'm just that----BAD.

The rest of the kids' heads join Dutch's out the sunroof. Carlos grins at them in triumph.

"Now," he asks, "how come I sound like that rapper, and how can I know the words and beats to that world premiere, never been heard before song if it wasn't my creation originally?"

"Like, duh," Mad Girl burns him, "it was leaked on the Internet last night. It ain't like we don't know nothin'. Quit tryin' to bring us down, Car-lows."

Learoy adds, "And you the one always braggin' about what a great actor you are. Course you can imitate it."

Bryan perks up. "Wait a minute. I think he's trying to prove something."

Carlos brightens: everybody knows Bryan always tells the truth.

"He's trying to tell us," Bryan continues, "that he's just as big a fan of Cripple Crip as the rest of us!"

The kids drop back into the limo laughing and shouting, "Put another bullet in it, Carlos is such a----*DICK*!"

The limo screeches to a halt at a backstage doorway in a clean alley, the momentum slamming Carlos face down onto the trunk, his chair on top of him.

The group streams from the car and primps before entering the building. Cripple Crip's beat up, old school wheelchair looks completely redone: the seat is cushy dark leather; scrolled side plates now adorn it; and everything's been coated in 24 karat gold, including the spokes which look like they've also been dusted with crushed diamonds. Even the new black tires gleam as he hand pumps his glinting chariot along.

Carlos glares at Pho and croaks through lips scrunched against the black trunk lid, "A little help here?"

Janice schmoozes into her cell phone. "Yes, we have arrived. Yes, I will surely tell my good friend," she winks at Cripple Crip, "that you are most appreciative of his agreeing to stop by on such short notice." Janice notices Carlos being lifted and righted by Pho. "Carlos, would you please stop your shenanigans! We are on a most tight schedule."

Moments later, weaving through corridors, the group joins various backstage officials who whisk them along. In low tones, Janice makes last minute arrangements with them. A voice over a PA grows louder as they move from the wings onto a darkened stage behind a closed curtain.

Moon bumps into an unmanned engineering station with a mixing board, computer, video gear, and expensive looking stuff with buttons and levers. She gets interested and starts feeling everything. For kicks, she unstraps the laptop from her back, logs onto the wireless connection, and starts messing around.

"And we are so pleased to announce that Black Handi-Rapper MC Cripple Crip will perform a benefit concert for the Muscular Degenerative Disorder Organization!"

While the crowd on the other side of the curtain goes absolutely nuts, Janice mouths a beaming *Thank you* to Cripple Crip, who nods magnanimously. She melts for the thousandth time.

"And now," the voice on the PA resumes, "as President of the Muscular Degenerative Disorder Organization of Western Valley City, I am pleased to say that Black Handi-

Rapper MC Cripple Crip is here, right now, to say hello!"

The curtain shoots up like a shooting up curtain should. The one thousand strong crowd, consisting mostly of kids afflicted with various types of muscular degenerative disorders, some on crutches some in wheelchairs, goes even more nuts than it did before.

Cripple Crip rolls forward smiling, embracing the adoration that threatens to burst the auditorium. The MDDO President, one Mr. Jay Cat, who possesses major floppy ears and huge round glasses, moves his well dressed self towards Cripple Crip, reaching out to shake his hand.

Moon works her magic to highlight them via remote spotlight. Yeah, it's weird, she's deaf-blind, no one knows how, but bats catch bugs in the dark, right? She's like that: she just does it.

Cripple Crip extends to reciprocate the handshake, then hesitates, startled. This is because MDDO President Mr. Jay Cat also possesses the longest, thickest, most scariest fingers ever possessed by a human being. These things look like so many mottled pepperoni sticks crimped together and stuck into a hamburger bun. Cripple Crip deftly avoids the handshake by grabbing the mic instead and continuing to the stage's edge. Mr. Cat ignores the slight, being all too used to it, poor guy, and shifts back to stand with the kids.

A chanting begins: "MC, CC, MC, CC, MC, CC, MC, CC, MC, CC..."

Cripple Crip basks in the limelight's glow as a different voice booms over the PA.

"And now," the new voice says, "MC CC is gonna bust us out a song from his album. Hey, MC, how 'bout a mix set? Let's hear you do some old school DeeJay Tricky type play. Why not do verse one from cut four, then jump to chorus three on cut seven, then finish with the bridge from cut five. All right, here he goes! Give it up!"

The crowd's mood waxes confused by the complicated intro, with three-quarters of them scanning their portable MP3 player menus trying to figure out what they'll be hearing. The warm voices filling the room wane to mute.

The group on stage looks about, seeking the voice. They part, revealing Carlos behind them, holding a second mic with his toes. They stare, wondering what he's up to.

"C'mon, MC CC," Carlos sort of sounds nice, but sort of not. "If this is *your* music, that *you* wrenched *your* heart out creating, then *you* should know it good enough to let it flow."

Cripple Crip stays cool and noncommittal. Carlos looks like he's won. Janice is pissed.

"OR," Carlos rolls forward until he is next to Cripple Crip, "could it be you can't get jiggy wit it," he lays down his ace high royal flush, "'cause it ain't your music?!?!"

Janice, now even more pissed, pissedly whispers in one of MDDO President Mr. Jay Cat's huge floppy ears. He stiffens, his eyes growing wide behind his huge round glasses.

"Security!" He cries suddenly, jutting a long, scary pepperoni stick finger at Carlos, "Security! Grab that kid! Get him out of here! He doesn't belong! He doesn't have a MDD!!!"

Four hugely limbed security guards, one from each corner of the stage, converge on a completely stalled out Carlos. Cripple Crip takes the mic dangling from the toes of the shocked, single dogged kid.

"Now hold on, Mr. J-Cat Prez," holding both microphones in one hand Cripple Crip peacefully raises his other hand palm out, causing the guards to stop in their tracks, "and hold on Mr. Rental Bike Boys. Ain't no need lettin' this get janky on us. If we don't keep it gangster then who will? I may rap about separation in my songs, but that's just my way of addressin' inclusion as my message."

The place warms again, tense shoulders relax, bodies lean forward, eager to hear that message.

"Who cares if this poor kid," Cripple Crip puts a hand filled with empathetic love on Carlos's shoulder, "gots an MDD, or a ADD, or...the VD. We all of us be one people, one world, and if MC Cripple Crip don't stand for dat, then he can't stand at all!"

So much love kindles in the room that the fires of compassion fill every heart. Folks can't help but reach out one to another, extinguish old grudges, and nod knowingly in recognition of the human condition.

"Well, heck, I mean of course I can't stand," laughter, chuckles, more nodding heads, *Ah, of course he can't stand.* "But shucks, go on and give it up," he's orating now, "give it up for all of us."

He's gonna bring it on home now, just you watch.

Moon starts fiddling with even more buttons and switches.

"We all need help. Every one of us is swimming together, trying to find a safe harbor in this sea of life," Moon makes a screen drop behind him; she starts a slideshow presentation that projects images as his backdrop. Cripple Crip's words sail us past the Statue of Liberty toward the Promised Land, "all of us ride the stagecoach of life together, bumping across this prairie of pain that is our existence," a new image helps his voice manifestively sweep our destiny across the Great Plains.

In the audience a sweet voiced, blond haired, blue eyed, young black girl starts singing *America the Beautiful*, with a phat beat.

"We throw each other ropes to hang onto, so we can all scale the mountains of understanding, and rise above an icy world gone cold with ignorance," flush against the next image he flies us safely over the crystal clear, snow-capped Rockies. Moon plays the controls like a virtuosa.

New voices join Blond Blue Black Girl, then more, and they swell phunky above those dope, amber waves of grain.

"Yes, we still help each other struggle across the great divide, and be nationwide even though we stuck fixin' our own busted bridges at home," he brings us to the Golden Gate, and all that's left is the infinite, glowing, hope-filled horizon. *America*, sings the crowd, *she's the beautiful bomb, facheezie on the reezie.*

Yep, he's gonna bring it on home, right now.

"And we are nothin', NOTHIN', if we are not together," that glowing horizon turns into stars; then the image pulls out and becomes the glorious Stars and Stripes waving bravely in the wind, "all of us, in harmony, in peace, a United Nation of Hip Hop!!!"

The---place---just---EX---PLODES.

Feeling the crowd's vibrations Moon bows.

The floppy eared, round glassed, scary fingered MDDO President Mr. Jay Cat strides forward, daubing tears from his eyes. The kids gather round Cripple Crip and Carlos in a semi-circle. They cannot help but link arms and sway back and forth.

Cripple Crip takes Carlos's foot in one hand, looks deeply into his eyes, and thrusts arm and leg together up over their heads in brotherly victory.

Carlos is truly confused. The curtain falls.

A Short History of G.R.A.S.S.

Ages ago, in another time long forgotten, with the last wisps of Industrial Revolution steam dreamily fogging over the final extinction of the Jeffersonian Agrarian Era, when most folks still lived on farms but noticed the earth being covered by pavement and buildings, and the mythical Romantic Age had slipped into the prim Victorian with Modernism merely a whisper away, and Twain's rhythmic tones were not yet trounced by Hemingway's anti-flowery, conjunctively spliced sentences, and Faulkner had yet to link his flowing run-ons into the beautiful music that they are, when men were men and women were women, in the good old days when America was still spelled with a capital A, by gum, and---ah fuck it, around 1900, okay?

At that time the property that would one day become Green Rainbow Acres State School was a milk processing creamery plunk in the middle of nowhere. Well, not nowhere. It was Valley City, but not the place we know now. Back then the entire locality was astoundingly gorgeous, and the sun shone sweetly on all of it, not just the hilltop fringes.

The G.R.A.S.S. creamery, named after the owners Greener, Reinvow, Ace, Sonny & Son, sat on what was a sublime centerpiece at the bottom of the grassy bowl: a beautiful, fertile, green pasture where big shady trees ringed clear, natural springs. Wandering the land freely, the dairy cows happily herded themselves through the creamery gates to graze and drink the cool G.R.A.S.S. spring water. Even then the black wrought iron G.R.A.S.S. moniker spanned the noble arch, marking the first real business in the city. In shipping its products the countryside over, the creamery was what first put Valley City on the map.

It was such a staple the saying went thus: "Valley grass was here first day, but G.R.A.S.S., indeed, is here to stay."

Then that paradigm shifted. In swept developers and businessmen who lacked any connection to the land, held no love or understanding of it, no memory of it. To them it was not rich dirt and soft loam and pastoral sustainability; it was profitable miles quickly crossed, harshly razed, and piteously pummeled to their will. Once financiers realized that Valley City stood at the center of outlying developing areas, it made perfect sense to turn it into a shipping hub and make sure the railroads ran trains through it. Overnight the land surrounding the creamery became annexed, subdivided, split up, eminently domained and righted away until the cows had nowhere to go and no way to get there. This left G.R.A.S.S., quite literally, on the wrong side of the tracks.

The passing of an era slipped by in the wispy blink of a foggy eye.

A creamery without milk is a mixery that cannot mix. And so the cutthroating started: Greener, ever the foresighted one, sold out to Reinvow, who was always just a dollar behind Greener. Then Ace, not wanting to be left out, bought up Reinvow, which made Sonny, who never quite understood reality until it passed him up, buy out Ace. By the time Sonny realized reality meant that a creamery without milk is a business that cannot biz, the only person left to sell to was Son.

Luckily for Sonny, Son was not a relative, which made it okay to screw him.

So he did.

Mr. Samosa Son was a good man, a man of the land, a man of his word. A stalwart Valley Citier his entire life, he'd never traveled farther than twenty-seven miles from his birthplace, which was a small shack a mile from the creamery. He herded the cows at six, won the creamery apprenticeship at ten, earned the second S on the G.R.A.S.S. moniker at twenty-five. Becoming the creamery's sole owner at thirty-five was, he thought, a dream come true. He signed the papers, emptied his bank account, and handed the money to a swiftly departing Sonny. Son ran to his little cottage, built by him next to the creamery filtration building, to tell his wife about their great fortune.

Son was a good man, yes, but not the brightest.

As he told the story, he watched his wife's face fall with every syllable that spilled from his mouth. By the time he reached his final phoneme, and she asked him twice to repeat that they had not a penny left for groceries, she handed him their one-year-old baby, packed her bags, and walked out the door.

He neither heard from her nor saw her again.

Son was heartbroken, but not completely broken. Over the next several years he struggled with the business, forced to downsize and live on less and less as the remaining grassy pastures were covered over. He fought selling parcels of creamery land the best he could, but he kept having to hatchet off pieces here and there, until all that survived was one large city block of beautiful greenery surrounded by ugly buildings.

It was then he started building the wall.

Using the last of the money gained from selling the land, he ordered brick and mortar and crafted, by hand, by himself, the ten-foot high wall to enclose the last beautiful place on the floor of Valley City.

He didn't do it for the cows. They were gone long before.

He didn't do it for the people. They stopped caring years before.

He didn't do it for himself. He'd lost the ability to think about that.

He did it for his daughter, Petunia.

When his wife thrust baby Petunia into his arms and left, Son stood slack jawed for forty-five minutes. Finally, he looked down just as his Petunia opened her eyes from her sleep. She smiled at him.

"Da!" she said. "Outside! Da!"

It was her favorite place, the outside, walking across the grass, dipping her hands into the cold spring wells, sipping that cool G.R.A.S.S. spring water, shading herself under the big trees. Son had followed her that afternoon without a care in the world. His daughter was his heart, if not his very soul.

As she grew, her world was the creamery and the land, the dirt and the sky, the grass and the wind. No matter what happened to Son, no matter how difficult the work, how little the money, how bare the cupboard, his day brightened when he saw Petunia with the sun on her curly hair.

So when Petunia grew old enough to see how the land suffered, Son knew that as a father he possessed only one way to shield her from the inevitable. In building that wall he protected the only beautiful things left to him.

Petunia also sensed the world changing, moving on. She watched the cows she loved get freighted away because there was no place left for them there. She saw the land she adored mistreated, dug up, egregiously used for empty monetary gain. Before her eyes the creamery had become stagnant. Her father's heart-wrenching work had slowly faltered, faded, and been forgotten.

Not so much forgotten, she thought, just ignored.

She apprehended all this happened because people felt better about themselves when allowed to ignore things they considered to be not useful. Petunia realized then why people created junkyards. She also realized that junkyards came in many forms.

When her father started building that wall, Petunia understood why. Even though it would allow the world to ignore what it had discarded, it also meant freedom. Freedom because when beautiful, discarded things end up ignored behind walls, those things are free to become whatever they can.

Petunia was most definitely a counterintuitive thinker.

At that time Petunia was well into her fifteenth year and smart as a whip, both by the book and by the street. She'd caught on years before that G.R.A.S.S. was not a growing concern, so she'd done her homework and researched alternative income sources. Her mind filled with possibilities. While she watched her father build the wall brick by brick, she lingered with thoughts of junkyards and discards and beautiful things.

Junkyard, Petunia thought, is just another name for a place where discarded things gather because they've no where else to go. Even beautiful things, like my father and me.

That was when she set out to find other beautiful, discarded, ignored people.

But first she went to the federal building and applied for a government grant. This happened way, way back in the day when The New Deal acted like a teenager: just wisely mature enough to have money and irresponsibly young enough to want to spend the hell out of it. She got her grant. A truckload of a grant, as a matter of fact. Like I said, she was smart as a whip.

She found her first discarded person and returned with him as her first client on a brisk, fall afternoon fading quickly to a dark, orange sunset. She led the eleven-year-old boy by the hand and proudly pulled him through the arches topped with the G.R.A.S.S. moniker.

Samosa Son sat cleaning cement from his tools after another long day's work. Laying down his trowel he strode up to them, sticking a rag in his back pocket on the way. He had no idea what Petunia had been up too and thought the boy appeared a bit young to be her first beau.

"Dad," Petunia said, "this is Moses. He's coming to live with us."

Son was taken aback, but he reached out to shake the boy's hand anyway.

The boy didn't react, didn't look up, didn't seem to know the world existed around him. Oddly, he chose this moment to begin spinning in circles and flapping his hands around his face, all the while emitting a high-pitched keening sound.

Son thought he couldn't be much of a suitor.

Petunia said matter of factly, "Moses has been diagnosed as an Imbecile. That's better than an Idiot but not as good as a Moron."

"Oh," was all Son could think to say.

Actually, Moses was not an Imbecile, Idiot, or Moron. He was, we would say nowadays, Autistic, or suffering from Autism, or suffering from an Autistic Spectrum Disorder, or suffering from a brain development disorder, though some argue it's actually a condition, as opposed to a disorder, a whole other universe of discussion. But Petunia took the boy in before researchers such as Hans Asperger and Leo Kanner got us thinking along those lines, so Moses had to settle for the Imbecile label. He never seemed to mind all that much.

As Moses spun away from them, spastically flapping his hands and erratically whining through his nose, Petunia looked after him, deep in thought, studying his every aspect.

Eventually she smiled, understanding something. She said to her father, "Look at him. The booby hatch people say he's lost with insanity, acting inhuman. I say he's spinning himself a dance, looking for a partner. And see his hands? He's waving at us, trying to flag down some friends. And listen: hear him singing? He sings us a song so he doesn't have to feel alone; he's hoping we'll chime in. He's just searching for himself in life, you know. Security. Isn't he beautiful?"

Son pondered a moment, then asked, "There more like him?"

"Too many," Petunia gazed miles away, "too, too many."

"And why, my little girl, do they need to come here?"

Petunia looked at him with a quiet smile. "Because, dad, they've got no where else to go."

Son mulled her words over, choked, then voiced a thought he'd never faced before: "Sort of like us?"

"No," Petunia's smile grew, "*exactly* like us."

A weight shifted from Son's shoulders; he stood up straight and picked up a brick. "Then I guess I best get this wall finished, for all of us."

"Yep," Petunia said. "We need to make sure we keep the beautiful in and the ugly out."

Son hugged her closely to him. After a bit they gathered up Moses, and the new family went inside to dinner.

Almost a Canto, Never a Kant

Gentle knight was pricking on the plain,
With mighty arms he searched to be another's bane.
Redcrosse Carlitos, knight errant oh was he,

A battled warrior, yes, full of chivalry.
Across yon verdant field he doth spied,
Fair maiden Learoymart, to stakes lashed and tied.
Now sped Redcrosse Carlitos down the grassy ways,
Found he ignoble Cripmago staunch with icy gaze.
Learoymart cries, "Redcrosse Carlitos, my love, do stay,"
Yet forsooth, never would Redcrosse cowardly dart
away.
Redcrosse to Cripmago, they each the other dare,
Lance to lance they joust, both swearing to not
forebear.
Steed to steed they dash, clash, and ram,
Redcrosse Carlitos Cripmago's soul doth damn.
Victory goes to Redcrosse Carlitos in this dance,
As impaled, Cripmago is, by the Redcrosse lance.

Alone at a small table facing a corner in the G.R.A.S.S. cafeteria, an intensely focused Carlos, ferociously wielding a menacingly deadly chopstick with his toes, bayonets his egg roll up against a Hing's Kitchen Chinese food container.

"Ha, ha, ha-ha-haaaaa!" He laughs grandiosely. "That's for stealing my songs!"

"Whazzit!?" Carlos mockingly imitates Cripple Crip. "Them's ain't yo' songs, beaner!"

Carlos's voice swells with indignant bravado, "Yes they are, MC Mickey Mouse! Now, *pendejo*, you will face the death of a thousand deaths!"

He sadistically toe flicks the skewered egg roll across the table top battleground; it expires dramatically under the viciously twisting chopstick.

Carlos voices Cripple Crip's agonies: "Oh, oh, I'm dyin'! Hep me, hep me! I be dyin'! Don't nobody loves me 'cause I done did Carlos wrong, and now they all loves him again, so here I be dyin' alone, hated, horribly hated, alones, and deads. Oh, my ass is done been capped."

Grinning shamelessly Carlos totally loves this, until the chopstick tips the food container back onto his foot, covering it in sticky orange sauce. He tries shaking it off, but it won't budge. He gives it an extra big kick that flings it up and away where it SPLATS! with its splayed flaps sticking to the ceiling. He looks from ceiling to foot. What a mess.

Noise in the room zones him back to reality. It has definitely been Chinese Food Night at G.R.A.S.S.: Hing's Kitchen boxes cover tables everywhere, and kids scrounge for leftovers. Roaming about are some of the fifty or so variously challenged youngsters who live here, ranging in age from about six on up to their teens. There are boys and girls with Down syndrome, several kids in wheelchairs, a few blind children, some others with Autism, and smatterings of other syndromes, disorders, and conditions. Even though they lack things beyond the basic necessities, they are all well cared for because this place is not a sterile, bare, rundown "facility." It's a comfortable, warm home, and they find happiness and security in their familiar surroundings.

What draws Carlos's attention is that they are all humming an MC Cripple Crip song, *Girl, You A Glock Stopper!*

They picked it up from the wall-mounted television currently ambushing Carlos's eyes and ears. On it footage from the day's publicity tour headlines the local evening news. Against his will he rolls over for a better look.

News reporter Candice Cotton appears on screen. She's his favorite, with her tight fitting neon dresses and awesomely tweaked hair. She fervently doles out tonight's lead story, live from the now deserted scene.

"Tonight's top story:" she burns, "There is a talented black kid in the inner city who has good morals! No, really! He's one of a kind! A real hero! He's Black Handi-Rapper MC

Cripple Crip."

"Oh Candice," Carlos mutters, "not you! Please, could one person not be a Cripple Crip zombie?"

Candice continues, "Black Handi-Rapper MC Cripple Crip, by the way, has been black from birth! Watching him socialize with all of those special needs kids is inspiring. Never has a black handi-rapper been so moving, and it's so inspiring because he is, after all, black. And he is so unique because in addition to being moving and inspiring and in a wheelchair, he's black!"

While Candice's whizbang reporting continues dimly in his mind, Carlos mentally fades into dark thoughts. His attention wavers in and out; his eyes focus blearily on different parts of the room.

A wall poster renders Cripple Crip giving the world a thumbs up, but then he scowls and flips Carlos the bird.

His vision roves back across the television and Candice clucking, "And Black Handi-Rapper MC Cripple Crip is not only black, he's black! And everybody knows the only good rappers are black rappers, and black and black-black and blackity-black-black-black..."

Then the chanting starts, oh the ceaseless chanting, the baleful chanting that's haunted him all day, bansheeing his mind. Now the children perform it, joining hands and circling, spinning him dizzy with a freakily perverse singsonging playground rhythm:

"MC, CC, MC, CC, MC, CC, MC, CC, MC, CC, MC, CC..."

Carlos completely retreats from it all to a place where blissful tranquility reigns. The poster stills, the television mutes, the children circle voicelessly. Silence wraps him within its poised peacefulness.

A sound raises a brow. Slow, squishy, gushy, perhaps how a piece of paper covered with sticky honey being lifted from a slick surface might play, were your hearing acute enough to pick it up.

He searches, certain it's the precursor to total insanity. He looks up.

One of the flaps on the food carton stuck to the ceiling completes its detaching, leaving it swinging from the other extremity. It hangs precariously right over him.

"Uh-oh," Carlos says.

Still staring upward, his foot jabs for the wheelchair's control stick. He hears the other flap separating with its own slow, slurpy sound. This one, he thinks, is more like how sweaty gum lifted from summer hot cement by the bottom of a flip-flop might clamor, were you an ant.

He misses the control stick.

The container's remaining appendage lets go. The fall begins.

Again he jabs the foot. Again he misses the control stick.

Somehow the little box rotates during its descent, instead of staying bottom side down. This does not make sense, Carlos thinks, because wouldn't the weight of the sticky sauce have congealed in the bottom, since it was stuck right side up to the ceiling? So how can this physics defying receptacle roll over in the air and land open side down?

He even has time to go for the control stick again. He misses.

SPLAT! The container lands square on his unturned face, the sauce ripping down his cheeks and neck and onto his chest and, oh jeez, in his ears and all that.

Carlos moans, voice muffled by the makeshift muzzle, "What a goddamn day this has been."

As he leans forward, the messy food box slumps from his face, glances off his knee, and plonks back onto his foot.

Carlos looks down. Kick it off again? Nope. Won't be

bitten twice.

He calls to a young boy in front of the TV, "Hey, Clarence, help a homeboy over here?"

Clarence, a blind, ten-year-old black boy with very dark, round eyeshades, rather dapper in a navy sport coat, white button-up, and red bow tie, turns to Carlos. "You require assistance, Counselor Carlos?"

"Yes, underling Clarence, I require assistance."

"Be right with you, sir." Clarence whistles through his teeth and calls, "Max! Here boy, Max!"

"No!" Carlos shouts. "Not the dog, man!"

Too late. Nails clack across linoleum as a sneaky, bright white, short haired, wolfish looking dog approaches Clarence. He's Max the Guide Dog.

On his way over Max greedily licks the inside of a stolen Hing's container covering his snout. Just before reaching the blind Clarence, he creeps it off his nose, cops a raffishly nonchalant expression, and innocently sidles up. He's a sly one.

Clarence takes Max's halter in his right hand and they start walking. When Max realizes Carlos is their destination he slits his eyes and curls his upper lip. Max enjoys giving Carlos a hard time. He especially relishes pissing on his spokes.

"How may I assist you, sir?" Clarence asks.

"Clarence, there's a Hing's box stuck on my foot," he relates the state of affairs. "Remove it and throw it away, please."

"Yes, sir." Clarence motions to Max, then orders, "Take it, boy!"

"No, no, no," Carlos flinches, "not the damn dog, man!"

But it's too late. Max chomps onto the container, clamping it down onto Carlos's foot, then whips his head back and forth like a great white shark ripping a chunk out of a walrus.

"That's it, Max," Clarence affirms, "good boy!"

"Naw, man," Carlos grimaces and tries pulling away, "not a good boy!"

Max bares his teeth, really getting off on this. His eyes say, *I like Mexican food, Carlos! Gimme a foot taco!*

All smiles, Clarence releases the halter and says, "Trashcan, Max, trashcan!"

Max pulls Carlos from his chair and drags him toward a trashcan across the room.

Carlos calls out, "Stop him, Clarence, stop him!"

"Now Carlos," Clarence says, looking in his direction, "if you were going to follow him to the trashcan why didn't you just take it there yourself?"

Max pulls, yanks, really works it while Carlos slides across the floor on his back.

"The freakin' dog has my freakin' foot! He's killing me!"

"Max is not a biter," Clarence wags his finger at Carlos's voice, "and I resent your trying to make him out to be something he's not. That's it. Max, drop."

Max lets go just as they get to the trashcan. He moves to Carlos's face and smirks down at him. Growling, Carlos jerks his head up so they're eye to eye. Max burps right up his nose. Recoiling from the odor, Carlos bashes the back of his head on the floor. Max smirks again.

"Come Max," Clarence calls. "Sir, I am always glad to assist you, but you cannot treat my dog inhumanely."

Looking back over his shoulder, Max winks at Carlos. Clarence takes the halter, and they move away.

Carlos raises his foot and catches the food carton on the trashcan's lip. It falls inside.

"Well at least that's done," he mutters.

Heaven and Earth

In the restroom off of the cafeteria, Carlos lifts his foot to the sink. Depressing the plunger on top of the faucet with the back of his heel, he makes the water run smoothly. He lowers his foot to rinse off the sticky orange sauce.

The plunger pops up before he makes it. The water stops.

He repeats the heel plunger press, this time holding it down a bit longer to get the water good and going. He jets his foot under the spout quick as he can. He makes it!

The plunger pops up. His foot is barely wet. The sink gurgles cutely as the water flees joyfully down the drain.

Staring down the tap, he pits his intelligence against the simple mechanics of a stubbornly overzealous return spring in a plunger valve. The bad luck kid is not a quitter. Armed, so to speak, with only a left foot in a world that favors right handed, four limbed people, he takes all challenges as personal battles he must win. That's the way it has been, the way it is, the way it will always be.

A single twinkling water droplet grips the end of the dulled chrome-plated spigot, wildly ridiculing him with its superb surface tension survival skills. Contemplating the situation he focuses on untying another knot in the endless string of complications that make up his every complex day.

His eyes never leaving the droplet, he slides open a drawer beneath his wheelchair's seat, gropes, then brandishes a gleaming screwdriver. Deep in his brain, somewhere within dark caverns packed with resourceful synapses, a light bulb flashes on.

Sharp breath intake; posture steeled erect; putting

the screwdriver on the sink ledge, Carlos lays his big toe along the side of his nose and ponders a moment. Crisis time ending in 3, 2, 1, now.

"Hey," he says meekly, "anybody in here can give me a...a hand?"

A silent beat passes. Someone, who *was* being stealthy, exhales loudly in the handicapped stall and flushes. Placidly, politely, the deadbolt slides to breach; the stall door opens reluctantly.

Pho, wearing a crisp, white martial arts uniform tied with a beginner's white belt, squeezes himself through the opening, his girth so wide and thick that turning sideways doesn't help much. He twists back and forth, getting wedged then unwedged, wedged then unwedged, emerging slowly, inches at a time. His countenance plays sheepish.

"Goddammit, Pho!" Carlos is angry. "How many times I tell you not to use the handi-stall? Are you handicapped?"

"Well, not officially," Pho answers guiltily.

"You ridin' a chair? You pushin' a walker?" Carlos fires. "Shoot, I'll settle for a cane. You got a cane on ya?"

"Nope," Pho says.

"Then stay out of my stall, you hear me?"

"But Carlos," the giant pleads, "I keep telling you I can't fit in the regular ones. They're too small."

"Don't care," Carlos shoots back. "Get a disabled sign tattooed on your forehead, you can use it. 'Til then, don't do it, or I go bobo keys on your ass."

"Sure, man, no problem," anything to get Carlos off his back.

"Now get over here and hold down this button," Carlos demands. "Unless you got a sink disorder syndrome or some crap like that."

Pho trods over, pushes the button with a big thumb, then steps back to give Carlos room. The button stays down.

Babbling brookishly and flowing fiendishly, water tears torrentially from the tap. It's nearly a Niagara.

Carlos looks from the water to Pho. Water. Pho. "You some kind of a smartass or somethin'?"

"No," Pho is puzzled. "Wa'sup wit you?"

Carlos shakes his head and rinses his foot.

Pho dares make conversation, "Hey, I'm wondering. How do you...you know...how you do it?"

Snagging a paper towel from the dispenser, Carlos wets it and wipes the orange sauce from his face and neck. "How I do what?"

"Well," Pho is delicate, "do you stand up, or sit down? And like, if you stand up, how the heck you hold it?"

"Damn, you a cold piece of work," Carlos reflares. "What kind of fool question is that to ask, fool?"

Distanced from the handi-stall violation, Pho toughens up, "I ain't the only one wants to know. Everybody wonders."

"Then I won't say. It's my mystery." Carlos snickers, shoots the grimy paper towel into a short trashcan. He grins at himself in the mirror over the sink. "Next time they ask, though, you tell 'em in the bathroom Carlos doesn't look one legged. Mofo gots two big ol' legs, straight up."

"Now who's the fool, fool? No way I'm sayin' that!" Pho hits the exit.

In the corridor they head the same way.

Carlos asks, "You helping Moon tonight with aikido class?"

"Yep," Pho answers, "I'm her huckleberry."

"I'm going that way too," Carlos says. "She texted that there's a glitch in her gizmo."

"Then you her huckleberry too," Pho smiles.

Pho pushes through doublewide doors and they enter the G.R.A.S.S. occupational therapy room. A busy therapeutic playground, it's an awesome place, the kind few ever get to see.

First off, there's thick, multi-colored padded mats secured wall to wall and floor to ceiling, with padded ladders, padded supports, padded bars, padded doohickeys, and padded pads everywhere. A few odd looking platform-like contraptions and trapezes hang by rubber-coated chains from sturdy, overhead beams. On the platforms, kids sit or kneel and spin until they get dizzy. Other kids hang from the trapezes, stretching their muscles and feeling the positive pull on their joints. Kids with crutches try walking without them; they laugh when they fall flat on the cushions.

Across the way a padded stairway leads up to a padded ledge where a little girl stands with a basketball. Leaping from it she shoots the ball into a tub ten feet away. In a burst of happy squeals she splashes into a plastic ball-pool, making the shot while others cheer for her.

Far over everyone's head a boy races across the room on a zip-line. When he gets to the other side he drops onto a pile of thick, blue mats.

This place is designed for G.R.A.S.S. clients to integrate mind and body. Here they work on developing coordination, improving muscle development, finding their bodies in space, pushing their physical limits, and having a damn lot of fun doing it with minimal risk of being injured.

Moon's aikido class is off to the left in a small *dojo* area she created. She prepares to demonstrate the heaven and earth throw, *tenchi nage*, on a senior girl student while a small group of kneeling children watch. Moon wears a white *gi* similar to Pho, but because she's a black belt, she also has the black *hakama* over her pants.

As the student moves forward, Moon sweeps her with one hand low to earth and the other hand high to heaven, easily unbalancing and toppling her. Moon takes her down, all the while exhibiting aikido by another of its titles, The Art of Peace. She controls every movement, guiding the student to the mat as if she is a bird Moon loves too much to harm. At the last moment, effortlessly Moon releases her. The girl rolls happily somersaulting and immediately rises from the mat eager to face Moon.

Carlos and Pho head her way.

Sensing their presence, Moon single claps to her subordinates, indicating it's their turn to mentally review the techniques for a moment. She moves a few steps and takes Carlos's outstretched foot to trace-talk with him.

Carlos as Moon says, "The projector isn't projecting. I can't figure it out. Can you give me a foot with it?"

Carlos trace-toes on her hand, "No prob, Moonie Girl."

Returning her attention to the class, Moon claps twice for the students to all line up and kneel. Pho bows onto the mat and faces her. They bow to each other.

"Now sensei and I will demonstrate *ukemi,*" Pho explains, "which is how to fall properly. Watch us both carefully. I'm the initiator so I take the role of the *uke,* while sensei is the *nage.*" Pho winks at the kids. "As *uke* my main job right now is to not get my butt broken!"

The kids giggle. Moon raises an eyebrow, sensing their insubordination. They stop immediately. A boy and girl sneak looks at each other, *How does she do that?*

Carlos rolls over to a small stand that holds Moon's laptop and projector. He fiddles around for ten seconds and the projector flashes Moon's presentation onto a wall. It is text on a background of tea leaves and Japanese lettering. It reads:

The techniques of Aikido are neither fast nor
slow, nor are they inside or outside.
They transcend time and space.

To injure an opponent is to injure yourself. To control aggression without inflicting injury is the Art of Peace.
Morihei Ueshiba

Whip crack quick, Pho moves on Moon. Completely relaxed, she pivots on him even faster, blending with his motions as if she's quicker than time itself. She takes control of his momentum, his attacking energy, by meeting him rather than backing down in any way. As he tries grabbing her wrists she adapts to become one with him, and he's off balance before he even knows it. With little effort she throws him to the mat. Pho shows his skill by rolling out of the fall gracefully.

He stands quickly to address the students, "Remember, we always use technique, not strength. That's how sensei can throw big me!" He pounds his chest and the kids laugh. They love seeing the little Moon put the huge Pho on the ground so easily, believing they might be able to learn how.

Moon ends the class traditionally, bowing first to the *shomen* wall, where hangs the photograph of O' Sensei and under that his shrine. Next she faces the students and they all bow to each other, saying and signing, "*Domo arigato gozaimashita*." *Thank you very much for what has happened.* The students break and thank each other separately before scrambling away.

At the projector Carlos advances Moon's slide show, which flashes a "Slide Show Over" message onto the wall. He closes the program and sees the laptop's desktop image spring up. Carlos freezes, his mouth dropping open for the umpteenth time today.

The image on the wall is a photograph of the shelves behind Moon's bed in her room, the shelves that hold her handmade, three-dimensional puzzles of the gang. Carlos gapes because there's a new one.

Front and center, with all the other figures surrounding it, beams a puzzle statuette of Black Handi-Rapper MC Cripple Crip.

Carlos rolls from the room, slamming his way through the double doors.

Moon takes Pho's hand to trace-talk. "What's up?" she asks. "I felt an angry vibration."

"Carlos saw the new puzzle on your desktop," Pho traces back. "You really think Cripple Crip's earned a spot up on your shelf already?"

"He's just a lonely outsider," Moon answers, "wanting to belong to something like what we have with our group."

Pho is doubtful. "I think all that dude wants to belong up with is my Janice."

Moon tugs gently on his uniform. Knowing this signal well, he kneels to put his face close to hers. Like rose petals in a warm breeze her fingertips caress his face, reading it to verify the emotions she suspected she felt in the stiffness of his hand and the vibrations from his voice. The intimate face-read tells her what he is really trying to say.

She takes his hand again. "Is it him bothering you," she traces, "or is it really Janice?"

"It's messed up watching her dig that guy and breakin' my heart all over again," Pho traces back. "If he wasn't around, I think we'd be together again. Plus, I'm sure he's gonna hurt her. I just want him gone already."

"We all experience things we'd rather not see," Moon responds. "I've been dreaming about wanting a girl to take her top off!"

Pho considers, then traces, "Wow. Kinky!"

She gives his hand a hard pinch.

"Sorry, sorry," Pho scrambles his fingers. "But don't worry too much. Your dreams always have a way of working out for the best, you know?"

Moon releases his hand. Pho takes a step to the wall, closely studying the picture that stars Cripple Crip. He thinks.

One Chapter Short of a Dozen

Off at The Dark, Bryan, Mad Girl, and Dutch lie on their backs, their heads resting in the small, dimly lit square formed by the sun shining down through the skylight resting on top of the ugly, really ugly, black, four-story parking garage. Vague patterns painted by the Sunflower's leafy shadow caress their faces and the ground around them.

"One, two, three," Mad Girl counts, "go!"

Each of them blows steadily upward, making three leaves flutter in wind they would not otherwise feel.

Dutch poops out first, raising his hands to his temples and groaning, "Head rush! Oh I'm dizzy." He goes into a coughing fit. "I gotta stop smoking."

After lasting several additional seconds, Bryan rasps proudly, "I beat your ass again, Dutch!"

Mad Girl ends last, breathing slowly, gracefully, nonplussed by her efforts. "Next," she says, "shallow breaths in, short bursts out. A full minute this time, boys. One, two, three, go!"

They begin again, the three leaves bobbing rhythmically up and down. Dutch struggles to keep up, his cheeks quickly blooming crimson; Bryan's facial features exaggerate marvelously, turning him into a large lipped blowfish huff-puffing in and out; Mad Girl's an Olympian, taking it all in stride.

Dutch quits early again, once more grabbing his temples, gasping, "I just can't do it, yo. I'm gonna spew."

Bryan works it all the way with Mad Girl. They stop together.

Mad Girl scowls at Dutch, "You the one said you'd help me with my Lamaze techniques. Stop being a whiner."

"Yeah," Bryan joins in, "stop whining, whiner."

"I can't handle all this air, yo." Dutch closes his eyes.

Bryan gloats, "I win! I get to be your coach, right Mad Girl?"

"Sure, Bryan, you win," she says.

"Awesome! I wanna be there when he comes out." He's excited. "Do you know if it's a boy yet? I want him to be a boy like me so I can play with him."

"Nope," Mad Girl shakes her head, "don't know if him or her's a girl or boy yet."

"That's cool, but I want a boy." Bryan goes on, "He's gonna be retarded like me, right, so we can be twin brothers together, right?"

Dutch chuckles.

"I don't think so," Mad Girl responds. "Besides, you already got Dutch for your retard twin brother."

Dutch stops chuckling.

"But," Bryan protests, "Learoy said your baby would have problems for sure."

Mad Girl's face sharpens to defense mode. "What'd she say?"

"She said," Bryan speaks without craft, merely reporting the facts, "since the father was 'such a lame assed, glass dick suckin', motherfuckin' moron,' and you are 'such a skanky, dirty pearl, crack ho', ripnut skank ho', that baby will fo' sho' come out all messed up. Snap, Snap.'"

Dutch chuckles again. "She called you 'skank' and 'ho'

two times."

"I'm goin' bitch slap you two times you don't stop that laughin', Duuumb-tch," Mad Girl warns.

Dutch can't help it, "It's funny, you gotta admit, it's damn funny. Whoo! That girl can surely dish up the smack, yo."

Mad Girl moves amazingly fast: leaping up, she spins on her left foot with her right foot headed straight for Dutch's still laughing face, both hands automatically supporting her protruding belly.

Dutch's own dexterity proves useful. He rolls out of the way just in time, jerking to his knees. Mad Girl adjusts her aim in mid sweep and plants her foot solidly in Dutch's ass. It's a hit, a very palpable hit.

"GOOOAAAL! GOOOAAAL! GOOOAAAL!" she shouts victoriously.

"Dee-yamn, gimme a break, bee-yatch," Dutch complains.

"I'll break your trifling ass," Mad Girl strikes again.

Dutch gains his feet, dodging her. He's quick, playing the lithe mongoose to her bulbous striking cobra.

"Besides," he says, dodge, swoop, "your bein' mad at me," hop left, "when you oughta be," jump right, "takin' it out," shoot, got him hard in the shin, "on her, yo."

In a classic flamingo pose, Dutch balances on his right foot with his left leg lifted and bent at the knee, his hands cradling his injured shin.

Mad Girl stops, her eyes bulge wildly, her face beats beet red, her whole body trembles in rage. She's charging her battle batteries, the familiar deadly wind up to the full blown Mad Girl Tempest.

Bryan approaches her. "Mad Girl," he says, "Dutch and Learoy are your friends."

At break point moments like these she can always go

either way. This time she hesitates, willing herself to stop the fury. In a twinkling she pops on a frighteningly sweet girl, all is rosy as can be smile. She bats her eyelashes and cocks her head cutely.

It's really creepy.

Her bottom lip quivers. "A'ight," she says in an odd, low voice. "Friends. Yes. I'm gonna forget all about what you said she said. I'll wait. Then, at just the right moment, Learoy will know just how much I love her. I'll show her."

Still holding his shin, Dutch freezes, searches her face. He suddenly looks horrified. "Yo, Mad Girl, really, you don't gotta play that way---"

She stops him with a palm swept out before his face. She bats her eyelashes again.

Bryan gawks at her as well, previous experiences reminding him that her words do not always match her inner feelings.

"Okay," Dutch says, as if talking to a person about to jump from a bridge, "that sounds great, Mad Girl. We'll just do some more breathing stuff, won't we Bryan, or something, and talk about something else."

"Okay," Mad Girl says brightly, "let's do something nice, and fun. I know! Let's go find Learoy, and we'll all be friends together."

She stride-waddles off from the Sunflower to an exit. Dutch and Bryan's eyes meet. Dutch lowers his leg gingerly to the ground. They shrug at each other, look after Mad Girl, look at each other again. Then their eyes flash wide in realization. As one they bolt off after her.

Bryan stops, sprints back to the Sunflower, gives it a quick pet, then jams off into the darkness.

Chapter 12

Love, Love, Love. When did it start, what was its genesis? It addles brains, ruins lives, survives all punishment. It simultaneously eliminates and creates hate, driving the world to distraction. Without it, babies cry and men whimper; with it, babies cry and men whimper. It generates war, death, enemies, yet brings peace, life, friends. It can be cruel, kind, idiotic, wise, bad, good, heavily hot, or coolly platonic. It's a game for gamblers who can't help but risk all for the fleeting chance of it. Love, Love, Love.

Back in the olden olden days there was a belief in an entity called Lady Fortune. She was fickle, deciding a person's fate on her whimsically spinning wheel that brought either happy life or dismal existence. Sounds like just another name for love to me.

The power of love, the book of love, young love, sweet love, tough love, free love, lost love, found love, love is blind, love hurts, love stinks, love is all you need. Billions upon billions of words, mega-upon-mega-tons of paper, carvings on trees, writings on stones, countless edifices lost in time. Where did it come from?

Better question: Where is it going?

It's a mystery, this thing we call Love.

Sunlight streaming through the window at WE NAIL YOU! BEAUTY SALON falls on a tight trio: Janice sits sexy in a cushy chair, a rainbow explosion of shiny sleek colors; Cripple Crip perches on a salon chair, his head an afro-explosion of hair bristling up on end because every dread's been unlocked; and Learoy is a whirling explosion of hands moving roughly, as if wanting to tangle Cripple Crip up in pain, as she works to get his hair back into its dreaded splendor of yore.

"So's I told 'em," Cripple Crip expounds, "they best take their wack hairdo artist somewhere else or I'd get all kinds a ugly on them. Now they let me do what I want. That record-label dude, and all his boss mans, they know I'm head man now. And that, my stunning ladies, was all that."

"That ain't all that," scowling Learoy scowls.

"It is very much indeed all that," starry eyed Janice shines.

"Ain't no big thang," Cripple Crip quips.

"Like yo' wang," Learoy cuts.

"Learoy, dang!" Janice snips.

"She just wants to play," Cripple Crip nods.

"And you just be gay," Learoy smirks.

"Learoy, call it a day!" Janice continues quickly, "I love your personality, CC. You possess such self-dignity, and power. I adore dominant men."

"Yeah, girl," Cripple Crip purrs, "you got it straight. Listen, cakes, do me a favor?"

"Anything," Janice certainly means it.

"I don't trust them record geek types with fixin' my doo or picking my threads. Uh-unh," he shakes his head for emphasis. "There's a store on 158th and 143rd that's got this fly shirt---"

"I'll get it for you," Janice responds before he's finished.

"You will?" Cripple Crip flashes his disarming smile. "Girl, you the best. Just mention my name. They know what I want."

"Just like me," Janice spins on a crutch and floats on clouds to the door, loving that CC needs her. Before exiting she looks back and asks, "You'll wait for me to get back before you depart for the mayoral ceremony, won't you?"

"Baby," Cripple Crip glows, "I'll wait fast forever until your resplendent return."

Janice's pale face turns red as she crutch-dances out the door.

Cripple Crip grunts in satisfaction then fastens his eyes on Learoy's face via the mirror's reflection.

"Now that we alone, Learoy---"

"Unh, unh," Learoy yanks his hair hard to avert his gaze, "don't start up, MC Dripple Drip."

"Hey, you wrong about me, baby. I'm not like you think." He shifts to sincerity. "I'm not a hard gangster anymore. I caught the wrong end of a stray bullet, so my peeps sent me away from L.A. to start life over again, here with my auntie in Valley City."

Learoy ferociously works his hair. "So."

"So...so you don't have to be all tough on me," he talks back, firm but not too. "I'm just tryin' to make it in a world where black men rarely succeed. I wanted you to do-up my doo because we the same. We both got talent. I finally got my shot at the big game, but what opportunity you got?"

Learoy stops her fingers in mid-braid on one of his dreads, surprised that he turned the subject from himself to her.

"Learoy," he continues, "you impress me. I never met a girl like you, so if I talk all hard it's 'cause I'm intimidated by your beauty, the beauty you have on the inside. Learoy, you've got the prettiest heart I've ever seen."

Learoy pretends something's in her eye and blinks it out. "You tellin' big ol' lies, MC Thin Spokes. You best go spit that smack at some other bimbo 'cause it ain't working in this house."

"This ain't no game to me," Cripple Crip speaks softly.

Learoy spins him around in the salon chair, piercing him with her eyes. "You stop that talk now, right now! I've heard this before and was tricked by it once, but never again."

"Tricked?" Cripple Crip shows concern. "It wasn't by me, so why you takin' it out on me?"

"No," Learoy looks away into her memories. "It wasn't you. It was this boy, François. Art student scholarship boy from France, livin' large uptown. Found his way downtown here, looking for industrial influences, he said. He got industrious, sure did."

Cripple Crip asks gently, "What happened?"

Caught up in her moment of confession, she continues without thinking. "I was way sprung on him. He said all the right things. Got me right in the heart, and I fell, not all the way, but damn close." She takes a breath, looks him in the eyes, "Bad thing is while he was working on me to give it up, he was already getting busy with Mad Girl. Got busy with her in all kinds of ways."

Cripple Crip understands. "It's his baby, right?"

"Most surely it is," Learoy affirms. "Mad Girl and me were best friends before. I lost my heart and my friend to him. We're getting a little better, but will it ever be the same? I think not."

"I feel you, Learoy," Cripple Crip responds. "But I ain't no François."

"How do I know that?" Learoy asks.

"Because I'm sharin' wit you what my mamma told me just before I left," Cripple Crip says. "She spoke of how my heart was in the right place, and when I found my perfect woman I needed to share my heart thoughts with her, just like I'm doin' here."

"You best not be fooling with me." Learoy looks back into his face, intensely searching his eyes. "That's what my mamma used to say to me, to share my heart thoughts. How'd you know that?"

"I didn't, Learoy," he says. "I had no idea of that. But it shows me maybe we're meant to be."

Learoy looks at him long and hard. He smiles assuredly up at her. Then, like a veil finally being lifted, Learoy suddenly sees the charm everyone else has been unable to resist. Her face reflects her heart crumbling inside, sending the message of surrender that shows in her eyes.

"But, what about Janice?" she asks.

"Janice. Yeah, she's cute and everything, but, you know, I'm only down with sisters." He laughs a little. "My mamma was a Black Panther. She raised me to love, respect, and honor black women."

"You just playing her then. Just like François played me and Mad Girl." Learoy puts her dukes back up. "I knew you were up to no good."

"No, baby, no," Cripple Crip says. "It's not like that. I can't stop her from liking me, can I? What am I supposed to do? Tell her to hate me?"

Learoy considers this. "I'm going to think about what you've said. But just you know, I'm keeping it locked up, way locked up."

"Any chance I can get me the key?" Cripple Crip asks.

"This ain't no hack 5-0 station. This is prison, and the warden's got the only key." Learoy smiles, slightly.

"Maximum security?" Cripple Crip likes the metaphor.

"More like death row. On lockdown." She allows her smile to grow, just a little.

He smiles bigger and gives her a special double wink.

She spins him to face the mirror and starts back in on his hair, with a difference this time. Whereas before her look was stern and her fingers worked fiercely, now her touch is gentle and her hands move with compassionate care as she gazes at him with hesitant interest. It all sounds so logical, but...well... maybe...

How Many Is a Baker's Dozen?

Valley City City Hall: The sun shines sweetly on this beautiful structure; the fresco-covered and portico-filled white dome seems to float along with the puffy white clouds drifting across the pure blue sky.

The sun also shines sweetly on the broad marble steps that sweep out from beneath stately, grooved pillars and cascade down to the perfectly paved and striped street. Buzzing with excited carnival animation, two thousand people cover the stairway, sidewalks, and barricaded thoroughfare. The young and old, the privileged hilltop fringers and butt crackers, the lawyers and hotel workers, doctors and trash collectors, stockbrokers and burger flippers, all mingle and mill. Even Crazy Billy Butt Cracker is here, fully dressed, staring at his broken cell phone, intently waiting for an important call. All attendees, save a few, wear variations of MC Cripple Crip's prison stripes T-shirt from the album's artwork. Those finding themselves lacking the prevalent style quickly snap one up from the numerous vendors hawking their wares. The CD's phat beats solidly thrump the pavement from strategically placed PA woofers, stirring hearts and vibrating soles in the movement of the moment.

People dance and laugh, talk and smile, reach and touch in a real celebration. Everyone anticipatorily hopes to glimpse their idol who, according to the huge banner stretched over the building's giant brass portals, will be receiving the Key To Valley City.

Up under the pillars: "ex"-crack-addict Mayor De La Gente huddles with his posse, which includes his five shark-skin suited, thick necked personal ruffians as well as dapperly dressed hilltop fringe dwellers, such as the ugly, really ugly, black, four-story parking garage builder Mr. Biggs who is sided by his loophole-finding attorney neighbor friend. Also attending is, of course, the ever-present-at-public-events-that-attract-the-press African-American Congresswoman Charlene Rivers.

The honorable "ex"-crack-addict Mayor De La Gente is the spitting image of that actor, the one who was in like three thousand Mexican movies, usually wearing a funny hat and sporting that quirky mustache flanking each side of his upper lip; you know, he was the Mexican Charlie Chaplin whose career spanned like fifty years wherein he made lots of black and white films as well as color, mostly comedies but also what appear to be dramas, maybe; you recognize him as you flash by Spanish stations and watch him for a second before moving on; beloved by millions, not sure if he's dead now or not. Yes! You got it. That guy!

The music quiets as "ex"-crack-addict Mayor De La Gente approaches the podium placed at the top center of the marble steps. Down on the street, right at the base of the grand stairway, boxed by purple velvet rope barriers, taking it all in, Dutch and Bryan squat on the front fender of the ultra-decked-out-jet-black-shiny-as-hell-stretched-and-overly-hyphenated limo. Janice and Learoy stand, popping out of the sunroof, basking in the glow of rubbernecking spectators wondering who they might be. Mad Girl and Moon lie on the trunk, their backs against the rear window, lounging in the sun. Pho patrols the perimeter, giving the hairy eyeball to any who so much as look at the car.

Carlos is noticeably absent.

Janice spruces up while jabbering at Learoy: "Did you see how great he looked in that shirt I delivered? And did you note the way he thanked me in such a heartfelt fashion?"

"Sure," Learoy cedes. "His hair looked pretty good too."

"Oh, yes, Learoy," Janice politely yields, "of course it did. But surely it was not lost on you how he romantically held my gaze when I handed him the shirt, how our fingertips kissed, how he so eloquently called me his 'tighty whitey boney pony.' I just know he verges on being all mine! Wouldn't you agree? I am compelled to express my gratitude, Learoy. Were it not for your assistance with my new look, he wouldn't have given me a second glance."

Hearing this, Pho glowers up at her; she skips her eyes over him to avoid seeing his pain.

Learoy stiffens. Her lips tighten, trapping words she isn't ready to let spring. She gets out a stilted, "You're welcome."

"It's pretty amazing," Bryan addresses Dutch, "how some people turn their lives around."

"Yeah," Dutch nods, "Cripple Crip sure's done it, yo."

"No, I mean that mayor guy," Bryan motions his head upwards. "I saw him scorin' crack last week on 120th and 5th Street. Now look at him!"

Clearing his throat over the microphone, "ex"-crack-addict Mayor De La Gente silences the fading music and the crowd. He begins his practiced oration.

"My name may mean 'from the people,'" his slight Spanish accent lends him an air of authenticity that he loves exploiting, "but really, I come from the streets, which is why I believe we should celebrate the inspirational stories of the ghetto. Black Handi-Rapper MC Cripple Crip reminds us we can change our futures. All we need to do is be ourselves, be true to ourselves, and be honest with everyone around us. Only then can the real, trustworthy person we are deserve the honor of success. The person we pay tribute to today embodies all of those ideals. So, for everything that Black

Handi-Rapper MC Cripple Crip has accomplished, and for what he represents to us all, I hereby give to him The Key to Valley City."

He holds up a gold, radiantly glowing, ornately scripted skeleton key that must be four feet long. He pauses, looks down at the limo, then side to side. Finally, turning to the rear he watches one of his big ruffian doofs shrug his shoulders. He peers down at the limo again. Bryan smiles broadly and gives him a wave.

He covers the mic, whispering to an aid, "Where the hell is this guy? I got other crap to do..." Naturally the PA picks it all up.

Overly loud in the silence, Crazy Billy Butt Cracker helps by making a call, "You can't see the president now. The turtles are naked in the shower! Yes, to Sweden, but my blunderbuss only shoots top hats!"

Out of nowhere the thomp-thomp-thomp-thomping of a police helicopter swooping down from above blasts the area with noise and wind. Hovering over the crowd, an authoritative cop voice using measured tones drones from its loudspeakers: "THIS IS THE POLICE! THROW DOWN YOUR WEAPONS AND PUT YOUR HANDS BEHIND YOUR HEADS! REPEAT: THROW DOWN YOUR WEAPONS AND PUT YOUR HANDS BEHIND YOUR HEADS!"

Putting the key down, "ex"-crack-addict Mayor De La Gente places his hands on the podium and assumes the spread-eagle position, sighing a resigned "Oh man, not again" through the mic and out over the PA. Behind him, in a scattering of dropped snub-nosed revolvers, his five oafish posse ruffians comply with the orders.

A small portion of the crowd scampers away, but most, smarter than their city leaders, look up in expectation.

They are not disappointed.

The chopper's speakers thunder shotgun blasts

followed by machine gun bursts, the recognizable opening melee from the album track entitled *I Shoot Cops 'Cause They's My Bitches!* Fog billows thickly from the bottom of the ghetto bird, whirling wispily in the spinning blades' downdraft. Spinning red lights mounted to the chopper's underside churn the mist red.

Emerging from the glowing miasma on a cable attached to his glossily golden wheelchair, MC Cripple Crip swings downward, poppin' all manner of upper body Hip Hop dance moves: Tuts, Puzzles, Hand Tricks, Waves, really getting into it as he raps.

All y'all ballers see my heat on da street
I'm the new squad, I patrol a new beat
Shot to the top by fighting tooth and claw
And now, baby, hear me rewrite the law
I got style, moves, and riches!
I shoot cops 'cause they's my bitches!

A white flash ignition fires and all four tires on his wheelchair spin, flaring and sparking like Fourth of July firework pinwheels. He finishes bustin' his moves with Hat Tricks, freeing his newly styled, colored and beaded dreads, then Frisbee flings the fly red hat straight at Janice and Learoy in the limo.

The crowd nutties it up. Crazy Billy Butt Cracker snaps pictures with his busted phone, laughing foolishly.

Janice and Learoy both grasp for the fly red hat; Learoy clenches the bill, Janice clasps the back band. There's a struggle, a pull, a snarl, a curse. Surprise grows in each pair of widening eyes when the hat flies from their claws into the crowd. A bug-eyed young boy dressed as a Cripple Crip look-a-like, sans wheelchair, snags it from the air and runs off with it.

Janice and Learoy look daggers at each other, then crossly cross arms in a standoff.

Mad Girl laughs at them, howling like a hysterical hyena. She grabs Moon's hand and gleefully finger-taps her palm, trace-talking to fill her in on the fun. Bryan and Dutch exchange big eyed looks that say, *Oooooooh, did you see that?*

The helicopter lowers Cripple Crip onto the top of the steps just as the wheel fireworks die. With the flick of a lever Cripple Crip releases the cable and rolls smoothly to the podium.

Looking up at the chopper he thanks the completely Caucasian crew with a Black Power fist thrust in the air. Pilot and co-pilot pop him thumbs up while three additional crewmen high five each other and wave down at him. Their looks all say, *Ah, that rapper and his cop shooting songs...ain't he a card?* The chopper twirls away, back into the sky.

Straightening up and running his hands through his hair, "ex"-crack-addict Mayor De La Gente tries playing it off. Behind him his ruffian boys scurry to pick up their handguns and slip them back under their coats. Mr. Biggs looks as if he may have soiled himself; his attorney neighbor friend takes a single sidestep away. A shocked African-American Congresswoman Charlene Rivers quivers and trembles like Tina Turner at the end of her Acid Queen scene in *Tommy*.

"Ah, MC Cripple Crip!" "ex"-crack-addict Mayor De La Gente regains his official voice. "You make a grand entrance, don't you? *Muy especial!*"

"Big playa's got to play big plays when he's playin'," Cripple Crip asserts, his mic already tied into the PA system. "So, Señor Mayor, I'm here to pick up my ki." Lowering his voice he questions, "Shouldn't a transaction of this nature be more on the down low?"

"Why no," "ex"-crack-addict Mayor De La Gente looks puzzled. "We always deliver keys in public so everyone can show their admiration for the recipient."

"Well I s'pose Valley City ways is different," Cripple Crip looks around, "but whenever I've scored a ki in the past we didn't broadcast it. P'raps I should get this deal done quick and roll on outta here."

"Yes, onto that!" "ex"-crack-addict Mayor De La Gente gives his throat another official clearing, then talks in the high speech reserved for such occasions and spoken only occasionally by occasional occasioneers: "Heretofore, notwithstanding, and forthwith: whereas Black Handi-Rapper MC Cripple Crip represents so very much to us all, lifting our souls ever higher for us all, beating the very pulse in the hearts of all, standing for honesty, truth, and justice for all, I hereby proudly, for us all, present you with The Key to Valley City!"

He raises the giant, gold key over his head for all to behold its glory.

Cripple Crip zips on a what-you-tryin'-to-pull face.

Slowly, "ex"-crack-addict Mayor De La Gente lowers the key to him. Every inch closer it gets, Cripple Crip's expression changes incrementally.

Oh, he realizes, it's a "key," not a "ki," like gettin' a prop, not scorin' a deal. Damn, what was I thinkin'? Of course. A key.

Cripple Crip receives the token and brandishes it over his head shouting, "It's a key ballers, a key! Fooled you all too, din't it?"

The crowd cheers him on. Camera flashes reflect brilliantly off the new diamond freshly embedded in his left, gold-clad eyetooth. He waves down at the limo where Janice and Learoy elbow and nudge, each vying to edge out the other while struggling to retain *I'm the one for you, CC!*

smiles.

Janice blows him a kiss. He gives her a wink in return.

Learoy remembers something. She smiles big and blows him a special double kiss.

Cripple Crip smiles even bigger and gives her a special double wink.

When he glances away, Learoy looks pissed at Janice; Janice looks even pisseder at Learoy.

Oh My Gosh, It's This Chapter Already! How Exciting.

"Feel a little better now, Samosa?" Off at The Dark, Carlos tips a metal can and trickles water into the Sunflower's small, dirt-filled pot. "Going dry ain't a good thing. I'll check with Bryan on the scheduling and see who screwed up."

Carlos sets the watering can down then gently toes a broad, green leaf. He looks up at the fading light filtering through the aperture in the ceiling.

"Oh my God," he groans dramatically, "it's getting dark. They'll be coming out soon!"

Slamming his foot to the wheelchair's control stick he whizzes away, slaloming between a bench, a slide, a tree pillar. Taking aim he kicks a tetherball on the way past, a perfect smack that wraps it tightly around its pole.

"We must gets home, precioussss," he rasps while racing to the exit door, "away from all the nasty fakes friendsessessss. Backs to our caveses, yeeessss precioussss."

Nearing the exit he expertly sends the chair into a

broad, sideways slide, ending with his back handles smack up against the dark gray door.

Voice low, he commands an imaginary squad, his bright eyes shifting back and forth: "Croft, you break left. Bourne, angle right flank. Master Chief, watch our backs...what's that? Me?" He smiles wistfully, tilts his head, a far away hero look filling his eyes. "I'm straight up the middle, babe, takin' everything they got and more. You know, the usual."

He pulls back from his reverie. Sharp breath intake; posture steeled erect; Carlos lays his big toe along the side of his nose and ponders a moment.

"On my mark, prepare for bloody, painful, inevitable death. Crisis time starts in three, two, one, now!"

In reverse he bursts through the door with all his might, quick-spinning around to face his enemies, screaming, "We give Hell! We live Hell! We are Hell!"

Across the street, under the thick, leafy tree limb sprouting out over the G.R.A.S.S. wall, the gang stares at him over Cripple Crip's limo, quietly amused at his grand exit from the ugly, really ugly, black, four-story parking garage.

Carlos freezes.

The limo's street side back window glides silently down, and Carlos's favorite person, all smiles and luster, pops his head out in greeting.

"'Sup, fellow wheel-bound rapper? Those's some biggy moves. Thought you was poppin' a cap in my ass fo' sho', you comin' outta there all gangster. Damn."

Cripple Crip turns away to continue the conversation Carlos interrupted, "A'ight, ya'll. I'm off. Thanks for being there today...and for bein' so chill to me and everything. Moonie OG! You plannin' that helicopter drop today was bomb! You best be ready to engineer things live at my benefit concert tomorrow night. We'll talk tomorrow."

Mad Girl trace-talks the message to her. Moon gives a thumbs up with her free hand.

"Don't forget, CC," Janice trills in, "we need to review your entire schedule first thing in the morning! Tour dates, promo shots, charity interviews...all T's dotted and all I's crossed, I always say, with humor of course."

"Straight up, publicity manager girl, you got it." He switches to Learoy, "And Learoy, remember what I said about hair and make-up, you the one. You---the---one."

Learoy eagerly swipes the spotlight from Janice, "No doubt, CC. I'll be in the house."

Cripple Crip looks to Pho and Dutch next, "I know you two know what's up, Mr. Security and Mr. T-Shirt Merchandiser!"

Pho nods. Dutch pops a snakebend arm-move and says, "Word!"

"It's all good in the 'hood then. There's front row seats for all y'all too, so you can catch part of the show while you takin' care of my business." He turns to Carlos and smiles, "You too homey! It's gonna be a show you do not want to miss, no way."

Learoy and Janice, in shrill unison, lean forward and wave, "GOOOOD NIIIIIIGHT CEEEEEEE CEEEEEEEEE!"

They look hard at each other: *You're too much!*

The limo's windows roll up as it moves forward. Suddenly it stops, and a window descends again. Cripple Crip calls out, "Hey, Carlos."

Carlos looks at him, wondering what's coming.

"There are two kinds of people in this world, my friend," the philosopher returns, "those with real playa' moves and those who just play. You play."

The limo shoots away, leaving the gang and Carlos re-evaluating each other through the twilight. They hold a second, then start breaking up.

Carlos rolls across the street. Learoy, Mad Girl, and Dutch move to his left along Truth Avenue, heading towards the Hope Alley Flophouse where they live. Bryan and Moon go to Carlos's right, stepping to the tall G.R.A.S.S. gates. Janice and Pho travel that way too, but they pass the gates, progressing up Pain Street, she crutching her way back to the secret life no one asks her about, he slowly skateboarding to his grandmas' house where they wait to feed him dinner and make sure their gigantic grandbaby has made it through another day unscathed.

Bryan holds the gates open for Carlos before muscling them closed behind him and lowering the medievalish security bar. The wide iron strap is more than ample protection from the outside. The clunk it makes when rammed home sounds like safety.

Bryan trace-talks with Moon as they walk toward the main building, "Let's see what's up for dinner." He turns to Carlos, "You want to sit with us?"

"Naw," he responds, "I'll check it later."

"Okay," Bryan smiles, "See ya. Let's hit it, Moonie!"

Carlos rolls toward the far side of the grounds, heading to the three-story dorm building, weaving along lighted, curving paths bordered by grass and hedges. It's a large landscaped area with gazebos for sitting, open areas for play, and scattered tables with benches. Old growth trees hover over the ancient cool springs that provide the facility with all its water needs.

It's a welcoming park setting---no, more like a secret garden setting made for kids to roam and grow. Sheltered by the giant ten-foot walls, nestled in the twilight's final gloaming, the place is idyllic.

Carlos pauses to take it all in. Relaxing serenity.

With a SHRIEKING battle cry, a lithe, green clad figure leaps into the middle of the path, landing in a ninja crouch.

Carlos yelps and bounces up on his butt, scared totally, completely shitless.

The menace twirls a staff, causing the row of needled spikes strafing one end to whistle through the air. Slowly, the tightly wound form rises into a combat ready pose.

Quicker than quick the perilous person pounces, stopping the razor teeth a bare inch from Carlos's face!

Carlos screams like a little girl.

From under a green pith helmet the figure liberates a thin, tin can burst of "Hee-hee-hee-hee-hee"s. Then, in the heaviest of Chinese accents, he speaks: "Carwos, you no come by get green tea rike I say! You pay now, wif you rife!"

"Dammit Ching!" Carlos exhales, "What you doin' jumping out like that? Give me a heart attack spinning that rake all kung fu at my ass."

"Hee-hee-hee-hee-hee," Janitor Ching titters. "New rake, get today. Stirr shiny. You rike?" Lowering the rake, which suddenly looks much less formidable, he takes a step back and bows low to Carlos.

A mysterious ancient of ancients, Janitor Ching has been at G.R.A.S.S. since time out of mind. No one's quite sure from whence he sprang, or what he did before, or if a before ever even existed for him.

Elusive rumors surround him like smoke circling opaque mirrors, but one fact proves manifestly clear: he possesses infinite wisdom. He can wire a building while quoting Confucius, Mother Teresa, Einstein, or Bob Marley; watch him rebuild a toilet and one learns the Ming Dynasty's views on porcelain and proctology; he'll pinky split a two-by-four while tenderly applying herbs to a skinned knee; and (not meaning to stereotype, but) he's the best gardener in the world. The truth is, if there is anyone keeping G.R.A.S.S.'s facilities up and running and the grounds in perfect order, Janitor Ching's the guy.

He inexplicably appears anywhere at will, but he domiciles deep in the bowels of the main building, in what used to be the creamery's huge, underground refrigeration units that he has converted into living quarters. Down there, under a giant portrait of Chairman Mao---to whom he bears much more than a striking resemblance---he houses his tools, his herbs, his arts, and his secrets. Kept at his fingertips and brought forth whenever needed is anything one requires in a pinch, as the kids have discovered many times over the years.

"Yeah, sure, Ching, I rike your rake," Carlos shrugs his armless shoulders. "But you can't jump a cholo like that, okay?"

"Okay, I no do," he gives Carlos an affected wink, "not before tomorrow, hee-hee-hee-hee-hee."

"What are you doing out here in the dark, anyway? Don't you never stop working?"

"Oh no," Janitor Ching's lined face grows serious, "work never stop. Growing things grow, so arways need Ching. I here now find eating bugs on flowers. Boss Rady's flowers. No good. I kirr, DEAD! In morning, you come down basement, you get speshawl tea. You need."

"Sure, okay, okay. Late." Carlos rolls on.

Janitor Ching calls after him, "And you terr you friend Dutch he no say my name Ching-Chong-Ding-Dong-Ching-Chong-Ding-Dong-Ching-Chong-Ding-Dong behind back! I catch him, I kirr him dead!"

"Yeah, sure, whatever," Carlos replies.

Making the dorm, Carlos chugs up the ramp and goes inside.

Back in the commons, Janitor Ching weaves his way through flowerbeds, whispering to himself in singsong Chinese.

Let's sprint quickly now, leap high, and take a bound over the G.R.A.S.S. wall---and, while vaulting it in the dim light, catch a freeze-frame glimpse of Samosa Son's handprint on the wall's cement cap with the name "Petunia" forever inscribed in his long gone palm---to the sidewalk outside.

Upon landing, Cripple Crip's limo ambles into view, slowly prowling along Truth Avenue. Follow until it brakes and stops at the curb just past Hope Alley. See the lights cut; hear the engine stop. A back door clicks open oh so gently.

Rolling out of the limo in a completely charcoal colored wheelchair, Cripple Crip is got up all in black, and even though it's pretty much dark out now, midnight shades cover his eyes. He pops in a black rubber mouth guard so that when he smiles his normally gold and diamond sparkling teeth reflect no light.

Dude is in stealth mode.

Moving up the alley he scoots from one shadow to the next, ever wary of the slightest noise that might alert him to the happenstance of a passerby.

It's silent rolling.

On the other side of the tall green wall bordering the alley, a light flashes on in a third-story window of the G.R.A.S.S. dormitory.

Cripple Crip halts in a recess and looks up at it.

In his room, Carlos flips his curtains wide then foots open his window for some fresh air. He peers across the alley at the flophouse where Learoy, Mad Girl, and Dutch live.

Turning around he weaves through the tangle of half-made gadgets and electro-crap madness to his ultra-custom DJ Battle Coffin and PA next to the TV Gamer Shrine area. Reaching it he gazes down in reverence, genuflects as if he's in church, and solemnly lifts the smoke-tinted plastic cover back on its hinges. Punching buttons he fires up a solid drum 'n bass beat. Catching hold of the groove he deftly places big toe to turntable and joins in, scratchin' and rappin'.

MC/DJ Carlos lets his art flow. He's good. The sounds and words fill the room and spill from the open window.

Girl, I ain't your mollywopped boy,
When you with me I ain't no toy,
So hear me give you the real talk,
If you dis' me and take that long walk,
I'll keep rollin' on my 4 wheels,
I love you, I do, that's the real deals.

Outside in the alley, Cripple Crip pricks up his ears.

Please girl, don't you go,
I want and I need you to know,
That I'll roll right after you,
I love you, I do...

Drawing pen and small notepad from a coat pocket, Cripple Crip writes down Carlos's song fast as he can.

Girl, you swore we'd never grow apart,
You won me straight from the very start,
So I'll roll my 4-wheeler past the dark part,
Down the cold sidewalk to your warm
hearrrrrrrrr-t.

Cripple Crip finishes writing and resumes his original purpose: sneaking up to the flophouse. Parking under a window whose sash is raised an inch, he pulls out a mini, submarine-style periscope. He extends it upward until it's even with the window.

He looks through the eyepiece and sees: Learoy's

bedroom through the window.

Learoy's there wearing a white T-shirt and super snug hot pink tights. Like these things fit so tight and stretch so thin they're almost invisible, clinging to her calves, hugging her wondrous thighs, caressing that firm, apple-blossom, pumpkin butt that goes on and on for blessed days and days. I mean her backside ain't nationwide or nothin', it just pushes the road to perdition with its load of perfection to just this side of too far.

The Reveal: With her rear to the window she's bent over, stretching, with her head between her knees.

Shoot. I think I just had an accident in my pants.

Cripple Crip almost does too. "Damn!!!" he whispers.

In her room, Learoy muses to herself. "Hmmmm," she murmurs, "it's getting all hot up in here. Maybe I should take off these tights before my next set of butterfly stretches."

She straightens up, putting her hands to the waistband.

Cripple Crip grins. This is just too good. Looking up, he sees a building pipe just above the window. Thinking quick, he stands up in his chair.

Yep, he *STANDS UP* in his chair.

Blast the blaring Plot Twist Klaxon three times. Repeat, Repeat, Repeat: He *STANDS UP* in his chair, like with his legs.

With a spring denoting the speed of a cobra and the reflexes of a bird, he leaps and grabs the pipe. Now at window level, he looks in.

Learoy seems to have changed her mind because her tights are still in place.

Cripple Crip's disappointed, as am I.

But, no, wait, she's changing her mind yet again! Hooking her thumbs into the waistband, she bends forward slightly, her shapely, heavenly, heart-shaped, perfectly formed, outstandingly agile, sexier than all hell rump pointed right at me---I mean pointed right at the window.

She starts pulling the tights down, slowly, sexily, as if it's a movie or something. Oh man, she's wearing a neon red thong that gathers the thin straps at the top into a lacy, ruby red heart!

Cripple Crip pants. I'm feeling faint.

She bends over even farther. This is just really, really, really too good---

"Hey!"---what's this Carlos yelling about somethi---"Hey you!"

A stark, bright FLASH! of light hits Cripple Crip. He turns his head and sees Carlos up in his window holding a camera.

Another harsh FLASH! blasts Cripple Crip and bathes the alley.

Cripple Crip drops and hits the ground. He looks around wildly, decides, then dashes down the alley pulling his wheelchair behind him, performing a decidedly odd rendition of ghost ridin' the whip.

FLASH! FLASH! FLASH! FLASH! Carlos captures it all in strobe light fashion.

Learoy, now in a robe, slings her window open and thrusts her upper body out of it, screaming at Carlos, "You! You skinny assed pervert! You tryin' to take nudey pictures of me! I'm callin' the cops!"

"No," Carlos is ruffled. "No, it was Reggie---I mean Cripp---"

To the right and up a level from Learoy, Mad Girl sticks her head out of her window, "That's right, Learoy, he a biiiggg ol' peeerrrrvy-boy! I seen him lookinnnn' at you, him all touchinnnn' his self and ge'innnn' all hot on it! I seeeennn it all. I did! Carlos is a peeeeper! Carlos is a peeeeper! He's trying to snap me too. Knows I'm doing my Kegel exercises right now, and he's trying to look all up in my wild thang!"

A little to the left and one floor up from Mad Girl, a bare chested Dutch appears at his window, furiously pulling up his pants. "Hey! Carlos!" He's abashed rather than annoyed, "You weren't, you know, taking pictures of my place, were you, yo? Like, if you were I wasn't doin' nothin', yo. Like, I've had this rash, yo, and I was applying the medication ointment to, you know, down there, yo. I gotta rub it on, yo, so like I know it might have looked like something else, but it was not, absolutely not that, yo..."

"Ho'd up ho'd up ho'd up!!!" Learoy thunders. "Carlos: YOU---ARE---A---DEAD---ONE---LEGGED---BEANER---PERVERT!"

She SLAMS! her window shut and disappears inside.

Carlos looks at Mad Girl. Throwing her head back she cackles like a jackal while retreating and slamming her window shut.

Carlos shifts his gaze and locks eyes with a gaping mouthed Dutch. They hold a second. Dutch snaps his mouth closed, drops his eyes guiltily, raises a hand to say something but changes his mind. Slowly, quietly, he slides his window shut and gently twists the security clasp. He meekly draws the curtains together, tucking them in carefully to eliminate any pesky openings.

Carlos looks up and down the alley, dejected once again. Glancing down at his foot, he studies the camera there. Suddenly realizing what he's got, he smiles way big and closes his glassy portal on the night.

Even with the window closed, his maniacal Ho! Ho! Ho! laughter vibrates the metal trashcan lids down in the alley below.

"HIGH DAWN": a Screenplay

FADE IN:

EXTERIOR AERIAL SHOT - VALLEY CITY - DAWN

A rosy, pre-sunrise glow mutes its way through the spiraling fog playfully clinging to the hilltop fringes of Valley City. Down below, the swarming vapor stalks the streets more thickly, the murky buildings becoming dark, lurking figures in the as yet dim morning.

CARLOS'S ROOM - SAME TIME

A small, green shaded desk lamp switches on; a foot snaps a cool digital camera onto a dock station; toes press buttons on a printer then dial a phone; a set of photos slides into a nondescript 8 ½ x 11 brown envelope; the desk lamp switches off; the front door closes and snicks shut.

BRYAN'S ROOM - A SPLIT-SECOND LATER

CLOSEUP: A groping hand kills a buzzing alarm clock and switches on a bare-bulbed lamp atop a red, milk-crate nightstand.

WIDE SHOT: Bryan sits up in bed rubbing his eyes. A threadbare, green and blue Bizz The Space Man comforter covers his lower half. He puts on his awful looking, thick framed eyeglasses and looks around.

BRYAN'S POINT OF VIEW: The room is bare save for several variously sized and colored basketballs scattered about. It's a place where the occupant never tarries or pursues solitary endeavors because life is better when you're out with friends.

WIDE SHOT: Bursting from bed, Bryan hop-skips to the closet, bounds into some clothes, grabs a dark blue basketball, and heads out the door.

DUTCH'S ROOM - A NANO-SECOND LATER

CLOSEUP: An unlit bare light bulb hangs by a frayed wire from the ceiling. Two hands reach up and jiggle the bulb. It sputters to life then glares meanly.

CAMERA PULLS BACK TO REVEAL: Dutch standing on an upside down, five gallon bucket beneath the bulb. He steps down and moves out of camera frame.

His room is a mess of cracked, yellowed walls with a wavy, drooping ceiling. An un-sheeted, dingy mattress decorated with a thin, crumpled blanket huddles on the floor in a corner.

CUT TO: A full-length mirror on a wall surrounded by pictures of iced-out black rappers clipped from magazines. One larger poster stands out: a rapper holds a Grammy in the air. His head has been replaced with a photo of Dutch's face.

Dutch leaps in front of the mirror, imitating the Grammy rapper's pose for the thousandth time, using his afro pick in place of the award.

DUTCH

(to imaginary crowd)

Yo, listen up! Even though I roll with major playa's like MC Cripple Crip and all, I haven't dogged my roots, yo. This one's for all my little peeps out there! Keep dreamin' on the big time, yo, and some day you can be like me, yo!

EXTERIOR - TRUTH AVENUE - SAME TIME

The heavy mist creeps mysteriously over the world.

Wraithlike, Carlos appears, riding down the sidewalk.

Against the morning dampness he's donned a faded green, Eastwood-style gunslinger poncho with zigzag stripes and short-tasseleed edges. On his head rides a battered, dark brown, flat brimmed Stetson hat.

Straight backed and stoic, he trots his wheelchair through the thickly layered fog, dissolving as it wafts closed behind him.

JANICE'S ROOM - A REGULAR-SECOND LATER

CLOSEUP: A lit, ornate, glittering crystal chandelier hanging from a fleur-de-lis patterned, copper-plated ceiling.

START 360-DEGREE SLOW PAN OF ROOM FROM CHANDELIER'S POINT OF VIEW: The pristine room reeks of stuffy old money. We see: plush drapes; a pink canopied princess bed with silk covers; a 15th Century Italian tapestry; a master bathroom with a huge, glassed-in shower/bathtub/Jacuzzi combo and gold-plated fixtures; a walk-in closet with clothing filling its corridors; posh dressers, overstuffed chairs and pillowed couches; a brick and tile fireplace twisted up like Picasso stopped by to build it; classic and modern paintings adorning walls; vases and sculptures commanding shelves and small tables.

END 360-DEGREE SLOW PAN, PUSH CAMERA IN ON: Janice, sitting before a large, ebony vanity, staring at herself in the oversized, round mirror.

She turns. Scanning the room, her melancholic expression communicates her feeling that nothing here connects to her real life. This perfect dream cage contains not a single hint of her true friends, yet it begs her to never leave.

A crisp professional knock sounds from the other side of her paneled, doublewide doors.

BUTLER'S VOICE
(off screen)
Breakfast is served, Miss Janice. By the by, your parents send you their warmest regards from Tuscany.

PHO'S ROOM - A MINUTE LATER

CLOSEUP: A lit, round, rice paper lamp hangs from a white cord.

QUICK PAN ACROSS THE WALLS: Pho's graffiti images cover every wall. Tags, throw ups, lettering, pieces, characters; it's a mishmash exhibit of his extraordinary artisanship that shows he's a master of various styles. Even this chaotic practice work is colorful, well executed, and complex. Spray cans, stencils, tips, brushes, and his private design/writing binders all rally in corners of the room like soldiers ready for action.

PAN UP TO CEILING: Up there the orderly pieces are different. A large smiling portrait of Janice dominates the center with smaller satellite likenesses of her orbiting it. Each was obviously created with love and care.

WIDE SHOT: Pho lies face up on his futon holding Cripple Crip's CD case while staring at the ceiling. Rising, he flicks the CD case across the room, grabs his skateboard, and exits.

EXTERIOR - 5th STREET aka SKID ROW - SAME TIME

Perched just over the sidewalk, the flashing green neon cross of the Jesus Saves Mission eerily colors the fog. Its intermittent electrical buzz is the only sound for blocks.

Emerging from the fog, Carlos passes under the cross. It stops flashing and goes dead. Reining in his mount, Carlos eyeballs it. The darkened cross hangs threateningly over him. A silent, eternal moment envelops him with the ghostly fog.

A black cat SCREECHES on a nearby window ledge, arches its back, hisses, then springs in front of him and runs off into the mist.

Raising his foot, Carlos makes the Horned Toed Claw sign to ward away bad luck.

Buzz-sputtering back to life, the cross resumes its flashing.

Carlos exhales and rides on, once again vanishing into the foggy murk.

LEAROY'S ROOM - A MOMENT LATER

It's black as pitch. Nothing is visible.

A noise: Learoy snores loudly. Suddenly, her breathing catches. There is a silent pause---

---interrupted by one, short, beefy FART.

The snoring kicks back in.

MAD GIRL'S ROOM - TWO MOMENTS LATER

CLOSEUP: A lit, clip-on shop light hangs onto the handle of a purple boom box. A thin, strong finger presses a button. The concerto "La primavera (Spring)" from Vivaldi's *The Four*

Seasons plays brightly.

MAD GIRL
(off camera)
Time to wake up baby!

START SLOW PULL BACK: With spotlight and boom box remaining in foreground, begin the slow reveal of a large, gray and black graffiti piece on the wall that the spotlight is set up to illuminate.

MAD GIRL
(off camera)
This is Vi-val-di. He ain't much my style, but you'll like him. And Mozart, and that Beethoven guy.

CONTINUE SLOW PULL BACK: Reveal Mad Girl stretched out on the floor cuddling her big belly with her hands, her head turned toward the image on the wall, which is still unclear to us.

MAD GIRL
You'll go to that Catholic elementary school uptown, then onto Valley Grace Prep on the Westside. After that, college. Harvard, or Oxford, or one of those ard-ord places.

CONTINUE SLOW PULL BACK: Mad Girl sits up with her back to us, facing the image so it frames her. We cannot see the whole wall yet, but the image is beginning to look like some sort of X-ray.

MAD GIRL
And you will always, always, always know that you are loved, loved, loved.

WIDE SHOT: Mad Girl remains in foreground framed

by the image, which we now see is a beautiful, graffitied sonogram of her baby that she created to cover the entire wall. The baby is on its side, turned towards her, staring out. The baby's expression is wisely secure in the knowledge of Mad Girl's love.

MOON'S ROOM - A FEW MOMENTS LATER

A ceiling light, a floor lamp, a table lamp, and a shelf lamp, all of which are unlit.

Faint light tries squeezing past the closed curtains. Moon sits up in bed, frazzled. Like the last time we were here, her sheets are askew, and her short green hair is tangled.

Once again she's had her "Lesbian Nightmare" where she cheers for the girl to pull her top up. Moon's confused expression asks, *Am I gay?*

Curious, she reaches up with both hands and touches her own breasts. She shrugs. Hmff. No big deal.

EXTERIOR - DRY GULCH ROAD COMMUTER TRAIN STATION - A TAD LATER

HIGH/WIDE CRANE SHOT: The fog shrouded Dry Gulch Road Commuter Train Station platform sits a few steps above street level. It's long, narrow, old fashioned looking, clock-topped with an awning and benches under it and the tracks beyond. A dozen sleepy, blue-collar type commuters on their way to work sit on the benches awaiting the six a.m. train's arrival.

PUSH IN: We weave through the mist until discovering a lone, swarthy featured, dark bearded, sombrero-wearing man sitting on the right side of the station steps. He cradles an acoustic guitar, its case opened at his feet to receive donations.

The sun, at last, peeks through the mist, landing a warm beam on this figure. He tips his sombrero back, closes his eyes, scratches his bristly black beard, basks a moment, then strums his guitar to sound a crisp, honest major chord.

CUT TO: The sidewalk vanishing into the fog. As if breaking through from a parallel universe, Carlos's trail-worn, poncho and hat-covered form plods solidly into view, stopping when he catches sight of the train station.

CUT TO: Sombrero Guitar Man strikes a second practice chord, this one in a fuzzy, devious minor key that assaults the air.

CUT TO: The opposite sidewalk vanishing point. Through the thinning swirl of mist, Cripple Crip appears astride his golden wheelchair mount, skittishly stopping short to do his own reconnoitering.

Cripple Crip's duds are straight off the dude-ranch rack: The brim of a white leather Fedora slants down to cover his face; a long-tasseled white leather jacket is zipped up tight; white leather chaps drape over white snakeskin cowboy boots. It's really just a bit much even for him.

WIDE SHOT: Carlos and Cripple Crip size each other up across the hazy void.

Cripple Crip shifts in his chair, coiling like a rattler.

Carlos sits stolid as a rock, moving nary a muscle.

The clock atop the station awning ticks to six o'clock high. It begins pealing out loud, well spaced BONGS. Off in the distance, the train's whistle wails. On the platform the waiting passengers stir.

CLOSEUP: Sombrero Guitar Man's hands start expertly picking and tapping out a Flamenco-flavored number. The music fills the area.

PULL BACK FROM THE HANDS: We see Carlos and Cripple Crip start their slow, steady, showdown walk.

The fog dissipates more quickly now. The sunlight intensifies. The train's whistle yowls again, much closer. The clock BONGS for the third time.

Carlos and Cripple Crip continue their gunslinger stroll.

The clock's second hand sweeps past the number six. It BONGS again.

CLOSEUP: Sombrero Guitar Man's bearded face. His eyes remain closed. He grimaces in artistic rhapsody as he ratchets up the music's intensity.

WIDE SHOT: Carlos and Cripple Crip reach their respective ends of the subway station platform. Separated by twenty feet now, they halt and sight in on possible weaknesses.

From the station platform, a bandana-wearing older female passenger eyes Carlos and Cripple Crip. She nudges the custodial-type, middle aged male beside her. Looking frightened, they steal away behind a closed ticket kiosk, peeking out from behind it to watch the action.

The other passengers also notice the wheelchair duo squaring off, and they all take action. Some hide under benches; others dodge behind pillars; a man dives in back of a trashcan. One by one, like prairie dogs popping out of holes, they peer out from their hiding places.

CLOSEUP: Carlos's face. He narrows his eyes while his tight lips rise at the corners to form a self-assured, semi-smirk.

CLOSEUP: Cripple Crip's face. A nervous tremor betrays his bravado smile.

WIDE SHOT: Carlos surges ahead strongly. Cripple Crip dawdles forward in little jerking movements.

The clock gives a final BONG. Sombrero Guitar Man plays on.

Reaching the center front of the station platform, Carlos and Cripple Crip stop. Six feet of cold, hardpan sidewalk separates them. On the platform, hiding, peeking, and quivering, the passengers await the outcome.

Sombrero Guitar Man, lost in his own universe, begins a rapid succession of pluck-tapping mixed with wild strumming and chaotic runs up and down the guitar's neck. He creates a marvelous golpe, picado, and rasguedo fusion for his huge, melodramatic, out of this world musical climax.

SERIES OF EXTREME CLOSEUPS:
Carlos's witheringly wise, world-weary eyes.
Cripple Crip's guilefully gleaming, guilt-gilded eyes.
Carlos's mouth breaking into a toothy smile.
Cripple Crip's mouth dropping open in shock.
Carlos's eyes again, this time in a victorious, mirthful squint.
Cripple Crip's eyes again, this time wide in fright.
Carlos's foot reaching for the bottom of his poncho.
Cripple Crip's left temple: a single trickle of sweat slides down past his ear.

SNAP CUT TO: Sombrero Guitar Man slapping his hands down onto his strings, instantly stopping the music.

Carlos. With a flourish he whips the front of his poncho up over his left shoulder. At his right hip he's packing the nondescript 8 ½ x 11 brown envelope.

Cripple Crip. He nervously unzips his leather coat and opens it wide.

Stone-faced Carlos stares down Cripple Crip's blustering facade.

Beyond them the train rumbles into the station with its whistle bawling.

Sombrero Guitar Man opens his eyes, taking in the two chairslingers for the first time. With a huge grin he sits back, tugging at his beard, settling in to enjoy whatever the showdown may bring.

CARLOS

There are two kinds of people in this world, my friend. Those with loaded cameras and those who run. You run. It's time to stand and make your play, son.

Cripple Crip plunges his hand to his inside coat pocket.

Quicker than lightning, Carlos swipes his foot to the envelope at his hip and draws, pointing it at Cripple Crip.

Cripple Crip's hand remains inside his coat. Too slow. He stills all movement.

CRIPPLE CRIP

Looks like you done got the drop on me, Slim.

Cripple Crip glances down at the hand in his coat, looks back at Carlos with an expression that begs permission. Carlos nods assent. Cripple

Crip slowly draws his "iron" and holds it out butt first for surrender. It's a very fat roll of hundred dollar bills.

Carlos hawks and spits at the ground.

CARLOS
I won't cotton to your money. You plum rustled my life. I reckon I want it back.

CRIPPLE CRIP
Your life? I'm living the life you never had nor never will fetch, lil' buckaroo. This fistful of dollars here is just a gift, a favor I'm doing you. But there's a time limit on it.

CARLOS
Yup, but the timepiece is a tickin' for you, REGGIE, not for me.

With a fancy twirl, Carlos holsters the envelope back at his hip. Reaching in he draws forth a photo and holds it up between his toes.

CLOSEUP: The 8 x 10 photo is grainy and dark, but it does contain the vague form of a wheelchair sitting in an alley.

CRIPPLE CRIP
(sniggering)
Not much there, High Plains Drifter.

Carlos remains unfazed. He holds up a second 8 x 10 photo.

CLOSEUP: This one is clearer and shows Cripple Crip hanging from the pipe outside of Learoy's window.

CRIPPLE CRIP
That's a fiddle faddle nothin'. I tain't even took to my feet, Josey Wales.

CARLOS
I'll wager the little lady will hanker to know what you were doing outside her window.

Cripple Crip laughs.

CRIPPLE CRIP
That floozy slommack trug ho' slut don't mean diddly to me. Go ahead and show her, Pale Rider.

Carlos fights back his anger at Cripple Crip's words about his woman. Taking out the third, fourth, and fifth photos, he fans them between his toes.

CLOSEUP: One photo is of Learoy's rear end as seen through her window. Another is of Cripple Crip's upper body with no implication he could be standing. The last is a vague, blurry form in the alley, but nothing in it can be made out.

CRIPPLE CRIP
Looks like your aim was a might off, Bronco Billy. But I'll give you fifty bucks for the one of Learoy's derrière.

CARLOS
Knew you'd say that, but that dog won't hunt. You've got the wrong pig by the tail: these five shots mightn't a turned out, but you don't know how many I blasted last night. In the envelope could be one more that the newsy paper boys'd just love to print in

today's late edition. That'd put you in an awful bad box, reckon so?

Cripple Crip halts his gloating.

At the platform, the train's whistle shrieks its departure signal. The passengers file onboard, ignoring the boys now that they know there will be no gunplay.

Holding all five photos in his foot like a poker hand, Carlos plays his ace in the hole.

CARLOS

I know what you're thinking - Did he take six shots or only five? Well, to tell you the truth, in all this excitement, I've kinda lost track myself. But, being as I used an Olympidak Straight Shot 44 MagnumPlus, the most powerful camera in the world and could blow your fake persona clean off that wheelchair, you've got to ask yourself one question: Do I feel lucky?

Carlos pauses for that single, slow, stupendous beat.

CARLOS

Well do ya, punk?

A loud, booming, Middle Eastern voice shatters the moment.

MIDDLE EASTERN VOICE

(off screen)

Oh, yes-yes-yes, very nice. Well, are you of the lucky feeling, you hairy-dirty punk? Very nice, very-very nice.

Swarthy featured, black bristle-bearded, Sombrero Guitar Man steps up next to Carlos and Cripple Crip. I reckon he wasn't Mexican after all.

SOMBRERO GUITAR MAN
(beaming down at them)
A thousand pardons my friends! Watching and listening have I stood by so far, but take the mounting tension any longer I cannot. Intervene I must. In my beloved homeland of Persia we have a saying for this situation, drawn from the ancient teachings of Abu Ali al-Hasan himself. Thus, 'When two dance along the sharp edge of Occam's Razor, one must be prepared for the cut.' Yes-yes-yes, that is it, very-very nice, wouldn't you agree?

Carlos and Cripple Crip stare up at him with a complete absence of comprehension.

SOMBRERO GUITAR MAN
Oh yes, I see. Put another way, 'When two caravans gain the desert oasis at the same time, one group will still only have dust for drink.'

In lost unison, Carlos and Cripple Crip shake their heads.

Sombrero Guitar Man leans forward and speaks softly and slowly so they understand.

SOMBRERO GUITAR MAN
As my beloved mother used to say, 'One of you has the other's camel by the balls.'

The boys look to each other for understanding.

Carlos cocks an eyebrow. Cripple Crip shrugs in response.

CRIPPLE CRIP
What's he talkin' 'bout?

CARLOS
I don't know. My mother's dead.

The train's whistle screams its all clear, final, final departure signal. A train worker actually steps onto the platform and yells---

TRAIN WORKER
All 'board!

Distracted, Carlos looks over at the commotion. Cripple Crip seizes the opportunity and launches his chair forward. He snags the pictures from Carlos's foot with one hand while snatching the envelope with the other. Without stopping, his quick hands skedaddle-roll him up a wheelchair ramp towards the train.

CRIPPLE CRIP
Ho'd up the train! Ho'd up the train!

Carlos gallop-rolls after him.

As Cripple Crip nears the train, he shoves the photos and envelope under his legs and whips out a railway pass, flashing it at the train worker who waves him in. Cripple Crip bumps through the doors just as they begin sliding closed! The train worker steps in behind him.

Trailing behind, Carlos reaches the train. The doors whisk shut in his face.

CARLOS
Wait! Wait! Hold the train for me too!

TRAIN WORKER
(mouthing the words through the window)
WHERE---IS---YOUR---TRAIN---PASS?

Carlos puts his foot up to the window in utter futility.

CARLOS
I...I don't have one...

The train thunders and jerks forward, the windows sliding by before Carlos's big toe. He locks eyes with Cripple Crip, who smiles big and waves the pictures and envelope at him. The train departs the station. Left alone on the platform, Carlos's hat gets blown from his head by the locomotive's back draft.

Walking up behind him, Sombrero Guitar Man gently places the hat back on Carlos's head.

SOMBRERO GUITAR MAN
(comforting him)
You played the game very, very well, but who knows who will pay the price in the end. Only time will tell.

Gathering his composure, Carlos sits up tall in his saddle, spurs his chair around, and grandly rides away from the showdown at Dry Gulch Road Commuter Train Station.

FADE TO BLACK

A Murder of Patchwork

Unraveling the last of the fraying, misty wisps, the sun peeks down to spy Bryan bouncing his dark blue basketball off the Hope Alley Flophouse steps.

Stopping, Bryan draws a breath in through his nose and grimaces at the smell. "Foggy mornings smell like piss," he says. Quick-dribbling the ball between his legs, he cheers, "Yahoo! Kobe Bryan be in da how-wouse!"

Dutch pops out of the flophouse front door, morning spry and bouncy fresh, carrying a cardboard box under his left arm while plastering his cell phone to his right ear. That funky white boy's spittin' game for somebody on the line.

"Yo, tha's right, baby. That's me. PIMP: Paper In My Pocket. Word up, yo." Then he flies low and slick, "So how's s'bout it? I got an extra ticket. Center, front row." Pause, then defensive, "No no no. See, it ain't like that!" Pause, then, "No, not like that neither! Shanicileena, baby, Cripple Crip's my man, baby, he's got my back." Pause, listening intently.

"Hey, Dutch," Bryan tries breaking in, "you seen Learoy?"

Putting the box down next to the steps, Dutch gives Bryan a slit-eyed look while dashing a shush-up finger to his lips. "Baby, baby, baby, no, that wasn't my fault that time, yo." Pause. "Oh. Your mamma's sick. Again? In the hospital? A'ight, a'ight. Maybe next time. Late. Yo." He hits end, then hits a speed dial button.

Bryan asks again, "So have you seen her?"

"Yo, Bryan, can't you see when a man's busy puttin' his women in line?" Dutch returns the phone to his ear, gets his playa' voice back on, "Yo, Jazmirella, girl, what up?" Then comes a shocked look and, "Yo yo yo, don't hang up! Really, girl, that was not my fault that time!" He holds the phone away and a voice, way beyond enraged, crackles loudly from the earpiece. "Jazmirella, Jazmirella, Jazmirella," he calls out, "that fake I.D. was pristine. PRISTINE. I don't know why the cops took it from you." The screaming voice quiets. The phone goes back to his ear, "Jazmirella?" He whips it away as another aural assault assails him.

To Bryan he says, "Now that was a dirty trick." Looking down at the phone, he cops an attitude, "Okay, okay, okay, I hear you. Look, yo, I'll call you back once you calm yo' ass down, yo. You stick by the phone and wait till I get back at you."

The earsplitting screaming kicks up a notch before ending abruptly. She hangs up.

Dutch quizzes the phone, "Jazmirella?" Nothing. He shrugs at Bryan. "Dropped call. Reception here sucks, yo. She wants me, I know it."

Bryan peers at Dutch through his awful looking, thick framed eyeglasses. "She does? But you're such a loser!"

"Playa' hata'." Dutch hits another speed dial button. "Yo, Yo, Yo. Celestiniqua! Girl, wuzzup wich you, yo?" He strolls off up the alley.

Hearing footsteps, Bryan turns to the door smiling, hoping for Learoy.

Mad Girl pops out carrying several plastic shopping bags full of trash.

At the sight of her the joy runs from Bryan's face.

Mad Girl sees his reaction and frowns. "Well good morning to you too, Bryan."

"Hi Mad Girl," he tries brightening up. "Have you seen Learoy?"

His question only makes it worse. "No," Mad Girl raises her voice and looks up at Learoy's window above them, "I ain't seen Miss Balloonie Boobies yet today. I'm not her secretary." She tromps to the trashcans several feet to the left of the flophouse steps.

"Boy, Mad Girl," Bryan fires back, "it's just a question. I wanna see if she wants to shoot hoops with me. Friday mornings that's our thing."

Mad Girl pounds the trash bags into a can. "In case you forgot, me, you, and Dutch are practicing Lamaze this morning."

"Oh, yeah," Bryan looks down, embarrassed.

Dutch returns from his short promenade up the alley, phone still at his ear. He's accompanied by a spiky haired, baggy clothed, Hispanic looking teenage boy whose most outstanding feature is his sparkly purple, high-top cross trainers, complete with spotless barcode tags dangling from eyelets.

"Okay, okay, Delondarae," Dutch says into the phone, "but I got to say again, yo, that was so not my fault! Really! And I'm sorry to hear about your cat being sick, yo. Maybe we can go out another time---hello? Hello?" He looks at his companion. "Man, another dropped call! I'm tellin' ya Rudy, this alley sucks for reception, fo' sho'."

"Whatever, Dutch," Rudy rolls his eyes, "just show me the stuff already."

"Got it, yo, right here." Dutch hunches down, opens the cardboard box, and pulls out the merchandise.

It's a SportsMeUp shoebox. From it he draws forth an awesomely fly shoe whose satin red finish twinkles in the morning sun.

"Original packaging, original paper, check it out." Dutch is the super salesman, "Not even laced up yet, yo."

Rudy takes the shoe and inspects it, "You screw me again, Dutch, I'll get you."

Dutch is all hurt innocence, "Rudy, Rudy, now that's

cold, *compadre*. I told you, that was not my fault that time! Those HoopDog High-Pump Air-Traction Actions were pristine. PRISTINE! Not my fault one faded out."

"Faded? Dutch, they were different colors out of the box, asshole," Rudy slices back.

"I swear, Rudy, I swear, on my mother's grave," Dutch crosses his heart, "in the box they were identical, yo, IDENTICAL!"

"Here," Rudy jams a wad of bills into Dutch's outstretched hand, grabs the shoebox from the other, "take this and spare me the woo wop, YO." He walks back up the alley.

"Pleasure doing business with you again, *amigo*," Dutch says. "Tell your *tio* I said *hola*."

"Up yours, Dutch," Rudy says without looking back.

Mad Girl stomps up and gets in Dutch's face. "Yeah," she says, "up yours, Dutch! What you doin' out here hustlin' when you supposed to be ready to practice Lamaze wit me and Bryan?"

"Lamaze? Yo. I am too busy for that. I gotta hustle up some Benjamins and find me a woman for tonight's concert, yo." He checks the time on his phone. "And I got to hurry. I'm meetin' up with CC in an hour. He's gonna sign a bunch of shirts for me to sell later, yo."

A new voice spins all three of them around: "You're meeting up with CC?" It's Learoy in the flophouse doorway. She's stone-cold hot in Greek sandals strapped up her calves, a stretchy black leather mini-skirt, and a fire engine red belly shirt that she must have been born in because there's no way she yanked that painted-on thing down over her spectacularly sumptuous torso.

"Yep," Dutch is sure, "that's right. That's what I said, yo."

"That's just funny," Learoy says, "'cause he's meeting

me in an hour at the salon to do-up his hair."

"Well, yo," Dutch reasons, "I guess he forgot he made plans with you, yo."

"You think he's meetin' up with stupid, ugly ol', white bread you, and passin' up on," Learoy flourishes her hands from head to toe, "this beautiful black gift of femininity?"

"Yep," Dutch says it again, "that's what I said, yo."

Learoy barks laughter at his idiocy.

"Learoy," Bryan steps up to her holding out his ball, "did you see my new ball? I brought it over to show you."

"Quiet now, Bryan," Learoy's sharp, "I'm tryin' to make a point to Dutch-for-brains over here."

"But Learoy," Bryan's hurt, "we haven't shot hoops together for a long ti---"

"Just shut up, Bryan!" Way sharp this time.

He turns away.

"Hey," Mad Girl says, "don't talk to him like that, bitch!"

"Don't you tell me how to talk, skank!" Learoy shoots back.

They lean in. Words roil beneath the surface as blazing eyes dare the other to say the worst, each of them aching to annihilate the enemy over old business. Perhaps now is the time to finally have it out.

The sound of running footsteps breaks the silence along with a howl, a yell, and what can only be the hollow THUMP! of someone being slammed up against a wall.

Learoy, Mad Girl, and Bryan whip their heads around.

Dutch is being held by the throat up against the flophouse by a large-ish sort of young-ish black guy. He wears a doo-rag on his head, dark blue Dickies work pants, black work boots, and a thin, dark blue shop coat. His huge hands sprout from enormous wrists.

"Dutch," his voice is low and menacing, "you

nutmegged my ass. I'm gone cut you."

Dutch struggles to get his voice out. "Whoa, whoa, wait up, wait up, yo." His face turns red. "Ice Tray, my man, my main man, how you doing, yo?"

"Don't start with me, Dutch," Ice Tray is cold, "don't even."

"Man, Ice Tray, really, you gotta believe me, that was totally not my fault last time," Dutch fights to get the words out. "Not my fault at all, man. I thought the stuff was pristine. PRISTINE! But you know how it is, yo. Jello stepped on it after Tran, who stepped on it after Boxer and Sammy. It was definitely, totally, one hundred percent NOT my fault!" He drags in a long, slow breath. "Besides, I can make it up to you. Just let me breathe, gangsta, let me breathe."

Ice Tray loosens his grip. "Now you talkin' like a man who knows what needs sayin'. Say on."

"Listen, Ice Tray," Dutch talks low, "I got something right here."

"What?" Interested just enough, Ice Tray releases him. "You got the Chronic? Some Dank?"

"Better than that," Dutch kneels down to open his box.

Ice Tray jams a hand into his coat pocket and points it at him. "Slow," he says.

"Ice Tray!" Dutch is shocked. "Stop that. I ain't packin'. Homey don't play dat. But, what I am packin' is this." Dutch opens the box and draws forth a small, brown paper bag and shakes it. There's something in there. "Behold," he continues, "the new stuff: Shepherdess Herb, Ska Pastora, the one, the only, Lady Salvia. Totally bomb, and still totally legal."

Ice Tray rolls his eyes. "Dutch, that ain't new and it ain't nothin'. But, if that's all you got," Ice Tray snaps up the bag, "then I'll take it." He walks off up the alley.

"Okay, all right, yo," Dutch calls after him. "You can

settle up with me next time. Better yet, no charge this time. That's right, no charge, my brotha'! And hey, give a big shout out to that beautiful wife of yours."

"Up yours, Dutch," Ice Tray says without looking back.

Dutch's phone rings. He takes it out of his pocket, looks at the caller ID, then answers: "Yo yo YO yo yo Mei-Ling! What's shakin' girl! No no no no, now that, seriously, I mean SERIOUSLY was NOT my fault that time..." he turns away and walks up the alley, continuing the call.

"Messin' with folks like Ice Tray," Learoy mutters, "That retard's gonna get us all killed some time."

"Learoy," Bryan says, "Dutch might be slow, but he's not retarded. You shouldn't call people names like that."

"That's right," Mad Girl jumps in. "You're all the time callin' people names, even before they get borned! Like that talk you talked about my baby comin' out all messed up!"

Learoy gives Bryan a look, then Mad Girl. "I say what I say," she folds her arms dramatically, "*when* I want, *about* what I want. Especially when it's true. Now, I am leaving here because I got to go open the shop for CC, because *HE* is coming to see *ME*!"

"Is that so?" A new voice spins this trio to the street side of the alley. It's Janice, newly arrived. She's got herself all made up: her hair stands gelled six inches high, spilling back down into glittering, sparkle-beaded braids; the hot yellow dress clinging to her body matches her lipstick, eyeliner, and rouge as well as the spike heels below; her crutches are cleverly veiled in red tassels. She's an awesome sight.

"That's odd, Learoy," Janice goes on, "because truth to tell is that he, even now, makes his way to meet yours truly. Namely, me. By the way, those sandals are exquisite."

"Hi, Janice!" Bryan smiles at her.

"Good morning, Bryan," Janice returns the smile.

"Now, Learoy, what is your confusion about CC's agenda this morning?"

"Confusion's on you," Learoy comes back. "I'm square here, no doubt. I'm meetin' up with him at the salon at eleven to do-up his hair."

"But, Learoy," Janice says calmly, "he is 'meetin' up' here with me at eleven to go 'do-up' autographs at the MDDO Pre-Concert Event."

"What?" Dutch returns, phone in hand. "Can't be, yo. He's signing shirts for me at eleven so I can sell 'em later. Both you girls are wrong, yo."

Mad Girl shouts, "Dutch! You're comin' with me to practice! Why can't you get that straight?!"

"Learoy," Bryan tries again, "since Cripple Crip is going with Janice, will you come play basketball with me?"

"Bryan, I said already," Learoy lectures, "I don't have time for that today, and yes, CC is coming to see me."

"Anyway, Bryan," Mad Girl scolds, "you're coming with me and Dutch!"

"Learoy," Janice says, "you really must give up this delusion that CC is coming to see you. It's just not in the cards."

"It be in my cards," Learoy quips.

"Well, there's some missing from your deck," Janice smiles.

"I'll deck you, you don't quit that tone with me," Learoy scowls.

"Hey," a deep voice that can only belong to the gigantic Pho sounds. "No cat fights, ladies, you both just look too nice." With Moon lightly riding on his shoulders, Pho sidles up on his board, smiling at Janice.

"Pho," not wanting any complications, Janice is arctic, "I do not need your assistance at present, thank you. I can handle Learoy."

Learoy scoffs, "You gonna need to handle stitches too!"

"Learoy," Janice says, "your worn out threats grow tiresome. It's time for you to either, as they say, put up or shut up."

It's silent as Janice and Learoy stare each other down. Building now for days, their confrontation threatens to pour out in front of everyone.

Pho reaches up and lowers Moon to the ground in front of him. "Okay, who's gonna fill us in on the happenings here?"

Mad Girl rushes over, eager to stir the pot. Grabbing Moon's hand she trace-talks, tapping fingers to palm at a mile a minute. "Bryan's waitin' here for Learoy, sweet as he can be, then Learoy treats him like dogmeat---"

"Hey!" Learoy shouts.

"---while Dutch gets busy screwin' everybody under the sun---"

"Hey!" Dutch shouts.

"---then Miss Priss shows up talkin' her smack---"

"Just you hold on a minute!" Janice shouts.

"---and all I want is to do my Lamaze so my poor baby has half a chance to make something of itself in this world. But these haters hate my baby and want me to fail so they're abusin' me!" Mad Girl wells up, on the verge of tears, but the malicious glint in her eyes shows it's an act.

Pho sees it clearly. "Mad Girl," he says, "stop fillin' Moon's head with your stories."

Dropping Moon's hand Mad Girl closes on Pho. "I don't care how big you are, I can bring you doooowwwwwnnnn, Pho Bowl!"

Learoy gets to Moon and grabs her hand to trace-talk her side of things. "Moonie, don't pay no attention to Mad Girl. 411 is Mad Girl's all kinds of jealous of me 'cause

Cripple Crip digs me---"

"SO!" Janice erupts. "The truth is out! You are trying to steal my boyfriend!" She crutches over and grabs Moon's other hand. "Moon! Learoy is lying and she is attempting to steal CC from me! I had him first!"

Moon tries following both conversations coming at her from each hand.

"Janice," Pho says over Mad Girl's head, "CC is not trying to get up with you. He's just using you to---"

Janice drops Moon's hand and joins Mad Girl in front of Pho. "You wouldn't know shit about it, Pho!" Janice cusses, taking her anger out on an easy target. "Stop trying to control my life! Fuck, I feel like you're stalking me or something! Get over your obsession! I don't care about you anymore! Just drop dead, okay? We're through!"

Something clicks within Pho. "Fuck you, Janice." He says it so coldly it's weird. "I'm your friend, not your stalker."

Learoy still has Moon's hand, keeping her up to date. "Yep, Janice, Pho is right! CC don't want your flat chested, skinny ass! He wants a real woman," Learoy thrusts out her breasts, "like me!"

Mad Girl attacks Learoy. "You are not all that, Miss Lame-a-roy, not all that at all."

"You just pissed, Mad Slut," Learoy's ready to go the extra mile to hurt whoever gets in her way, "'cause CC is one man you know you can't steal from me. Not with that big old baby belly you got going. Cripple Crip is not François, Mad Pig, and you will not get him from me!"

"Well at least I got a baby to love!" Mad Girl shouts back. "But I'll say this: You and Cripple Crip's baby will come out all screwed up and just be another loser in a wheelchair! He'll get all up in your business, and I hope you have MC Lea-Cripple Crip to deal with!"

Carlos's voice makes them all turn. "Mad Girl," he

says, still in his hat and poncho, "you want someone born disabled, to hurt her? And Learoy," he looks up at her, puzzled, "you're hookin' up with Cripple Crip? Already?"

"That ain't none of your business, Spoke Man." Learoy drops Moon's hand, leaving Janice to take over with the trace-talking, "An' you got nothin' to say to me until you give me those pictures you were taking of me last night, pervert!"

"Check it, Learoy," based on his day so far, Carlos has nothing left to lose, "the world doesn't revolve around you. I wasn't taking pictures of you, you ugly mud duck."

"Mad Girl, I must agree with Carlos," Janice says scornfully, "how dare you insult someone for being physically challenged! Especially a brave person such as Cripple Crip who has overcome so much to climb to such great heights!"

"Janice," Carlos says, "stuff it, okay? I am so sick of your always talking like you're so high and mighty! Tell you what, you stick up for your crutch crowd. I'll handle the wheel-people."

"Yeah, Janice," Mad Girl jeers, "listen to Chair Boy here and stuff it."

"You too, Mad Girl," Carlos says to her. "Shut up. FOR ONCE, JUST SHUT UP!"

"Hey," Mad Girl says, "you want to throw down? Right now, Tenderfoot! We'll go toe to toe, just me and you, Car-loser!"

"Nobody's fightin' nobody," Pho grunts, "not while I'm here."

During the jumble they've ended up in a fuming circle. Angry faces vie to get their jabs in; everyone wants to win no matter what it takes or what winning even means. Anything can happen.

Learoy challenges Pho, "Mind your own business, Pho! I'll fight whoever I wanna fight!"

"This is my business!" Pho is loud. "And Learoy, if just

for once you'd shut that never ending smack hole of yours maybe someone else could talk sense into your fat head!"

"You tell her, Pho," Janice says.

"Janice," Pho looks at her again, "I already said fuck you, and I still mean it. I don't need your help."

Janice's face turns evil. "I never loved you!"

"Good," Pho returns, "and CC doesn't want a diseased twig like you."

That rocks her; Janice's face goes blank.

"You tell her, Pho!" Learoy burns to cause pain. "Janice, you'll be dead before you ever get a new man---we all know that!"

Recognizing she just stepped over the invisible line, everyone but Learoy winces.

Janice looks at her. "Damn you, Learoy." Single tears streak down each cheek. She flings her own dagger. "Okay, sure, I'll be dead, Learoy, and away from you. Oh, hey, just like your mom, right? Didn't she kill herself so she wouldn't have to deal with your meaningless life?"

Even with the bright sunlight streaming down, the alley suddenly turns dangerously cold, frozen, still. They've gone way past Taboo Land; the group knows it should stop, but it doesn't.

Mad Girl wants more, "Yeah, Learoy, she blew her brains out because of you! Isn't that what the suicide note she left said?"

Learoy looks straight at Mad Girl with red, glowing eyes. "Mad Girl, I hope your baby comes out a stupid retard like Bryan and Dutch, a useless cripple like Carlos, an ugly monster like Pho, and then dies a slow, sick death like Janice is going to! Then YOU will know what pain really is."

They bleed on all sides now, but no one steps in to staunch the flow.

Mad Girl's eyes bulge wildly, her face beats beet red,

her whole body trembles in rage. The battle batteries charge, powering up for the full blown Mad Girl Tempest.

It's really creepy.

With bottom lip quivering she vindictively grinds out her words, "That's fine, Learoy. I'd rather have my baby dead than be screwed up like any of you here." Knowing she shouldn't, she strikes a final blow, unable to stop the words, "You know what François told me while we were doin' it, Learoy? He said you called him your Frenchy Franny, and we just laughed at that behind your back." Learoy's stricken look confirms the nickname, and her old wound deepens. "He never dug you one bit. He said you a cold, lonely girl who wou-int ever find no one. Ever."

Carlos can't believe what's been said. At a loss, he addresses Learoy, "Bryan's stupid and I'm useless? Learoy, why are you even our friend then? And can't you see that what you're doing to Janice is what Mad Girl did to you?" He decides something about her. "You're a total hypocrite. You should just go to Hell." Then he looks at Mad Girl. "If you're not going to love your kid no matter what, I don't know what to say. Ain't that what your dad did to you, just left you?"

Learoy lashes out, craving to get the last word because somehow that means she wins, "So somebody finally said somethin' that gets under Mr. Steely Carlos's skin, huh?" Her voice is choked, tight, injured, "The tough Mexican *hombre*! The Lone Wolf! Mr. Big Sky Dreamer! What's the problem? Is it too hard knowin' we see you stuck in that chair even though your imagination tells you you're not?"

Carlos looks at her with glassy bitterness. "I see what you see. I know I'm in a chair. But hearing your *friend* put you down about it still hurts."

Bryan throws his ball at the trashcans as hard as he can. The clatter echoes the frustration playing across his anguish-filled face.

"Hey!!!" He yells. Bryan doesn't meet anyone's eyes, he just looks off to his right. "You're all hating each other and fighting. It's just stooopid. You're all being so dumb!" He can't hold back the tears as he chokes and sobs. "I hate this! I mean, like, I'm the dumb one. *I'm* retarded! *WHAT'S YOUR EXCUSE*?"

Bryan lowers his head and runs off down the alley.

Mad Girl pops her mouth open to say something, stops, puts a palm to her eye to squelch the water gathering there.

Learoy stares at her own feet. She stifles a sob by taking in a shallow breath and holding it.

Her body trembling, Janice adjusts her stance on her crutches.

Pho twists a wheel on his skateboard.

With tears dripping freely from his chin, Carlos stares after Bryan.

Her face a show of confused emotions, Moon steps into the middle of the circle, absorbing the tension filling the air. Moving slowly forward she reaches out to place her fingertips on Carlos's forehead. Sliding downward, she finds his tears, following them until her palm cups his chin and catches the rain. Sadly, she raises her wet hand and cradles it to her heart.

Silence binds them, until Dutch's phone rings.

Everyone looks at him, annoyed by the interruption.

Before answering Dutch pauses. Looking at them all in turn he says, "Wait, yo, this is not, seriously, totally, pristinely, NOT my fault."

He spins away and walks off, talking quietly into his phone.

Learoy makes the next move. "I've got an appointment."

A few steps behind her, Janice says, "Me too."

Mad Girl grabs Moon and drags her away. "C'mon Moon. I'll get you up to speed," puckering her face at Pho, "the way I want too!"

Carlos and Pho give the lonely moment time to pass.

Carlos speaks quietly, regretfully, "You got anything to add?"

Pho squats, picks up the blue basketball that rolled to his feet, bounces it.

Finally he answers. "Let's go find Bryan."

Love & Rubbish

On Bryan's trail up Hope Alley, Pho slow-glides his board next to Carlos. He gives him the once over. "John Wayne, right?"

Carlos sighs. "No. It ain't John Wayne."

Pho chuckles. "Didjya' shoot any Injuns?"

"Jesus, Pho," Carlos rolls his eyes. "Shoot 'Injuns'! You talk smack that way you get popped for being racist. You have to say it right, fool."

"How?" Pho asks.

"What?!" Carlos shrieks. "Don't say 'How' about them! That's not the way they spoke. That's racist talk too!"

"No, Carlos," Pho says, "I was asking *how* do you say it the right way."

"Oh," Carlos eyes him with suspicion. "Native Americans, that's how."

"Okay, Mr. ACIOU," Pho says, "thanks for the diversity lesson. Whassup? Why are you got up like that?"

"Long story," he answers. "Clint Eastwood."

"What?" Pho's puzzled.

"The outfit. It's not John Wayne," Carlos says, "It's Clint Eastwood."

"How?" Pho asks.

"Don't start up with me again, Pho!"

Pho laughs at him. "Eazy Weezy! I mean *how* is it Clint Eastwood and not John Wayne?"

Reaching the Hope Alley T, they hang a right up Stink Alley, which runs along the backside of the G.R.A.S.S. lot. Stink Alley's not the real name, just the one it earned because it is lined with big, boxy dumpsters belonging to the ghetto projects on the side of the alley opposite G.R.A.S.S. There must be fifty filthy dumpsters crammed all the way up Stink Alley to where it ends at Pain Street. Seems like they are always full too, hence the stench.

Yet even as the boys round that corner, one can stop and spot, if one so chooses, a single gracefully lined, old fashioned, cylindrical trashcan resting at this end of the ugly dumpsters. Further, if one looks closely, that perceptive person's peering peepers will just make out the worn, scripted lettering on the container's attractively curved side: *Hamilton Truth Rubbish Haulers*. Although Hamilton Truth Rubbish Haulers went defunct decades ago, this svelte, 50-gallon, oil-drum type receptacle remains at attention, its single handle out, saluting the alley and ready for duty, Brother. A relic it is, from an era long bygone.

Carlos and Pho stop a moment, scanning up and down for Bryan.

Pho shakes his head. "I can't take it no longer."

"Hey," Carlos says, "we only just started looking for him."

"Not Bryan. Janice. She's making herself into a cheap ho' for this guy." He frowns. "Like, we broke up and she can date and all, but he's gonna hurt her."

"Of course he's gonna hurt her. You know he's really eyein' Learoy. Maybe he's already got her." The harsh words from moments before still sting. "I hate her right now, but she's MY girl...I mean, I been working it, you know?"

"I know, I know," Pho shakes his head. "But he's a famous rapper---"

"Homes," Carlos shakes his head, "I keep telling you he's not. Okay, yes---*now* he's a famous rapper. But he stole it. He doesn't deserve it. It's gotta end."

"How long you going to go on about that?" Pho's tired of hearing about it.

And Carlos is tired of hearing that sort of question. Something's got to be done, but what? He looks inward.

Sharp breath intake; posture steeled erect; Carlos lays his big toe along the side of his nose and ponders a moment. It's decision time in 3, 2, 1, now.

"Listen up," he says, "I got a plan, but I need your help. If it works, it'll prove I'm right and it'll get rid of Cripple Crip. You down?"

Pho shows no hesitation, "Cool whip. I'm down. What's the plan?" He and Carlos continue on up Stink Alley.

It's an interesting story how the Hamilton Truth Rubbish Haulers trashcans became single handled after starting out as standard, dual handled cans.

You see, there once lived a goodly man named Hamilton Truth. He collected the rubbish along Avenue E, which ran the full length of Valley City, end to end. For years and years he held the city rubbish contract for that single, long boulevard, and the work supplied him with as much as he needed or wanted.

His slogan read "*Truth* Rubbish *refuse*-s to let your trash *lie*---around!" That got a literary guffaw every time.

Back in the day there existed a rubbish hauling guild, aptly named the Rubbish Hauling Guild of Valley City, created by independent waste haulers who contracted with the municipality. Hundreds of these guild members worked together, carving up the city's districts and streets in a manner equitable for all. These astute refuse collectors shared a spirit of comradeship, treating each other like family, like Brothers, without greed or competitiveness. In their deep wisdom they knew the work was plentiful, and that it would always be there.

As they often said, with a smile, "Where you see people, there you see trash!"

These were fine, wholesome days of honorable sanitation work. The Brothers took pride in their careers, treating their customers well while building honest reputations handed down through generations. This era also boasted customers who knew their collection men by name, customers who taped envelopes to cans come Christmas time with a little something in them for Gus and Jeremy, or that nice Hal; customers unafraid to tell a co-worker around the water cooler that, "Heck, my rubbish hauler's a swell, standup fella."

Come a Friday eve with the last load dumped and the dusky horizon streaking the sun's lower half, the debris transporters could be seen pulling up to Big Raul's Tavern. There they gathered to fellowship, sing songs, tell whoppers, shake hands and slap backs, all the while shouting toasts to the health of all. Outside, huddling on the street, their battered, trustworthy, plywood-sided trucks rested after the long week, whispering their own ancient tales of yore.

Symbiotic and harmonious, living as a stout Brotherhood of trash carter professionals, times were good and all was right with the world.

Pho's shocked voice interrupts, rudely, from twenty yards or so away: "*That's* your plan? You gonna spring *that* at the concert tonight?"

"Shhhhhh!" Carlos looks around. He emits a super loud, hoarse whisper, "Don't let anybody hear you!"

"Dude, you're wack." They go on the move again, hopefully to some place far away.

There once was an evil man named Alexis Pain, a big city sanitation slicker from "Up North." He had cobbled his garbage empire together by invading cities to undercut local competition and drive them out of business. Each time his filthy blitzkrieg ended, he'd hire the starving collectors back for scrap pay. He derived great pleasure from this, calling it his Brother Buster Plan.

Like litter in the wind, he eventually blew into Valley City. Slithering into City Hall, he bought expensive lunches and gifts for the council members and the mayor, "ex"-alcoholic Mayor Howie White. Snaking their attention, he disparaged the backwardness of small potato trashmen driving dirty, beat up, plywood-sided trucks that smelled. Why have that when, for just a little bit more money, his shiny bright trash trucks would do a better job and streamline the city controller's bill paying process.

Plus, he said with a devilish wink, Pain Sanitation would fork over certain "benefits" to the esteemed city leaders that the old school trash boys could not.

In another wink, shiny bright Pain Sanitation trash trucks magically appeared overnight. Then shiny bright Pain Sanitation trashcans cloned their way into driveways, side-yards, and alleys all over Valley City, replacing the charismatic mishmash of independent hauler receptacles.

Bryan's blue basketball rolls up and bounces off the single handled Hamilton Truth Rubbish Haulers container. Pho swooshes up on his board and grabs the ball. Must have gotten away from him just as he was conveniently disposed of further up the alley. Alas.

He calls back to Carlos, "But Cripple Crip will be on

stage in front of thousands of fans. How you gonna make him do that?" He cocks an eyebrow. "You can really make him do that? How? How?"

"Shush yourself and get back over here," Carlos is up the alley forty yards, obviously wanting Pho to keep quiet about whatever trivial nonsense they keep discussing. Pho bounces the basketball and takes off toward him. Thank God.

Alexis Pain did as he'd done elsewhere: with a wink and a nod here, a lick and a promise there, the garbage contracts came his way. He broke the Rubbish Hauling Guild of Valley City, fragmenting that once stout Brotherhood, forcing them from their plywood-sided trucks of honor into the trucks of Pain.

They had no choice. They needed to make a living, and, as the story so often turns out, they had no where else to go.

Friday nights at Big Raul's Tavern grew somber. The once self-reliant, professional collectors became sullen trashmen in bondage. Instead of proudly pulling up in their own trustworthy vehicles, now they walked there, heavily, after parking the shiny bright Pain Sanitation trucks back at the yard. Their battered, plywood-sided trucks disappeared, disintegrating into parts, collapsing into scrap metal, each to its own demise, nevermore to be seen whispering together at the curb outside the tavern. Singing and hoisting a few as Brothers-in-arms turned into drowning their sorrows as sheepish prisoners of Pain.

The passing of an era wasted away in the wink of a goatish eye.

Finally, the only freeman rubbish hauler left was Hamilton Truth, and only because his cousin, a city council member, wouldn't completely cower to Pain. Sure, Hamilton's Avenue E route got whittled down on either end, leaving him with only a thirty block run through the center of Valley City.

And yes, he struggled, always just a day ahead of being broke. Still, he made it somehow, holding his chin high and retaining the glint in his eye.

Things should have ended there. Winning all but one of the city's refuse hauling contracts should have quenched Alexis Pain's fiery thirst. But no. He, like all hungry vultures, wanted it all. Not even a single small route could be ignored and left out of his wicked realm, and Truth became an excruciating thorn in Pain's side. Consequently, in the abysmal certitude of his appalling turpitude, he devised a plan so devious, so deceptive, so incredibly heartless, it gained its own name.

The Handle War of '57.

It's a funny thing about trashcan handles. Generally speaking, trashcans come factory equipped with two handles attached to their exteriors, near the top, placed at opposite sides of their 360-degree circumferences. Oddly enough, during most types of debris container manipulation one handle becomes superfluous because people tend to not use the grips conjointly. In fact, 98.6% of the time, scrap receptacle controllers utilize only a single grasp when dragging containers to preferred locations. As far as being emptied, waste can voiders also use a single handle in their hoisting method, ignoring the second appendage completely. Measured at a rate of 96.1% frequency, people will seize a single hold, lift the smaller can to the larger receptacle's edge, then move the free hand to the trashcan's bottom, raising that beyond horizontal to empty the undesirable contents.

So why two handles to begin with, one might ask?

It is due, of course, to the laws of chance. Upon approaching a trashcan in search of optimal grasp locations, the possession of two handles creates a fifty-fifty probability that one grip point will present within easy reach. This saves the person time because he or she need not rotate the container to find a handle prior to initiating litter carrier movement.

To the layperson, the time conservation appears minuscule. To the refuse professional, however, readily graspable handles that eliminate vessel rotation save hours in a day, days in a month, months in a year, and years over a lifetime.

By way of evidence, the time analysis study entitled "Refuse Receptacle Handle Positioning: Maintaining Significant Sanitation Sanity," conducted by Geoffrey K. Klyde, PhD, of the University of California at Los Angeles, proves the point well. In double-blind field study observations conducted April 16th through June 21st of 1952, Professor Klyde's investigation proved that, on a per diem basis, refuse sanitation technicians gained a cumulative average of 4 minutes 36 seconds (+/- 5 seconds) each day when trash receptacle handles were configured in positive graspable positions.[1]

It's an old saying in the rubbish biz when one sets the can down: "Handles Out! Brother is Stout!"

"Bryan!" Pho calls.

"Bryan!" Carlos yells.

---

[1]Cylindrical trash receptacles were of like length and girth, while weight to height ratios were strictly enforced for the duration of the study. Time readings were based on atypical ten-hour shifts with rubbish technicians collecting 869 cylindrical receptacles (+/- 20) per shift. The study did not account for handles positioned at greater than 86-degree angles from curbside placement. Data gathering was postponed during three consecutive days of steamy, dripping wet weather running from May 3rd through May 6th due to "slick handles" conditions skrewing [sic] timed data. Throughout the observations only hard discharges were counted using the following steps: Refuse Technicians were required to: a. maintain tight, positive handle stamina; b. attain total lift erection of cylindrical receptacles; c. consummate trash insertion by marrying the cylindrical receptacles' smaller openings with the larger boxes' lips, climaxing in the rubbish contents ejaculating from the cylindrical receptacles into said larger boxes (without dribbles). False grabs and empty receptacle tips, also known as "shooting blanks," were deemed impotent and aborted from the study.

Dammit.

They are way up at the end of Stink Alley now, far, far away where it meets Pain Street. Can almost not even hear them anymore.

"Bryan!" Carlos yells again. "I need your help with something!!! Where are you?!!"

So, you might ask, why the Hellation does this ancient Hamilton Truth Rubbish Haulers trashcan in the alley here sport only one handle? Excellent question; I salute your superior ability to remain focused.

As you may recall, Alexis Pain generated The Handle War of '57 because he wanted, nay, craved, the last remaining rubbish contract in Valley City that wasn't his. Now, Valley City sanitation contractual language at that time clearly stated, in Article 7, lines 55-64, that rubbish haulers must duly, and with utmost expediency, collect refuse on assigned routes on their scheduled days. Failure to do so would result in rescission of their contract and "permanent suspension of said contractor's services including, but not limited to, disbarment from the Rubbish Hauling Guild of Valley City."

In other words, pick up the garbage on time or you'll trash your job.

Alexis Pain decided the best way to steal the Avenue E route was to create a situation where Hamilton Truth breached his contract. To achieve this goal, he sent forth his decrepit minions into the night. No, these were not stout Valley City Brothers by any means. These were outsiders, depraved and twisted "Big City" trashmen. Yes, they'd once been honorable refuse runners, but years of servitude to Alexis Pain's will had changed them, transformed them, mutated them into traitorous wretches whose souls were no longer their own.

As they stole about, slinking here and there covered

by cowardly darkness, they ground handles off of Hamilton Truth Rubbish Haulers trashcans.

Not both handles, mind, just one. Dreadfully dishonorable and most dastardly! Particularly despicable because once the one handle plunked metallically to the ground, they then broke the ultimate Brotherhood Sanitation Code:

They *purposely* turned each can so the remaining handle was *AWAY* from the street!!!!

A different old saying resounds throughout the rubbish biz for this transgression: "Handles In! Brother Has Sinned!"

It was a sin against sanitation.

When Hamilton Truth set out that next morning before daybreak, as was his usual wont, he reached for his first handle and his fingertips met only air in the darkness. Fumbling around for a handle to grasp, he harrumphed to himself, certainly puzzled when he found the remaining handle *firmly wedged up against a wall.*

He considered this odd because, since he was the only person running his route, he knew he always left his handles out. It was the Brothers' way, after all.

He shrugged, figuring that the outboard handle had simply fallen off. Chalk it up to a defective weld. One in a million. No big deal.

No big deal until he went for the next can, and the next, and the next, each time finding the same situation: missing handle, remaining handle turned away from reach.

Most assuredly, "Handles In! Brother Has Sinned!" ran through his mind a thousand times that day.

Searching for handles, rotating cans, then carefully placing them "Handles Out! Brother is Stout!" for the next run became onerous torture. By his second hour on that first day of madness he was already seven hours behind schedule.

It slowly became the longest day of his career. Out until midnight, he stopped only when his exhausted eyes batted closed for good. He fell asleep in his truck, knowing he'd hit the road within a few hours in order to catch up on what he'd been unable to complete.

It was foul play for sure. The whole situation stank of it. Pain, it must be Pain! All that night Truth tossed and turned, his mind filled with Pain.

A single thought gave him slight solace: he'd made sure all his cans were "Handles Out!" when he left them. At the very least this meant he would not spend precious time rotating them again.

But Pain stayed ahead of him on that one. That same night, when the streets and alleys cleared, Pain's evildoers slunk out, rotating the cans so that once again they stood "Handles In!"

Those demon brothers sinned and sinned good, over and over, night after night, but Hamilton Truth was the one cast into Hell.

That was The Handle War of '57, when Truth, alone, fought against an army of Pain.

His hair went gray; he aged ten years in a month. Not just from working eighteen-hour days and still failing to keep up on his route, but from the sheer heartbreak of knowing, as he crawled out of bed in the cold, lonely, dark mornings, what awaited him. Every day he lived and breathed the betrayal and the horror that never ended, his head full of Pain, Pain, Pain. Sisyphus himself wept.

When the malevolent one saw that Truth would not give up, that Truth persevered, that Truth would continue fighting until the end, he launched his final assault.

Calling a midnight cabal of the city council, without Hamilton Truth's council member cousin, Pain tempted, lured, and seduced them into changing the name of Avenue

E. He was so bent on this change that he'd seen to getting the new street signs manufactured and had crews standing by to install them. Selling their souls once more, the council members approved the new name.

With another of his Luciferian winks, Pain made it happen overnight.

When Hamilton Truth went to work that next black morning, he had no reason to think he no longer ran rubbish on Avenue E. Not until he pulled up to the intersection at 12th Street, the only other road that ran the full length of Valley City, for his mid-route break did he notice the switch.

The junction at Avenue E and 12th Street, right smack dab in the middle of Valley City, was his favorite place in the whole universe. Two reasons existed for this:

1. The spot put him halfway through his route.
2. On one corner rested a place called G.R.A.S.S.

One hot July day long before, Hamilton Truth's rubbish truck overheated here. He cursed up a storm burning his fingers on his steaming radiator cap. On the other side of the tall, wooden G.R.A.S.S. gates someone heard the commotion and stuck her head out to investigate. Under the archway, seeing the odd man jumping around with his hands clasped between his legs screaming F this and F that, she laughed her head off.

That bright, lilting sound caressed his ears and calmed his heart. Looking over at her he couldn't help but laugh himself.

So, in laughter, Hamilton Truth locked eyes with Petunia Son on a hot July day in the middle of Valley City. That was all that it took.

She provided a bucket of water for the truck and a fresh, cool glass of G.R.A.S.S. spring water for him. They didn't say much to each other. They didn't have to.

That started an every day affair.

Theirs became a love spun round blissfully unfulfilled desire, a love spoken only from their eyes that said yes, you and me, togetherness will reign, just wait, wait until things settle down, until there's a not so busy day, a day when I'll ask you to come talk a spell somewhere.

A Someday.

Until then, this moment each day, with he outside the gates on the sidewalk and she framed by the entranceway, sufficed. They exchanged the cool glass of water, his glass, the one she kept on a special shelf in her room, the one she reached out and touched when moonlight webbed through her window. Then came the long, slow drink, his quiet thank you spurring her silent blush, the glint in his eyes waltzing her blossoming smile, the goodbye leaving each reassured their time would come.

Someday.

But this day, as Petunia opened the tall gates to replenish her fading hero, Hamilton struggled from his truck, urging himself to put a spring in his tired step and re-spark the glint to his dead eyes. Like one thousand times before, their fingers brushed electrically around the glass. In that moment, as always, Hamilton knew he would make it through another day if only because Petunia would be there.

Raising the glass to his lips, tilting his head back, he viewed the new street sign above his head.

That was when he saw that he now ran rubbish on *Pain Street*. The realization chiseled a final flake of freedom from his tender, aching heart.

Alexis Pain was a devious, impish fiend, a scavenger who well knew the habits of failing quarry. He appeared at that moment, having waited around the corner for Hamilton Truth's truck to stop, happy to view his victim's suffering.

Hamilton looked from the Pain Street sign into his Petunia's loving eyes. Those deep pools were stricken with grief for him and all he'd been through. From her he looked at Pain standing mere feet away, his smug eyes glowing with mirth.

"Pain," Hamilton Truth said, "I'm still here, ya bastard!"

Hamilton Truth took a step toward Alexis Pain, his face the color of blood red murder.

"So Bryan," Carlos says, "You know what to do at the concert tonight, right?"

Oh crap, they're back.

"Well," Bryan looks wary, a bit confused, "sure. But do I have to? Won't Learoy be kind of embarrassed?"

Pho answers to explain, and I hope he makes it quick, "It's hard to understand, but it's really for her own good. You'll see."

"But won't she be mad at me?" Bryan asks, and sure, he's got a point, but I really wish he'd just agree and get on with his life.

"I won't con you, bro," Carlos says, but maybe this would go faster if he did, "she's gonna be pissed. But she'll get it later. I know she will."

"Um...I don't know..." Bryan is still unsure and somebody better close this deal so we can get back to the story. Suddenly he glances around and says, "Hey! Where's my basketball?"

Oh Christ. I mean really. What the fuck.

Pho searches a second, then slaps his head. "We left if back where we found you. Here, let's get it."

Excellent! By all means, go! And take the wonder wheelchair boy with you, please.

Bryan scampers back up Stink Alley, Pho and Carlos hot on his heels, with Carlos yelling, "Bryan, you're gonna do it, right?" Cool.

Hamilton Truth took his step toward Alexis Pain but

stopped short as if he'd run into an invisible wall. He grabbed his chest with his free hand, letting loose a groan straight from his soul that shuddered the sidewalk beneath Petunia's feet.

She leapt toward him, a single, "Hamilton!" piercing her tight lips.

Somehow Hamilton turned to face her, his mouth working to speak, yearning to say the words he now wished he'd spoken sooner. But nothing came out.

They looked into each other's eyes. The special glass slipped from his hand.

For an eternity it fell; in slow motion it shattered, splintering both their hearts and all their unspoken plans into a million shards frosted across the indifferent cement.

Hamilton plunged to the sidewalk as well, already gone before he hit the ground.

Petunia knelt beside him, cradling his hands to her breast. She attempted to revive him, called for help, got someone to phone an ambulance, all to no avail. Then she cried and cried on that lonely sidewalk just outside the G.R.A.S.S. gates, knowing her one and only true love would never stop to drink of her waters again. Never.

Alexis Pain wasted no time in wriggling down to City Hall to snap up the now deceased Hamilton Truth's contract on Pain Street, nee Avenue E. He no longer needed to wait for the default occurrence. The death was the default. Gleefully dancing a whirling dervish he whistled a jaunty tune all the way back to his office.

The complaint calls started that afternoon. It happened almost immediately; you could even say in a wink.

The Pain Street trash stood uncollected, piling up quick as quick. Alexis Pain took the phone calls himself, swearing to the customers it wouldn't happen again or he'd know why.

The next morning he bleated orders to his workers. The formerly proud Valley City Brothers turned slavish trashmen stood silent by their shiny bright trucks. Pain now controlled the rubbish routes in all of Valley City, including the newly expanded Pain Street route, so you losers better get to grubbing it up.

Pain hissed.

The men flinched.

The trucks pulled away.

The complaint calls started again within the hour. The Pain Street trash remained uncollected, even though all other Valley City routes looked spic and span, spiccer and spanner than ever, as a matter of fact.

Odd thing was that not only were the Pain Street cans not emptied, the trash appeared to be piling up at thrice the rate. It overflowed into the streets, the driveways, the alleyways, the spillways, the gutterways. The residents grew confused at the mess and confounded by the smell.

Said Mrs. Calhone to a puzzled Pain on the phone, "I don't quite get it. Your shiny bright trucks are here every minute. But the trash is increasing, I'd say, like they're bringing it here instead of taking it away. What the heck is up with this?"

Indeed, Alexis Pain thought to himself, what the heck is up with this?

The next call hailed from downtown. On the horn a particularly anxious city council member shouted about the disaster on Pain Street and what the heck was up with this? Oh, by the way, numb nuts, what are all your trash trucks doing parked in front of City Hall?

Alexis Pain winged from his office to find the downtown streets blocked by shiny bright Pain Sanitation trucks. He also saw his trashmen at City Hall. Hundreds of them covered the broad, white, marble steps, from the stately grooved pillars down to the perfectly paved and striped street.

But lo, verily the sight said to all that these beings were no longer mere trashmen. For here loomed the powerful Refuse Brothers of old, their spirits shining bright after long days spent in shadow.

These men stood tall and proud together, clasping hands over their heads, chanting, "Hamilton Truth! Brother in Truth! Brother was Stout, His Handles Ever Out!" over and over and over again.

Alexis Pain hoofed it to the top of the steps to stand under the pillars with the very irate council members and the extremely irate "ex"-alcoholic Mayor Howie White.

Suddenly, the Brothers went silent. From amongst their numbers one stepped forward. A venerable old collector was he, an artisan who'd provided yeoman service through the years, a true Brother whose reputation remained unsmirched by rumor or recrimination.

"My name is Tomlinson Hamp," stated his loud, firm voice. "We Brothers collect in this place for action, and unload our request to you we will. By the handle, you'll not dump our claim and throw us away, or not a lid full of refuse will be collected in Valley City. Not a lid full!"

The council members shuddered. Alexis Pain looked frightened. The "ex"-alcoholic Mayor Howie White spoke up.

"All the world's a landfill, oh Brothers, and this one now be yorn," he said, showing respect by speaking in their own lofty tongue. "Toss your claim away we won't! We only hope the weight of the can be not too mighty to lift."

Brother Hamp cleared his throat and began: "12th Street is the only other road, besides that damned Pain Street, that runs the full length of Valley City, end to end. And where 12th Street crosses over Pain Street, our Brother Hamilton Truth liked that place best."

There he heaved a sigh and swayed until two strong Brothers lay rock steady hands upon him. More than one tear fell at the mention of Hamilton Truth's name again.

Collecting himself, Brother Hamp continued, "Mark us well: We demand 12th Street be renamed Truth Avenue in honor of Hamilton Truth! And until it is, not a lid full of litter will be hauled anywhere within the city limits. Mark us well on this."

The Brothers broke forth in hubbubs of approval that voiced righteous indignation.

Thoughtfully, "ex"-alcoholic Mayor Howie White answered, "Yes, goodly Brothers of The Handles, it shall be as you like it. But why do you pile on such a request? Why not change Pain Street to Truth Avenue in reclamation of your own?"

"Because," Tomlinson Hamp said, his voice rough as a gravel pit, "Pain runs all through Valley City, there's no denying it. Deep is that wound; never shall it heal. Such is life. But face Pain we can, long as we match it with Truth, for only then the throb can lessen." Here his voice reached a new timbre, and clear it rang, resounding all across the valley, "Rename the street so we never forget: Truth always crosses Pain, and that's what keeps our hearts clear of all the rubbish thrown at us by life!"

Then did the Brothers cheer long and hard in triumphant victory, and from those cheers came blessed relief, and from that relief laughter sprang forth, the healing laughter caused by witnessing the truth held within the pain.

The council members capitulated. 12th Street became Truth Avenue. Caught short on the can, what else could they do?

The refuse collection restarted. The people were relieved.

As they had in the before days, the Brothers again

held their heads high and met with honor at Big Raul's Tavern. The example of Hamilton Truth had breathed their lives back into their lives.

Then the Brothers revolted, took over Pain Sanitation, and became independent once again! And that devil Alexis Pain was never seen in Valley City again!!!

Well, no, not really. They kept the low paying jobs with him while Pain stayed gloriously rich and remained a total bastard. But he was a dick and everybody knew it, and the shunning was so harsh he hid in embarrassment! Actually, no, that didn't seem to bother him much. So, okay, the bad guys don't always get theirs. But that's not really what this story is about.

Not *this* story, at least.

And so this lone, round trashcan standing before us in Stink Alley, this Hamilton Truth Rubbish Haulers drum, its single handle proudly Out, stands as a testament to one man's valor in a cold world searching for its soul. In this beautifully rusted can, surrounded by large, ugly, boxy dumpsters, honor is found and honor is bound.

And if one puts a careful ear up to it, just at the rim, perhaps one will hear the long gone ring, the yesteryear shout that voiced the pride of an honest Brother staking his claim in the world: "Handle's Out! Brother is Stout!" In these immortal words one is truly inspired to live life to its fullest.

Carpe Handelum! Seize the Handle!

"Okay, okay, okay," Bryan says, basketball cradled to his side, "I'll do it, I'll do it!"

He blows by, followed by Pho and Carlos. They round the corner in the alley and keep going.

"Wooo hooo!" Carlos is amped up. "Tonight, Cripple Crip, watch out! We comin' to get ya!"

Oh yes, them. Thank goodness they worked all that out on their own.

EPIC-SKETCH

THE CROSSHAIRS

The sweetly shining sun halts at its zenith above the buzzingly bowlish Valley City.

Dropping a plumb line gaze straight down from up here reveals the crosshairs formed by Truth Avenue meeting Pain Street in the city's exact center. Well, you do have to tilt your head a little to make it look like real crosshairs, at least the way you see them in movies when the sniper sets eye to rifle scope. That's because neither Truth nor Pain runs in true north, south, east, or west directions, exactly. Each lolls out in kind of the middle of those compass points making it too vague to say they run true north, or true south, or true east or west, or anything true like that.

None of Valley City is true; it's painfully out of alignment.

It could be that Truth runs from west-south to east-north, sort of, and Pain runs from north-west to east-south, sort of. Since these are the main thoroughfares in Valley City, with all other streets branching off from them, the entire city grid tilts a tad off center. Accordingly, when looking at it from above, as we are even now, it's sort of like trying to read a timepiece with its numbers all switched counterclockwise a few tocks.

In other words, it's pretty fucked up.

This means one must further change one's point of view when taking a closer look at this place in order to see it as it is, or rather, to see it in the way it sees itself, or even furtherly rathermore, to see it in the way it wants to reveal itself.

It's sort of like suspending your own disbelief; it's pretty fucked down.

On a geographical level this could be why people sometimes mislay their sense of direction here, get off track, slip the cable, forget their way; it's always so easy to lose your bearings or your mind. In any case it's best to be tilted when you visit in order to see what's true and what's not, so you can see the difference.

Why? Maybe so you can start appreciating it, but that's only a maybe.

In the passing of several tilted tick-tock time lapse frames, the sun's chariot careens it away from us, plummeting and halting it again for our pleasure, to hang glowingly orbing out west, a sign day's end is near, that sunset's touch of dusky twilight will soon encroach, and everyone better get ready for the eventide's influx of mysterious night.

Ah, in a fleeting mist a short lived rainbow shines, its edge cutting sharp against the sky. Or maybe it's just a timely illusion.

THE HAPPENING

Before illusive time gets away from us we should descend for a closer look at the goings on down below.

Like a hawk we arc dreamily down, down, back and forth in easy handsaw motions, to see that up at the end of Pain Street, the city's activity lists a bit heavy. Gliding to that part of town the wind blows us up Pain in a north-north-west direction. It'll all end there, up yonder, and yes it's probably best if we're a little tilted for it. It's also permissible, while headed north-north-west, if we don't know a hawk from a handsaw.

Up there we discover enormous amounts of glowing tail lights, people parking, people walking, all converging on a certain building. Everyone from the beginning of Chapter Six is here: There strides the lawyer confidently, tickets in hand, saying no thank you to the scalper and waving a prosecutorial finger of warning; here walks the stockbroker, having already cheaped out and parked his BMW on a front lawn for twenty-five bucks, after negotiating the price of course; the doctor treads securely, no longer wearing the respected white lab coat yet still clothed with that calm air about him. The traffic cop directs the little old lady to the nearest entrance, and the previously well suited gentleman is dressed down and swaggering. The shoppers, their packages safely stowed at home, walk unfettered. The swanky cool men and women sip their purchased-to-go lattes while they stand in the long lines feeling the buzz, the build up, everyone pumped and ready to meet the thing to beat all things.

The MC Cripple Crip concert.

That's where we're headed, up to the end of Pain Street, to Valley City's own 37,000 seat venue, The Forena, at the north-north-west edge of town.

Atop the red carpet, under the lights, news reporter Candice Cotton, her hair the most awesomely type of tweaked, models the tightest, neonist, orangest dress ever. She radiantly ignites before the camera while eschewing her own brand of hyperbolic exuberance unmatched in the history of red carpetdomness.

"Tonight's top story:" she crows, "The morally righteous, one of a kind, giving, caring, ultra-spotless-honest role model, inner-city Black Handi-Rapper MC Cripple Crip will give his concert debut with his original songs! Here! Tonight! In front of a sell out crowd!"

Candice turns to rip "ex"-crack-addict Mayor De La Gente from his posse. "'Ex'-crack-addict Mayor De La Gente," Candice yells through the background noise, "are you looking forward to the show tonight?" She tilts the mic toward him.

He takes a half step back and totally checks out Candice from head to toe, his elevator eyes stopping at each floor for a lascivious look see. Behind him, his shark-skinned, thick necked ruffians jam hands into coats and scan the crowd for trouble.

"Well, *chica*," he says finally, leaning forward to the mic, "if the show is as good inside as it is out here we won't be disappointed." He slips a business card into her hand. Mouthing *Call me* he turns away. The goons fall in step behind him.

Holding the card Candice thinks about it before spotting and quickly grabbing the ever-present-at-public-events-that-attract-the-press African-American Congresswoman Charlene Rivers.

"African-American Congresswoman Charlene Rivers," Candice extols, "tell our viewers, please, how happy you must be to finally see an honest, hardworking, aboveboard, non-liar, black rapper from the inner city make the big time."

African-American Congresswoman Charlene Rivers elegantly lays the table for her college grad supporters with her refined, Harvard diction, "As I have stated many, many times in the past, this upstanding young man, this hero among us, this modern day Hercules, epitomizes the precise reasons that leave me feeling so very privileged to represent Valley City District 11 and its exemplary citizens." Without batting an eye she heaps the plates with down-home soul food in order to keep it real with a different part of her constituency, "But I gotta give a special shout out to all the good folks in District 11.2! I works hard, brothers and sisters, you know it, and finally this day comes shinin' down upon us. Praise the Lord! Because a me, we all stand hea' knockin' on the door to the Promised Land, free at last. Amen! So I says again to all my people, be they brothers and sisters, or Honkies, or Mezcans, or Orientals, or AAA-rabs, or even them Jew folk, that without me there'd be no young brothers like this one comin' up and representin' us." Dessert gets scooped up plain-style for another part of her voters, and she sprinkles it with "money drops," which is what she likes calling her tears, "So please, please, let's be minded in our clearness. We must...keep it steady...we must...stay the course...you betcha'. We must keep those donations coming into my re-election campaign." Sniffle sniffle. "Do your part to make sure this is not the last young, black rapper we see by keeping me in office! Bless you all, bless Valley City District 11 and 11.2, bless all honest, upright, truthful black rappers, and especially, God Bless America!"

Candice responds, "Thank you, African-American Congresswoman Charlene Rivers. Enjoy the show!" Into the camera she horks, "Now, here are some other reactions we've seen today at The Forena!"

Broadcasting on a TV screen placed in a liquor store window across the street, we see a snippet of Candice saying, "What a crazy bit---" just before the taped footage rolls.

The pre-prepared montage starts with massive crowds cheering and massive lines waiting.

An insert shot appears of that bug-eyed young boy from the Key To The City ceremony, the Cripple Crip look-a-like sans wheelchair. But now he's wearing the fly, red hat he scored after Janice and Learoy fought over and lost it. He busts moves like a pro while singing "*Put another bullet in it, I did your date at the----PROM.*"

Lamentably, Candice, who by all means is hot, busts what she must feel are a few moves with the boy. She's an imbecile. The young boy stops, grows even more bug-eyed, and backs away into the crowd.

Footage rolls on a big screen monitor perched atop a

tall stand set amongst the excited crowd milling about outside The Forena:

A shot of ten blinged out, ultra-white, blue haired grandmas chant, "MC, CC, MC, CC, MC, CC..."

A shot of ten blinged out, multi-racial, spiky haired elementary students chant, "MC, CC, MC, CC, MC, CC..."

A shot of Janitor Ching, wearing his custodial greens topped with green pith helmet, sided by the dapperly dressed Clarence with his guide dog Max and a string of the G.R.A.S.S. kids, heading into an entrance for the handicapped. Some kids face the camera, a couple of blind kids face away, some kids spin in circles from sensory overload, some spin in wheelchairs. There is a mixture of shouting, signing, and odd pronunciations of "MC, CC, MC, CC, MC, CC..." At the end Janitor Ching gives two thumbs up and says, "Clipper Clip! He da boom! Hee-hee-hee-hee-hee."

More footage rolls on a second big screen monitor perched atop a different tall stand set amongst the excited crowd milling about outside The Forena:

A shot of clean cut, tucked-in-polo-shirted, creased-khaki-wearing African-American college frat boys hoisting cheap cans of white trash beer.

A shot of tatted out, tilted-baseball-cap wearing, sports-jersey-clad, saggy-pants-donned, ghetto-trailer-trash white boys hoisting blunts.

A shot of the bandana wearing older female passenger from the Dry Gulch Road Commuter Train Station earnestly saying, "He brings us all together, umm, black, white, green, umm, messed up, not messed up, smart, stupid, umm, all of us. He is just a saint, a true modern day saint!"

Even more footage rolls on a third big screen monitor set amongst the excited crowd milling about outside:

A shot of the completely Caucasian cop chopper crew that dropped Cripple Crip off at the Key Ceremony. Standing together they gyrate their hips in circles, laughing while they sing, "*I got style, moves, and riches! I shoot cops 'cause they's my bitches!*"

Then on 100's of big screen monitors perched atop 100's of tall stands set up outside The Forena, the album artwork appears showing MC Cripple Crip in prison stripes, strapped and wired into that wheelchair converted into an executioner's electric chair while he gets zapped. Naturally the pithy slogan blazes there as well:

BLACK HANDI-RAPPER MC CRIPPLE CRIP:
THE SURVIVOR
and his NEW ALBUM
SENTENCED TO LIFE IN THE ELECTRIC CHAIR
BUY IT HERE TONIGHT!
AGAIN!

A montage of shots appears on the 100's of big screen monitors outside The Forena. In each scene fans do seizure-shakes as if they are getting zapped.

The place seems packed already. Looks like everybody's gonna make it to the show on time.

THE LIMO RIDE

The outside crowd noise silences as a very small TV screen fills our vision.

A Hispanic trash collector next to a shiny bright Pain Sanitation truck appears saying, "Cripple Crip's like my best friend. He's changed my life in the way no *Mexican* rapper ever could."

We pull away from the small screen, and by George we're cruising slowly up Pain Street toward The Forena in the overly-hyphenated limo. The kids are all here, even Carlos because Cripple Crip isn't. No one looks at each other.

Sombrero Guitar Man materializes onscreen saying, "The real thing is he! Seen him myself I have, with two of these eyes! I swear by Allah it is true! Cripple Crip is a GOD!"

The taped footage ends. Candice Cotton returns, her words spouting fanatically from her aglow face into the camera, "There you have it! The buzz! The excitement! Tonight's the show! Don't miss it! And make sure you come down with your phat beats on to blow it out!" She propels a Black Power fist skyward (even she isn't sure why). "Don't you forget: this concert is for all those special needs kids who idolize him. And never has a black handi-rapper been so moving. And he's so movingly inspiring because he is, after all, black. And he's so movingly inspiringly unique because in addition to being in a wheelchair, he's black!"

Carlos stares at the little flip down TV screen hanging from the headliner.

Candice clucks on and on: "And Black Handi-Rapper MC Cripple Crip is not only black, he's black! And everybody knows the only good rappers are black rappers, and black and black-black and blackity-black-black-black..."

Carlos reaches up and switches off the TV with his big toe.

Across from him, from under the screen, with no view of it, Mad Girl snarls, "Ask before turning it off."

Carlos inquires snidely, "Were you watchin' it?"

"Nope," Mad Girl grunts, "Moon was."

Carlos looks at Moon sitting next to him in the plush, way back seats sightlessly cradling her laptop. Next to Moon is Dutch, studiously counting a wad of dollar bills, and then Learoy next to the driver's side rear door, staring out the window. In front of Learoy a glum looking Pho reclines along the entire couch seat running up the limo's side. To his left, with their backs to the limo's front, ride Mad Girl, Bryan, and

Janice.

The after-effects of the fight in the alley pervade the atmosphere, making the limo's interior deathically quiet, tombitically silent, cryptically cool ice on ice. Such a short time has not healed these wounds.

Leaning his head back, Bryan upends a fancy crystal glass and noisily slurps through a straw, searching for the last drops of soda clinging to the bottom.

Finally finished counting, Dutch fans himself with the money. Not to anyone in particular he says, "A hundred and fifty Washingtons be good startup chedda for my T-shirt sales, yo. Gonna make a kill-ling too-night. Cripple Crip gave me the whole floor as my territory, yo. I might even be able to move out of the flophouse and score a better place. I'm down to move uptown. BOOYA!"

Everyone stiffens. Dutch silently trace-talks his thoughts with Moon.

From her corner spot, Learoy clears her throat. To no one specific she says, "Talkin' 'bout movin' on, I'm pullin' down an easy three G's doing hair and makeup tonight." She pauses before tentatively continuing, "CC wants me on tour with him. Says I'll write my own ticket after all this exposure. Be gone six months."

Bryan chokes on a droplet. Janice pats him on the back to help him stop coughing.

"Then I *might* see you, now and again," Janice says, focusing on Bryan. "CC *engaged* me to arrange *marriage* opportunities between charities and his appearances as *we* traverse city to city." She's loving the innuendoing way too much. “His *insider* I’ll be, *on top* of his *private*---schedule. Constantly. Only makes sense as the *intercourse* between us will be non-stop.”

Pho glowers at his shoes.

Bryan looks at Learoy as he catches his breath.

Formulating something so she's not left out, Mad Girl brandishes her goin'-on-the-offense eyes. Resting her firmly crossed arms on her big belly, she proclaims, "I'm ge'in outta this place too. Yeah. My *Tio* Ray says to come see him. Outta state. On a big farm. Lots of grass and clean air and crap. Good place for a kid. Not like the hole we live in."

"Learoy," Bryan can finally talk, "can I come with you?"

Looking guilty she tries smoothing it over, tenderly. "No, Bryan, you can't. You need to stay with your jobs at G.R.A.S.S., you know? They need you there. And I'll be back."

Bryan stares at her, rolling the words around in his mind.

Pho takes a breath. "My Ba Tuyen and Ba Thien been talking about getting back to Vietnam. You know how grandmas are; only been staying here for me. Maybe time's good for me to split too. If everybody's going out their own ways."

Carlos sits awash in this news. "Cripple Crip's taking you guys with him? But it's all a lie, he's a fake, it's not real."

"Carlos," Learoy responds without anger, just plain resignation, "the only not real thing here is you not facin' what's really happening. Reality's out the window if you look."

Carlos turns his head to see The Forena loom into view. There are the crowds, the monitors, the chanters, the scalpers, the lights, the posters. All the Really Shitty Shit is right in his face, screaming out the success of MC Cripple Crip.

"A wiser person, Carlos," Janice adds, "might regroup to gracefully ask CC for gainful employment. A technician of your abilities could be utilized to great extent out on the road. Who knows, perhaps he could help you make a name for yourself. You might begin by giving him a most contrite and heartfelt apology. Needless to say I'll put a good word in for you."

Dutch, who has kept Moon in the loop with trace-talking the entire time breaks in for her, "Sure, Carlos," Dutch as Moon says, "you'd be on my team running the show! Sound, lights, special effects," Moon lifts her laptop to show him, "it's all right here. I connect to the wireless in the tech booth and away we go. We'd be great!"

Carlos shakes his head, trying to make disappear this surrealistic scene of the world he thought he knew. *Apologize to Cripple Crip...?*

Looking directly at him Learoy says, "Time to man up and understand it's over for us here. All over. We've all got somewhere else to go."

"So it's like see ya'll later, have a nice life, don't need ya anymore?" Carlos asks. "That's what you're saying?"

"No," Learoy balks, "not really like that---"

"Oh," Carlos interrupts, "not *really* like that? Suddenly something *isn't* real to you? And I'm the one not seeing reality?"

Learoy goes sharp, "I don't need this, not from you Carlos! Not from any of you!"

"Fine then," Carlos says, "I don't need you and you don't need me and nobody needs nobody. Great. Now that's as real as it freakin' gets."

Learoy and Carlos stare each other down, their eyes fathomless, like still pools drowning unrevivable dreams.

Bryan works his mouth for the words he can't quite find, his feelings obviously making his stomach quake. Finally he has it.

"If you're all going away," he says innocently, "who's going to help me take care of Samosa? Who's gonna help me with the sunflower? And the puppet shows?"

Learoy and Carlos struggle; on each side a ripple on

the surface leads to a moment of pure seeking. Down below there's a flicker, a recognition of something, but neither will dive deeply enough for it. Too soon their eyes sink heavily away; the moment drowns alone.

Everyone in the limo, in his and her own way, silently tries deciphering the full significance of what Bryan's words might actually mean.

We fall out the top of the limo and hover there, watching it jet away from us up to The Forena's backstage doors, leaving the kids, who've only ever known each other, who've only ever known the world of G.R.A.S.S. and Valley City, alone with themselves while they contemplate that growing up is hard to do.

Hard because time doesn't allow for do-overs as it rushes tock tickingly by.

THE BACKSTAGE ENTRANCE

Two doublewide utility doors burst open to frame the kids in the backstage portal. A beefy guy wearing a black T-shirt blazoning the word SECURITY stands behind the check-in podium. They coolly group-saunter up to him.

Moon and Mad Girl trace-whisper in the middle of a private conversation. Mad Girl clicks her tongue: "Uh-oh. Dreamin' about that strippin' girl for three nights means it must be true. You're a lesbian, Moonie, no doubt. Congratulations!"

Mad Girl as Moon responds, "But I don't feel like a lesbian. How does a lesbian feel? How should I act?"

Mad Girl responds, "A cousin of mine's a lezbeaner. I could introduce you..."

Next to the security guy hangs a bulletin board labeled "Special Homies" with colorful, personalized backstage passes attached to purple lanyards pinned to it. The security guy doles them out. In addition to his pass, Pho gets a gigantic security shirt that he pulls on over his head.

The kids stand together checking out their cool new IDs. It should be a huge, uplifting event for them, but it doesn't ring true; the moment's tilted out of kilter.

"Well," Janice forces a smile, "this is it! G.R.A.S.S. kids make it big!"

Moving forward around a corner, they get whisked into the eye of true backstage bedlam, a place of pure Pandæmonium.

Floor to ceiling chaos becomes visible before them. Stagehands dash everywhere finalizing lights, splaying cords, patting mics, hoisting speakers, and tape, tape, taping everything down. Oversized props are winched, dragged, roped, fork-lifted and person-handled from here to there. A galore of big booty hoochie mamas gallivant in all stages of dress, from street-walking get ups to chrome-mirrored bikinis to Vegas showgirl headdresses, all of them hotter than demons from Hell.

In the middle of it all basks MC Cripple Crip, his golden wheelchair placed diademically high on a kingishly ornate throne, a gigantic, puffed up imperial crown atop his head. He barks orders down to the glossy, white-guy record exec from Behind Bars Records.

"You know I'm the real deal," Cripple Crip spouts, "and I been straight up wit you every step, so when I says I don't want no spinach wraps with pepper cheese that's just what I mean! Now be gone witchoo and go count up my money."

"No problemo," the bullshitingly savvy Record Exec Guy responds, "My new assistant, the freshly demoted Marvin Kibblestein, will get right on that."

"Sho' nuff," Cripple Crip snorts. "Now gets outta my way. You stinkin' the place all up with yo' squareness, man."

Record Exec Guy slimes away and Cripple Crip sees

the kids approaching. He beams way, way big. "Hey, big ballas, you finally made it! Hope the limo was to y'all's satisfaction."

Janice crutch-cuts her way in front of Learoy. She's a startling sight in her third outfit of the day, this one a blasting dayglo blue with sleek matching powder-coated crutches decked with gold spiderweb netting. It's obvious her bra is a bit padded under the thin fabric dress that hugs her boney frame, but the complete package reeks of a sexy lioness blatantly on the hunt.

She gives a seductive smile. "Exquisite, CC. All we lacked was," a pout for good measure, "you."

"Yeah, baby," he plays back, "I missed you too. Oh, Jani, sugar, would you do the most important thing tonight and find that MDDO prez to set him straight? You know that next to me you runnin' this show. You my main stage-managin' crutch girl, a'ight?"

"Anything you want, CC," Janice shamelessly writhes her body, "anything, anytime, anyhow, anywhere." She moves off to do her job.

He looks down at Moon. "Moonie OG! They waitin' for you in the control booth out yonder. Go make that magic majestical!"

Mad Girl as Moon responds, "Ready and set to go. Mad Girl's helping me out too. The gig is going to be fantastic!"

Mad Girl and Moon depart to engineer the show.

"Yo, your Crippleness, your main money maker man be in da howse, yo!" Dutch busts a move, Egyptian style. "I got the lettuce to make you the cabbage, my brotha', yo."

"'Sup, my cracka' wrappa'? They waiting for you too. Go round the side there," Cripple Crip nods the direction, "and give them the low down on yo' ho' down."

"Check, mate." Dutch gives a flourish before jive

strutting away. "Obama, out."

Cripple Crip addresses Pho next: "Biggie Man Pho. I told 'em I wanted no one but you up at that stage front. Those fans love me, but they all want a piece of me. You'll handle that bizness, a'ight?"

Pho plays a fake exuberance, "Yes sir, CC. Got your back all the way."

Cripple Crip moves a lever and the throne seat sinks, lowering him to their level. The gigantic crown stays behind, revealing that it's suspended from wires up above. On the way down he whips out a bouquet of two dozen red, long stem roses. "And you, my lovely African Queen, are here at last." Rolling from the throne he holds them out to her. "I give you these roses as a small token of what's in store tonight."

Melting beyond melt Learoy takes the flowers. "Thank you CC. They're beautiful."

"Like you." He switches to Carlos. "Yo, dawg, how you been? Seen any good Westerns lately?"

"Nope," Carlos answers, "nothin' but dramas."

"Well, as promised, you got the best seat in the house: Front Row. Center." Cripple Crip smiles with hidden meaning. "I want you, especially you, to have a picture perfect view of everything. You'll see *my* fans, *my* show, and hear *my* music in all its glory. Ain't that the biggity bomb?"

"Fo' shizzle, CC," Carlos is deadpan, "you a fo' real homeboy, straight up."

Cripple Crip lets slip a victorious smile. "You welcome."

"If it's okay," Carlos says lazily, "me and Bryan'll hang back here a bit to check your stuff out. A'ight?"

"*No problemo, muchacho.*" Dismissing them from thought he returns to Learoy. "Now, my woman, let's you and me go to my private dressing room to discuss, hmm, my look."

Learoy and Cripple Crip move off. Carlos stares after them to see Cripple Crip hook a thumb on her hip so he can dangle some loose fingers onto her rump. He looks back at Carlos and gives him a big wink.

Tick-tock goes the clock, faster fast as they walk.

THE PLAN

Carlos talks low. Pho and Bryan lean in to hear him.

"Okay," weaving his eyes side to side for eavesdroppers, "time to execute this plan into motion. Bryan, you remember what we talked about in the alley today?"

"Yes," Bryan answers. "I need to go find the biggest soda drink I can and take it back to our seats."

"Right," Carlos affirms. "The biggest one. Hopefully they've got some real tubs for sale here. And your instructions?"

Careful recitation: "Buy it. Dump it. Fill it with water. Bring it back to our seats." He stops to frown, "But can't I drink it so I don't waste the soda?"

Carlos dips his toes into a pouch and foots him a twenty. "Tell you what, buy two so you can sip on one and fill the other with the water. Good enough?"

Liking the new plan Bryan takes the money. "That's solid, Carlos. Late." He takes off running.

"You got the 411 on Cripple Crip's stuff?" Carlos asks Pho.

"Yep," he says. "Right this way."

Pho winds them through the continuing milieu of pre-show set up. Way backstage they approach a dark corner enclosed by black fabric stretched across a portable framework. Pho holds a slit open for Carlos to roll through, then ducks in behind him, tugging the material back into place.

The makeshift enclosure contains three wheelchairs. One sparkles with jewels that match Cripple Crip's kingly throne. A printed sheet of paper stuck to the seat reads SHOW OPENER. The second is the executioner's electric chair off of the album cover artwork. The printed sheet on that one reads PRISON SCENE.

The third wheelchair is an exact spitting image, ripped off clone of Carlos's lowrider wheelchair, right down to the shiny spoke wheels and custom, tricked-out handles. Carlos rolls to it and grabs the paper taped to the seat. He reads it out loud.

"*4-Wheeler On The Sidewalk To Your Heart*." He's livid. "Pho, I swear I just wrote this song last night, and somehow he's got it already. Damn Reggie, I can't believe you. You steal my raps, you take my girl, and now you even jizzacked my chair."

Peering out the enclosure, Pho clears his throat and taps his foot. "Piss and bitch later, Carlos. Get this business handled."

Seeing the sense in that, Carlos gets to work. His foot slides open a drawer beneath his wheelchair's seat then folds out a black, velvet-covered platform. From the drawer he removes a few odd looking tools, a shoebox-sized metal box with wires and strange looking gears sticking out of it, and what looks like a remote control device with a six-inch LCD screen and a springy, wire antenna. He carefully places each item on the velvet platform.

Pushing a green button on his wheelchair's switchbox, the seatback slowly reclines until he rests flat. With the flick of a yellow toggle, hydraulics make the newly formed platen descend low enough for him to look up under Cripple Crip's knock-off lowrider wheelchair.

Gripping a tool that looks like a fork with different sized eyelets attached to its tines, Carlos says, "This'll only take a minute."

Pho looks down at him. "You sure it's gonna work?"

"Yep," Carlos says, squinting up under the other chair, "better than I thought since he copied my chair. This gearbox'll hook up perfect, and this remote will control every move. Whenever I want I'll bounce the hydraulics and POP! throw him right up on his feet. He can't help but stand so he don't fall down! Human instinct, Pho Man."

Pho laughs. "And if Plan Remote Control Carlos don't work, then Plan Soda Cup Bryan spilling water down Learoy's front oughta make him *pop up*."

Carlos laughs too, "That's more like Plan Triple D Cup! Anybody within eyesight of her wet T-shirt contest after Bryan douses her with all that water is bound to become *erect*!"

"Man," Pho cracks up, "I hope it's not too *hard on* Learoy!"

"Nope, homeboy," Carlos laughs, "but it will most surely be *hard on* us!"

Tickory Tockery Dock.

THE CRITIQUE

Wait a minute.

That's their lame ass plan? Popping Cripple Crip out of his wheelchair in front of everybody? That was the big fancy covert operation they strategized in the alley? I, for one, am darn glad you allowed yourself to be regaled with the history of refuse collection in Valley City rather than being forced against your will to listen to their load of trash.

And if that doesn't work they're going to drench Learoy's chest with water? Like, okay, I'm definitely down for that. No doubt her freshly firm bazoombas swelling through wetted fabric, the perfectly shaped areolas crinkling with the cold, pencil eraser nipples straining the thread count, will make everybody take to their feet. Rolling hills of chocolate heaven. Mmmm hmmm.

But hold! Stay my soaring libido! Lest we forget, this young woman, this girl, is underage, only sixteen for juvies' sake! Now I'm no prude, but to expose her thus in public borders, no, forget borders, *is* criminal. Have we forgotten the law in our rush for revenge? Anyone (okay, not anyone, but certainly any male over eighteen unable to claim a position in the medical field) who sinfully spies her terrifically titillating Ta Ta's will, by definition, be (Gasp!) exhibiting pedophilic tendencies!

For shame.

Can I merely stand by contributing to the craven modern day societal addiction that yearningly commands the exploitation of underage girls as *objets de sexual*? Admittedly there exists a millennia-old custom of marching cute, attractive, nubile young females in the sex parade, and certainly today's enticing fashions, somehow condoned by said females' parents and guardians, garishly flaunt their pre and post nymphet jailbait bodies to the Nth degree.

What can save us?

Or are we already steeped in the dust, heaping ashes onto our heads, falling furiously into the pit of iniquity that swallows our very souls in the fiery maelstrom of taboo images flashing by our eyes in magazine page flips, on freeway billboards, and up on the screen at twenty-four frames per second? Are we already lost and ruined when the urges left burning luridly on our doorsteps are not of our own making? Certainly all adult males are *not* artists and madmen, not *all* are creatures of infinite melancholy with bubbles of hot poison filling their loins, causing them to cringe and hide at the sight of, say, Catholic School girls frumping by in short plaid skirts.

What can save us?

With neither braggadocio nor apology, ever remaining your most humble of servants, I answer the above question with a singularly single subject: Me.

Yes, I will protect us. Rest assured that as a highly educated, professionally trained, superbly vetted, exquisitely talented raconteur, I possess the artistic ability required to explicitly mix matter and art to properly convey Learoy's virtues without the content straying beyond acceptable norms. And as for becoming aroused by her, oh please. Tut tut. Pshaw. I am nothing if not clinical in my detachment, when needs be. Otherwise might you not freely, however mistakenly, judge me a sick and twisted thing, a disgraced and perverted Humbert Humbert as I bring what could be the most excruciatingly ecstatic, climactic moment ever written to its deservedly visual life?

So don't worry, you are safe in my hands. And hey, what the heck, I'm sure no writer of *The Brady Bunch* ever had sexual thoughts about Marsha until after she turned eighteen. Right?

But artfully back to the matter at hand. How, oh tell me how is Cripple Crip supposed to see Learoy from the stage, what with the lights shining up in his eyes, even if she is in the front row? And if she's backstage doing her job, then how will she even get to the front row for them to make this happen? Beware, mateys! Here thar be plot holes!

What douchebags these guys are. This has got to be the most childish plan in the history of childish plans. Mark my words: having not thought this through, the whole scheme proves fraught with problems making it doomed to failure. I mean sure, I'll try to help them if I can, but it's out of my hands. The characters are in charge here, not me. I'm just the lowly narrator.

Okay. Break over. Start it rolling again. For good or for ill, time always marches on.

THE CONTROL BOOTH

With crowd music pumping the house speakers, Moon and Mad Girl walk to the raised control platform set up on The Forena floor about mid-way back. A medium sized security guy nods them through as they walk up the ramp, hand in hand.

At the top of the ramp they enter the engineering station for the show. With its banks of twinkling equalizers, glowing computer screens, and slick little clip-on desk lamps, it looks like a compact mission control counting down to launch time.

Freezing in mid knob turn, two sound engineers look up at the girls. Faces heavily armed with hostility, they roll their eyes in proper *Damn, I wish we didn't have to deal with this* fashion.

One of them, a thirty-ish-ish bald white guy with round wire specs on his head and donut crumbs on his midsection paunch-shelf, says, "Okay, *little girls*, make nice and sit over there in the corner. Get out your Barbies and stay out of our way, 'kay? If you're good we'll buy you ice cream."

The other one, who looks one day past fourteen and three steps from the beach (and has *Chili Peppers* scripted across his neck) says, "Like, j'yaw! This whole, like, Wish The Dream True Foundation fantasy crap should, like, be nowhere near my radar screen. Totally bogus, dude. Makes me wanna spew."

Mad Girl starts losing it but Moon quickly trace-talks her down. Shifting emotions on the fly, Mad Girl bats her eyes and uses her most dangerous nicey-nice voice: "Sure, sirs! We just wanna see how you pros do it so we can help out the drama club back at school. We're doing *The Sound Of Music* this year and, well, we could sure use some tips!"

"Our awesomeness," Surfer Dude says, "will like, be

readily apparent."

"Yes, our awesomeness," Bald White Guy agrees. "Now park it, Suzy-Q's."

The girls take chairs in a corner. Getting to work Moon opens her laptop and starts keystroking, trackpadding, and touchreading the pop-up Braille screen that Carlos invented for her. Within thirty seconds she trace-talks to Mad Girl, who smiles and trace-talks back. Moon merrily pushes Enter.

The background house music switches to a cooler mix, the volume pumps up a notch, and the sound quality becomes deeper and clearer. The Forena house lighting wavers down and up, then glows with a new chill, purplish quality. The three giant big screens above the stage stream graphic designs that flow with the music.

The mood throughout The Forena improves. The crowd, almost all seated, cheers in anticipation of the show.

"What did you do?" Bald White Guy asks.

"Like, dude," Surfer Dude responds, "like, nothing. What did you do?"

Bald White Guy pushes, twists, and slides things, quickly growing frustrated. "Nothing I do makes a difference!"

Surfer Dude makes like motions and agrees. "It's all like, belly up, dude. Curtain's in, like, five. This is, like, really, really not good."

Messing with them even more, Moon's deft fingers on the laptop make their slick little clip-on desk lamps flicker and die.

Bald White Guy: "Shit."

Surfer Dude: "Really, like, not good."

Mad Girl trace-talks to Moon and they snicker into their hands.

And those tick tocks keep marching along.

THE STAR'S DRESSING ROOM

Cripple Crip's dressing room looks like the inside of a sheik's tent, strewn with carpets and throw pillows on the floor, filled with ornate lights and candles, hung with tapestries that create alcoves and hideaways. Learoy finalizes his look before a huge, lighted makeup mirror.

"So, my dark goddess," Cripple Crip says, "after the show tonight you will be mine, won't you?"

Learoy frown-smiles pensively as she works to get his face made up just right. "Be yours? On a date? Like goin' out somewhere?"

Twisting, he makes his move, kissing her full on the lips. Upon release he looks intently into her eyes. "Baby, I was thinkin' we'd stay in."

Learoy straightens. "Bit fast for my money."

"Aw shucks, Learoy, you act like you've never even seen first base before."

She works his eyebrows.

"Whoa," Cripple Crip's shocked, "you haven't, have you?"

"I told you before," bashfully self-conscious, "it's been way locked up."

He thinks back to what she said at the beauty shop. "Maximum Security?"

She's glad he remembered. "Yep. Death row on lockdown."

Gently he smooths her temple with his right hand. "I was hopin' I'd found the key."

She sighs. "This body's never been unwrapped before, by nobody. It's unseen, untouched."

He lets that settle in. "I like that, homegirl. See, a man like me, wantin' a wifey like you, I can wait for my good thing. No big thang."

"Wifey?" Learoy looks shock-pleased. "Did you just say

wifey?"

"Yes, lover," he says. "I'm in this for the long haul, not the short ride, straight up. Said it back at your shop, say it again: These are my heart thoughts."

Learoy flounces onto his lap, knots her arms around his neck, and kisses him like she just invented it. "I know this is too fast," kiss, "but I can't help but believe you," long kiss, "thanks for bein' okay on going slow with the heat," really long kiss, "but for now you've got my heart," kiss, "please, please don't hurt it."

He stops her with a soft thumb to her chin, their eyes so, so close. "Trust me Learoy, just trust me. It's an easy thing to do. Honesty is my middle name."

A rap on the door with a shout: "Curtain in five!"

Learoy jumps to her feet. "Five minutes! I still need to touch up the opening hoochie mamas! I'll see you in between sets, 'right?"

She runs to the door. Cracking it she turns, smiles big, and blows him their special double kiss.

He smiles even bigger and gives her their special double wink.

"I love you CC." She runs off, slamming the door behind her.

The five minutes quick tock by.

THE SHOW BEGINS

From the tip of Moon's finger to the length, breadth, and top arc of The Forena, the house lights go completely dead, instantly shushing the capacity crowd. A lone spotlight strikes a thin figure standing on stage.

It's Janice.

Her voice fills The Forena: "All too many of us know the anguish and pain of struggling through a life with slim hope of making it anywhere, let alone making it big. Tonight we celebrate life with each other!"

The crowd cheers.

She continues: "There is one among us, however, whose life now stands at our center stage, a true beacon to us all of what any single one of us might accomplish, as long as we strive to stay true to our own dreams! And so, without further adieu, let us 'give it up' for MC CRIPPLE CRIP!"

The crowd goes wild as the spot winks out, leaving them in total darkness again.

High on a wall above the big screens over the stage, on The Forena's huge scoreboard, red numbers blush to life on the main digital clock. It sets itself to read three seconds, then ticks down as the crowd counts with it, "3, 2, 1!"

A purple laser from above needles through the darkness to prick a huge, symmetrically cut crystal hovering over the black stage, making it glow. The purple light webs downward, its veins forming the outline of Cripple Crip's gigantic, puffed up imperial crown. Wavering and pulsing as deep, sexy bass beats rumble and build, the light eventually spreads throughout the framework of the towering throne.

Sitting in the sparkly jeweled wheelchair, Cripple Crip rises magically up through the throne until the top of his head meets the crown. He's all got up in the reddest of blood crimson leather.

"Brotha's and sista's, crippies and healthies, oldsties and youngsties," his voice exemplifies compelling emotion, "this is my clear message: Let no one steal your dreams! Let no one steal your hopes! Live ya' own life, create ya' own means! Be ya' own self and be all that is true! That is my own little dose of Brutal Honesty!"

The crowd rowdies it up as Cripple Crip blasts into his hit *Brutal Honesty.* The stage lights reveal his band, consisting of several jiggy percussionists, three mad deejays at their coffins, two jammin' bassists, four screamin' guitarists, three knockin' keyboardists, and a white jumpsuited, ebony sunglass wearing, goatee bearded, shaved headed, big, fat, iced out, totally mega-cool black guy with a green tambourine.

Cripple Crip raps like a king:

I said I'm Cripple Crip
Homeboy you better squeeze that grip
'Cause if you hesitate, it'll be too late
They call me Cripple Crip,
I took a bullet in the hip,
And one in the spine,
But I'm back and feelin' fine

A mini, tube-steel framed, graffiti-splattered roller coaster sets down on stage. Cripple Crip rolls his wheelchair onto it straight from the throne seat. U-bolt arrangements secure the chair's tires to the rails, and it bursts forward at break neck speed! He rides the coaster, taking its mini loops and twists and inverted turns in stride, all the while rapping and holding his hands over his head.

I tell it so straight, I be evolution
I'm a bigger threat than the workers' revolution
Speakin' the truth is my weapon
I's a gangster, and I's be steppin'
When you all hear me
You want to cheer me
So when you near me
You better fear me
'Cause I said I'm Cripple Crip
There ain't no bigger grip
Fightin' me is futile
'Cause my honesty is bru-tal

And oh damn, here come the first batch of hoochie mamas shakin' they bootaaaay! They're got up like sexy carnival workers who look ready to punch your ticket. Jiggling in the right places, they appear as silky clowns, leotarded magician's assistants, and short-shorted food vendors, all with major round butt cheeks pouring and cleavage spilling. They twist and turn around the roller coaster's skeleton construction, clambering up the sides, grabbing for Cripple Crip as he screams by. Some shimmy to the top and bend over so he can slap some asses as he passes; others mount spots where they start dry humping the rails. The three giant screens above the stage get a workout.

The music builds to an orgasmic pitch with the girls literally writhing about, doing that pelvic thrust thing they do where they appear to have hot, steamy, sexual intercourse with the air.

Of course the crowd, the grandmas and grandpas, the mothers and fathers, the teenage girls and boys, the adolescent girls and boys, the small children and the babes in arms, everybody, I mean everybody, claps and cheers their hearts out for more.

It's a joy witnessing such good ol' fashion, clean, wholesome, family entertainment, not like that smut they always show on the television box!

The main digital clock up on the huge scoreboard replenishes itself with ninety minutes to go. Then it starts counting down the show with a tock tick tock, backwardly pushing the time forward through the night.

THE FRONT ROW

The front row isn't really a front row in the traditional sense. For this show it exists as a clear space on the floor between the stage and the second row. In the middle of that sits Carlos, three seats on his left and four on his right. The screaming fans splay out behind him and flank up the loges above him, all 37,000 of them on their feet and dancing. Only he sits still, a silent observer in the eye of the hurricane.

It's as if the whole thing was designed to be right in his face.

There is movement next to him: jumping up and down on the seat to his right, waving his huge cup of soda over his head, Bryan has the time of his life.

"Oh my god, Carlos," Bryan shouts, "do you see what he's doing?"

Cripple Crip sings *Put Another Bullet In It* while swinging on a cable over a sea of fly girls on their backs who alternate between spread-eagle stretches and bicycle leg pumps.

Carlos nods his head, fiddling with his remote device.

"Hey, Carlos," Bryan shouts again when Cripple Crip flips his wheelchair upside down on the cable, grabs a girl by her ankles, and continues swinging back and forth. "The dude has awesome upper body strength!" Bryan yells at the stage, "Hey, hey, yeah, yeah! I did your *MOM* at the *PROM*!"

Carlos checks beneath Bryan's seat to make sure the other cup, a 164-ounce Forena Foamer full of water, remains unspilled. The 3-D face shot of Cripple Crip on the cup's side winks at him as he bends down. Carlos laughs, shakes the remote at it, and winks back.

The music cuts at the song's end to roaring applause. It dies down during a brief transition.

Bryan keeps dancing on his chair. "Cripple Crip is rockin' it!" His sweaty, matted hair sticks to his forehead; he's lovin' life.

"Bryan, man," Carlos the serious, "don't forget why we're here. We don't actually like this guy, remember?"

"Oh, right. But damn! The show's killer!" Bryan thinks a moment, all the while tap dancing his feet on the chair seat. "Okay, so we've got these cups, and you want me to get close to Learoy and spill it on her boobies, but when's she going to get here so I can do it?"

"Don't fret. Pho's got that set up." Carlos the self-assured. "He'll jet backstage to get her whenever Cripple Crip rolls the lowrider wheelchair. He's over there waiting for the signal."

Pointing his big toe he looks to Pho's station in front of the stage.

He's not there.

Carlos points and looks elsewhere, then elsewhere, and elsewhere again, each glance evaporating his confident smile just a trifle more.

Bryan is quick to say, "Hey, he's not there, or there, or there. Not much good if he's not there, there, or there, Carlos."

"*Ay, chingada!*" Carlos the mortified. "Where the hell did the guy go?" He snags his phone from its holder on the switchbox and texts rapidly with his toes. He hits send and waits for a response.

Carlos checks his screen for a return message.

Nothing.

Carlos checks again.

Nothing.

And again.

And again.

And nothing and nothing.

Bryan's dancing shuffles his chair up against Carlos. "Sit down would ya? He ain't even on stage right now."

Bryan looks down, embarrassed, but keeps moving his feet. "I can't! I gotta go so bad I'm gonna piss my pants."

"Didn't you go when you got the drinks?" Carlos the annoyed.

"Yep, but I drank both of them 'cause I got so thirsty."

"Hold it," Carlos cocks an eye, "you mean the soda in your hand is gone, and the one with the water under your chair is too?"

Bryan looks even more embarrassed. He shakes the colossal gulper he's holding. It rattles. "I still have ice."

"How you supposed to splash Learoy with freakin' ice cubes?"

Bryan's face wrinkles in confusion. Then he has an idea. "I better go get some more water in it?"

Carlos barely keeps his cool. "Yes. Go fill it up, please. Fill up both of them. And hurry! The show's starting again anytime now!"

"Aye, aye, Carlos!" Bryan scampers away with the cups.

Carlos scans the crowd searching for Pho. Suddenly Bryan is back, tapping on his shoulder.

"What!?" Carlos responds.

"Can I get another soda?"

"NO! Got no time to stand in line again. Just fill those with water!"

Bryan re-scampers off. Ten seconds later he's re-back re-tapping Carlos's shoulder. Carlos glares at him.

Bryan triple times the piss dance now. "Can I please stop and pee?"

"YES! YES! Just hurry!"

"Yep!" Bryan re-goes again.

Still surrounded by 37,000 re-screaming people, Carlos re-re-checks his phone for a return message, hoping time doesn't slip away from him.

But ol' man clocker, he jes' keeps tickin' along!

THE SIDE STAGE VIEW

Up on stage, tucked away behind a side curtain on the right, Janice watches her dream man wow the crowd. No doubt the greatest moment in her life was introducing him. Without the leg braces her knees would have buckled.

The opening set with the laser and the crown and the roller coaster blew her away. Seeing the show's intricacies backstage, how it all fit together with split second timing, popped her eyes. Her mind dialed through the phone calls she'd start making tomorrow to high profile charity organizations all over the country. International as well! As CC's publicist, people would most definitely take notice of her skill at talking up his talents. Establishing promotional opportunities for him would surely bring her a modicum of semi-stardom all her own.

Already slated for the morning was an exclusive interview with Scoop Johanson of the *Valley City Gazette*. *Rolling Stone* would not be far behind.

All that considered, she didn't mind when the hoochie mamas swarmed the stage and vied for her man's attention. And when he ogled and slapped their firm, round, upturned booties while speeding by on the roller coaster, she giggled quietly at his superb acting abilities.

However, if she were giving Scoop the scoop regarding their budding relationship, which indeed she was planning on doing, she would be compelled to talk to CC tonight regarding toning down some of his onstage antics. He wouldn't have a problem with that, not for his dear little "Jani."

Still, when he was up on the cable looking down at the hoochies on their backs spreading their bicycling legs she did her best, really she did, to not over-think the situation. Yes, it proved difficult watching CC leer down at them; perhaps he smiled and enjoyed it overly much. But wait, hold on there girl, do not forget, he is acting, correct? But some of those girls, those sluts, spread their legs a little bit extra and lobbed the hot air kisses at him a bit thick. Hussies. There would be a post-show upbraid of those bimbos. Straighten them out she would. Fo' sho'.

But all those jealousodic tendril tinges need be set aside. Exemplary selfless devotion wins the day. Professionalism's the key, after all, and professionals know the difference between onstage performance and offstage real life.

But still, however, all that considered, now, as she looks out at the show, she just knows CC is her guy and will never betray her. It's all just an act.

The next song rolls up. It's her favorite: *Girl, You A Glock Stopper!* She's convinced CC wrote if for her. He's so romantic.

The compassionate, dreamily engineered shotgun blasts intertwine with the opening skip beats, but it's the romantic bliss of the blended automatic weapons fire that truly transports Janice away.

Her hero, Cripple Crip, appears on stage (alone and she likes that). He looks just like the album cover, wearing his black and white prison stripes, strapped and wired into the wheelchair converted into an executioner's electric chair.

Part of the stage floor slides back and a gigantic semi-automatic pistol replica of a Glock 9mm rises. In deadly, gleaming black finish, the thing grows ten feet tall, stretching twenty feet from back to barrel tip. Moving in behind it, Cripple Crip's wheelchair rises up on a lift, stopping him at a level above the grip where he suggestively snugs his knees around the weapon's slide.

The crowd hollers and cheers as Cripple Crip points his faux manhood, leaning back and really hamming it up. Janice laughs along because it really is funny, if you think about it. Sure it's base, but there's nothing like a good ol' fashioned gigantic penis prop to get the yucks going, especially since he isn't, you know, making it all dirty and stuff.

The ringing gunshots lower while Cripple Crip croons to the slowly rising, melodic intro music that sounds of soft, misty rain falling on honey sweet violin strings:

Girl, you got a hold on my heart's lock
Girl, you make me stop in shock
Girl, you make me wanna rock
Girl, you the hottest on the block
Girl, you a Glock Stopper!

Then, oh crap, the real sick beats kick in and the band starts thrashin'. And look at this: Six of the hottest hoochie mamas yet, in way undersized black and white prison striped hot pants with matching thinly nyloned bodices, drop down from above to straddle the Glock. They start doing that cute pelvic thrust thing on the long, round, thick, barrel.

Cripple Crip gets jiggy wit it:

Girl, wrap your hands 'round my Glock
Girl, wrap your legs 'round my Glock
Girl, slap the clip into my Glock
Girl, go on and load up my Glock

The prison striped hoochies start going at it more, sliding up and down, some facing Cripple Crip and licking the air, some facing away from him and licking each other (Like on the face and ears! Get your mind out of the gutter! This is a *family* show.). Cripple Crip really, really lives it up, oh boy you better believe it.

Janice's jaw drops. No, wait, it's snapped shut. Here comes the frown and, wait for it, wait for it...YES! We have the crimson faced stink eye going!

Oh jeez! The front of the gun just "elevated" a bit, so

now the tip is tilted upward in the front like it's popping a boner. Ha!

Yes, I totally agree: That's gross.

Cripple Crip gyrates too, making the whole gun rock back and forth as he raps:

You get a grip on my Glock
You get a rip on my Glock
Baby load my Glock
Baby kiss my Glock
Baby rock my Glock
Baby shock my Glock
Baby aim my Glock
Baby shoot my Glock

O---M---G. While the prison-striped hoochie mamas viciously bounce their crotches on Cripple Crip's big ol' Glock, five new prison striped hoochies appear on stage. They strut to the side then bend over with their palms flat on the ground.

My, these ones are limber.

But that's not the best part: There are bull's eye targets on their ASSES! Damn, this is SO HOT!!!---in a, you know, really droll sort of way.

Janice is back to slack jawed again. Guess she's a little shocked.

Cripple Crip aims his Glock at the quite-limber-bent-over-target-assed girls. He's got the off-the-hook dope beats on now, and the music loops and loops like a thumpin' wild thing:

Make my Glock shoot!
Make my Glock shoot!
Make my Glock shoot!

Make my Glock shoot!
Make my Glock shoot!
Girl, you a Glock Stopper!

He aims, prepares to fire---

Janice looks down at her phone vibrating in her hand. She flips it open importantly with the importance of the freshly important busily looking important. Scanning the screen her expression changes from slack jawed to grim to astounded to irate within several seconds. Snapping the phone closed she stares out at the stage a moment before moving quickly away.

Something's afoot, and that scoreboard clock up there keeps shooting down the time like a Glock spitting slugs.

THE CONTROL BOOTH REDUX

"Go ahead Moon," Mad Girl trace-talks through her laughter, "make Cripple Crip's big old Glock bounce them ho's!"

Moon's body jerks with inward chuckles as she slides her finger up and down the laptop's trackpad. On stage the gigantic Glock bucks.

Behind them, arms crossed and resting on his revoltingly bloated paunch-shelf (the donut crumbs replaced now by yellow cheese speckled nacho fragments), Bald White Guy mopes, "Hey! Are you girls even in the union?"

Surfer Dude, who seems to have a firmer grasp on the situation, flicks his thumb from the carb to clear his bong. He rasp-whispers to keep his hit in, "Dude---just let---'em take---care of it. We get---paid---anyway---"

"It's the principal of the thing!" Bald White Guy stares at the girls, psychotically planning some type of revenge. "I'm calling our association representative!"

"Listen, loser," Mad Girl hurls attitude at him, "get

stoned with your pal or go pull your pud. We're busy here so back off! Moonie, put a spotlight on the hoochie ho' on the right."

Moon mysteriously works her magic with the lights, the props, the sound, the stage, all the time alternating between feeling the laptop screen, punching keys, and trace-talking with Mad Girl. They're rocking it.

They both react to the feeling of their phones buzzing. Mad Girl flips hers out to scan it. Moon forwards the message to her laptop screen where she touch reads it.

Moon reads her message in a jiffy compared to the slower Mad Girl.

"Holy shit!" Mad Girl as Moon says. "Did you get this message?"

Mad Girl struggles over the last few words, then shouts, "Damn, girl, we gotta jam!"

Moon cradles her open laptop as they stand to leave.

Surfer Dude's totally blazed on some chronically dank Barney. "Whoa, whoa, whoa, where're you going, like? Who's gonna run the...the thing, like?"

Bald White Guy thinks he's got them, "So! Couldn't handle the big time after all! Fine. I can still save this disaster. Give us back control of the show, and I won't get my union rep on you."

Mad Girl howls in their faces, "Look, dorkloids, we got things to do, but don't worry. We'll run the show by wireless. It's so easy even us little girls can do it. You Suzy-boys go play with your Ken dolls or your army men or somethin', 'kay?"

Surfer Dude starts laughing, he's so twistedly high, "Hey, man! She just totally, like, ripped on you for that Barbie comment you made when they got here! Remember that? Remember? Dude, she got you so bad!"

"Shut up asshole," Bald White Guy says.

Mad Girl and Moon vanish down the platform ramp.

They move quickly, as if the essence of the time is, or something.

THE MINI MAYHEM

This could go on and on here, with a lot of space taken explaining what Pho and Dutch did, but for time's sake suffice it to say that Pho got called away from the front stage area to help out with a brawl, which is why he wasn't there when Carlos looked for him earlier. So Pho arrives at this brawl, right, and sees a pile of people, literally, on top of some poor slob way down at the bottom.

Pho yanked people off the poor slob with each of them saying, "I got ripped off by that moron down there!" Whom do you suppose Pho found at the bottom of the heap hugging a mangled stack of MC Cripple Crip T-shirts and clutching a wad of crumpled bills?

Yep. Dutch lacked the math skills necessary to correctly make change, and when everybody finally had their fill of his belligerent behavior, they jumped him. He typifies, as you know, the worst possible amalgamation of stubborn and stupid.

Pho spent several minutes quieting the squabblers and straightening out the cash exchanges. When Dutch and he were parting, they each felt pocket vibrations.

Then came the outing of the phones, the scanning of the screens, the looking at each other.

"Holy shit!" Dutch exclaimed. "Do you know what this means?"

"It means we gotta book it," Pho replied.

Their emotions way past tense, they were finding themselves having to be dashing off side by side, runners participling a furtive tense clock that was performing its reverse tick tock.

THE YELLOW STREAM

Just as Bryan catches that blessed midstream feeling, where the stinging edge wears off because the teeth stop hurting and the flow feels like paradise, his phone vibrates in his pocket.

Not everyone---LADIES---will be aware of this, but when caught in an unstoppable stand up piss, digging a phone from a pant's pocket becomes a very delicate operation.

First and throughout, one must make certain the evacuating member stays properly pointed lest bad targeting lead to the Yellow Drenching. With that focus in place, the cautious sliding of the non-unit holding hand into the appropriate pocket can commence (Lucky for us Bryan is a right handed urinator who keeps his phone on the left, allowing us to forego the detailed instructions involving the Wet Time Hootenanny Switch). This downward pocket hand slide requires graceful motion as any displacement of the fly opening will block the on-tap appendage. Needless to say, at full bore fire hose pressure that occurrence will cause major dampage. With phone safely grasped, steely nerves rule the day during the slow, clenched-fist retraction. At this juncture strict coordination of each hand becomes of utmost importance as one can ill afford a wandering Willy when it's weeing.

With phone safely out, accomplishing the single-handed flip open is all that remains. Nevertheless, one still proceeds with caution so as to not accidentally let fly with the wrong hand, causing, in a worst-case scenario, the Golden Neighbor Hose Down. That is the ultimate urinal *faux pas*, I can tell you!

Bryan performs this bit of tricky business and does a smashingly fine job of pulling it off (so to speak).

Upon seeing the phone screen, he yells, "Holy shit!"

A happy drunk a few urinals down says, "That's what *she* said."

Giving it the quick double shake, Bryan stows the baggage and jets from the restroom.

Everybody is in such a hurry. Why is time so very important to them all of the sudden?

THE SIXTH ONE

Learoy's vision this evening is filled with makeup brushes, hairbrushes, lint brushes, mascara brushes, toothbrushes, shoe brushes. She's swept and touched her way up through every person in the show, only here and there catching glimpses of Cripple Crip in action.

Scoring compliments on her creativity from all quarters and being stopped by backstagers wondering why she's not on stage because she's so amazingly hot, makes it the time of her life. Knowing that it's only the beginning of a great career and that the love of her life will be waiting for her after the show, leaves her feeling as if it's a dream.

Itsy bitsy bothersome occurrences: more than one girl, caught up in the excitement and not knowing Learoy's designation as Cripple Crip's main squeeze, blathered away about how *she* would be the one waiting for Cripple Crip in his dressing room at show's end. Actually, about twenty of the hoochie mamas prattled on thus, but each time Learoy stayed a pro and let it roll from her shoulders.

NOT!

Put it this way: Learoy thinks she's being a pro and not letting it bug her, but with every third hoochie swearing she'd be the one "polishin' the chrome on Cripple Crip's dome," her dander got further and farther up, until she was fairly smacking the touch ups onto the girls and throwing them out of her way.

And now one of the girls, in her alluringly

splensexerous bikini consisting of three spaghetti straps, one for each nipple and a slightly wider flat noodle for down below, asks Learoy if she can step on it because "I'm goin' get that boy's nubbin a rubbin on my muffin."

That about does it.

Turning from her makeup station, Learoy heads straight to Cripple Crip's dressing room. Once inside she writes on the mirror, in red lipstick no less, LOCKDOWN'S OVER! WARDEN'S GIVING UP THE KEY. I'M ALL YOURS! L.

"Like to see his face when he reads that," she muses aloud. "Hmmm." Sweeping aside a tapestry hanging behind her, she steps into the compact space on the other side to investigate its possibilities.

Quick experimentation proves it's the perfect place to watch him discover the message. Happy with the hidden alcove, she sees a stool with clothes on it next to a small table.

"May as well be sittin' pretty when the time comes!"

She lovingly picks up the clothing, carefully placing each piece on the small table. The ensemble outfit includes a white leather Fedora hat, a long-tasseled white leather jacket, and a set of white leather chaps.

"CC," she shakes her head, "even for you this is really too much. All you missin's the---" she sees them "---white snakeskin cowboy boots." She stands the boots on the table next to the rest of the outfit.

A final item lies flat on the stool: a nondescript 8½ x 11 brown envelope.

A quick, unthinking toss lands it perfectly on top of the boots. Well, not perfectly. It rests just off center on the boot shafts, tipping to the right, the flap on the open end making the difference. Learoy pauses, her expression forcing it to settle flat. Almost works.

But it tips just a little more, then a little more, looking

like it's gonna slide off, but then it gets even better: the open end dips just enough for some pictures to spill out onto the table.

Five pictures, to be exact.

Damn and hot diggity! Tick and hot tockity! Leaning over, perplexed by the images, she picks them up one by one.

They are, of course, the photos Cripple Crip swiped from Carlos at the train station.

There's the grainy shot of the wheelchair in the alley. No biggy. Next is the photo showing Cripple Crip hanging from the pipe outside her window. That's an eyebrow cocker.

When she picks up the one showing her own fantastically gorgeous rear end, her ears steam. "Last night! Carlos! I knew it! But why's CC got it?"

The fourth shows Cripple Crip's upper body. Whatever. The fifth exhibits a vague, blurry form in the alley. Forget this.

Ho hum, it's just like before: five shots with no hard evidence of Cripple Crip being anything less than a crippled cripple.

Learoy flings them back onto the table, unsure who gets the first yelling for which reason. Carlos took the pictures, but CC has them, and he was peeping on her. Gathering herself to storm off, she pauses to think twice. Picking up the nondescript 8½ x 11 brown envelope, she spreads the opening and dips her fingers in. She does not come up empty handed.

It's the *sixth* photo, powerful enough to blow Cripple Crip's persona clean off his wheelchair. Yes-yes-yes, it's very-very nice.

The sight of it makes Learoy's jaw drop open like the bone there just turned to rubber. Then comes a lost look, a mad one, a sad one, a heartbroken one, until finally the rancorous venom filled one appears. Now that's more like it.

Using her phone she angrily clicks off a picture of the picture. Afterwards she works the keys harshly. Send.

Almost simultaneously, in different parts of The Forena, from stage side to engineering booth to brawl pile to bathroom, vibrating phones call the kids to enlightenment.

The time has come.

THE MOMENT OF FURTHEST REMOVAL

Alone in the front row, the remote control unit dangling forgotten from his toe tips, a wide eyed Carlos sits hypnotized by the show. He can't help it; it's just so staggeringly fantastic.

Cripple Crip gets major mileage from that executioner's electric wheelchair. On stage an explosive, smoke-filled, prison riot scene roils in flames. Fifty hoochie mama inmates scream from barred cells for Cripple Crip to save them. He speeds around piles of bloody, quivering, dying prison guards (previously shot by him) while dodging ten masked SWAT guys zinging down ropes with their machine guns blazing. Guess the song? Here's the flow:

All y'all ballers see my heat on da street
I'm the new squad, I patrol a new beat
Shot to the top by fighting tooth and claw
And now, baby, hear me rewrite the law
I got style, moves, and riches!
I shoot cops 'cause they's my bitches!

Behind Carlos in the second row, sitting next to "ex"-crack-addict Mayor De La Gente, one of the shark-skin suited, thick necked ruffians shouts to another one: "HEY BENNY! JUST LIKE THE ATTICA RIOT IN '71, REMEMBER? RUB OUT THEM SCREWS CRIPPLE CRIP!!!"

Charged with passion, the scene becomes a heart

ripping cliffhanger, a quixotic love story, a timeless high art picaresque adventure of good versus evil! Cripple Crip takes a slug in the shoulder, another in the chest, both arms, and the head yet! Mortal wounds spewing blood, he bravely frees the hoochie prisoners who beg to stay and help but---NO!---gallantly he waves them to safety (tenderly and lovingly accepting several lap dances during their jigglefest departure). His self-sacrifice leaves him held at gunpoint, cornered by the ten masked SWAT guys!

A frenzied execution chamber slams onto the stage. They wheel him to the electrically glowing and rattlingly snapping Frankenstein looking *mishegas* of hideously wired transformer boxes and generators.

A glass-domed copy of the Popemobile rolls onto the stage. Disembarking from it, a fully adorned look-a-like Pope pompously paces to Cripple Crip. The personification of pretentiously posturing panache, the Pontiff clamps oversized battery jumper cables to the ugly skullcap of the executioner's electric wheelchair. After performing a solemn Sign of the Cross---Father, Son, and Holy Spirit---he laughs evilly and throws a huge red lever!

Wires crackle, sparks fly, spinners spin, and lightning bolts (Yes! Lightning bolts!) strike the chair! Cripple Crip's skeleton glows through his skin, shaking the seizure while he gets zapped! With a final drawn out whoosh of sound and action and bedazzlement the whole Forena plunges into dead darkness.

Silence.

A single stark spotlight strikes a senselessly still Cripple Crip in his chair. It is so, so very sad. Oh the tears, they fall like rain.

The air above him shimmers and a dozen angelically clad hoochie mamas grace the firmament. Although white clad with feathery wings and golden halos, they are the most wantonly expressed cherubs to ever titivate this dimension. The band slowly edges back in with the sounds of heaven steeped in mourning and eternally bereft of hope.

The angels weep.

Two sexy seraphs descend to the fallen one. Gently lifting him under his arms, they waft him upward, electric wheelchair and all, just as a thirty foot tall Jesus Cross rises from behind. They set him against the rood in the crucifixion pose.

One of the masked SWAT guys drops his machine gun, kneels, hangs his head, and cries, "Forgive us for we know not what we do."

Cripple Crip breaks his silence to groan, "It is finished. Fans, into your hands I commit my spirit!"

A booming God voice rumbles The Forena: "This is my Son, whom I love; with him I am well pleased."

A multitude of fans snap their purple, glow in the dark *WWCCD?* wristbands.

The band smashes the sadness with jubilant trumpeting chords!

Cripple Crip jerks back to life, resurrected!

The two hoochie angels rip away his prison stripe outfit to reveal a robe woven of the whitiest whitey-white material ever seen in the history of the universe. The angel mamas lift him, leaving the electric wheelchair behind. He rises skyward with them, glinting all the while like the morning star on Easter Sunday!

Cripple Crip points an index finger downward. A slashy lightning bolt strikes the Pope! Exploding into flames he runs; with great weeping and gnashing of teeth he falls into a Hellish flaming pit!

The audience's reaction? Well, as Cripple Crip makes the ascension to Heaven, I shamefully throw myself at the mercy of the Reader's Court in pitiful confession that I, convicted and humbled dunce of dunces, lack the skills necessary to righteously scribe the crowd's ebulliently boiling reaction, other than to ignobly scratch out that it should forever be deemed the archetypal model of performance appreciation to which all assemblies should aspire. Forever and ever. Amen.

Carlos, realizing he is stomping his foot and cheering, forces himself to stop.

Mentally returning from the concert-induced fugue, he looks around to find Learoy, Pho, Janice, Moon, Mad Girl, and Dutch looking down at him, shocked at his reaction to the show.

Learoy's mouth moves, but the crowd is too loud.

"What?" Carlos shouts at her. "What?"

Shaking her head in frustration she texts him.

Carlos ditches the remote for his cell. Viewing its screen he sees what Learoy already sent everyone else: the *sixth* photo.

As if toasting for the nonce, the other kids hold their phones out so he can see that they all possess the same, damning evidence.

Carlos breaks into a huge, wide, shit-eating grin.

The cheers subside enough for them to converse.

"Yo, Carlos," Dutch declares, "he really IS your person-A!"

"Let's get 'em!" Mad Girl wants a pound of flesh, just for the fun of it.

"My doubts are gone," Pho determines to fail no more.

Janice and Learoy remain silent, their eyes shining spitefully from faces tinted with anger.

Mad Girl as Moon says, "Carlos, I don't know what you want to do, but I'm still running his show. Say the word we bring him down from here with my laptop."

A group nod affirms their collective desire for unified

vengeance.

Carlos smugly holds up his remote control device. "It's cool of ya'll to offer, but I got it covered right here. No back up needed."

Learoy breaks her silence. "We want to do whatever needs doin' to help you---"

"Help me?" Carlos cuts in. "Why didn't you listen sooner? I been begging you, all of you, for help! You made it clear every day, and in the alley and the limo too, that we don't need each other." His resentment runs deep. "Keep it real. I started this alone. I'll end it alone."

"Alone, huh. Then Bryan and his water cups are what, nothin'?" Learoy asks pointedly.

Carlos fails at not looking totally busted. "How'd you find out? Bryan?"

Pho's the guilty one. "I figured the plan changed with the picture. I told her to watch out for him. Hope it's copacetic."

"*Si, no problemo.* Plan's officially changed. No help." Carlos looks at Learoy, "Especially not from you."

Learoy blows up. "You major pissin' me off, Spoke Boy! Do that to me?!?! I will never, EVER let this one go, unnnh-uhhh. Thinkin' you could use MY body in front of ever'body so's you could be the big hero. You got any clue how much that sucks the big one Carlos?"

"Doesn't suck as much as friends turning their backs on you when you need them," he responds.

No one can hold his gaze at that one.

Movement. The kids see creeping green fog spill over the stage front. Moon's still doing her job. She takes the seat on Carlos's left.

Learoy plunks down on his right, still yapping up his ear. "Carlos, you ain't alone in the hurt here! We all well up in it. I fell for the playa' poser! He wants to marry me---"

"Damn, Learoy," he hits back, "you think I need to hear this right now---"

"You gonna hear it, One Foot!" she says. "You got no idea what I'm giving up to be sittin' here witchoo right now."

"Then don't do it," so very bitter. "Get up on stage and show him your chi chis without me, you---"

"You the one always axin' 'n beggin' to see 'em!"

"Wouldn't look now if they was the last nips on earth!"

"Hell you wouldn't!"

"Hell I would!"

Cripple Crip rolls out in the lowrider wheelchair clone. He looks tight.

Adjacent to "ex"-crack-addict Mayor De La Gente's entourage, Mr. Biggs (you remember, the ugly, really ugly, black, four-story parking garage builder) says to his attorney neighbor friend (the fantastic loophole-finding lawyer), "Wow! A lowrider wheelchair! How original! I've never seen one before. That's so cool! This cat is a GENIUS!!! GO CRIPPLE CRIP GO!!!"

Carlos and Learoy look back at Mr. Biggs, then down at Carlos's chair, then at each other. They almost smile but don't. Pride.

Cripple Crip waves down the applause, the savior silencing his disciples. "This next song," he says, "is for the ladies...I love you...just like I know you love me." Female voices rise and fall. "But I'm sending this one out to my special girl---you know who you are. You got my truly true, honestly honest, onliest only heart thoughts."

The female voices rise and fall again, each fantasizing that she's the one to whom he speaks.

Cripple Crip rolls to the edge of the stage and looks down at Learoy, "It's all for you baby, and it's called *I'm A 4-Wheeler On The Sidewalk To Your Heart*."

Learoy whispers viciously into Carlos's ear, "See! I

could be up there with him right now."

Carlos focuses on the stage. "You're still sittin' here ain't ya."

The song quickly segues from another of those slow romantic intros into an aggressive fast beat with words to match:

Bitch, you better not walk away from me!
'Cause I'll roll after you,
I love you, I do

Carlos clasps the remote, his toes poised on the toggles and trigger.

From out of nowhere, like a speeding projectile, more agile than one might expect (his motor abilities honed due to his love of basketball), Bryan, still on his mission, gripping a sloshing, full 164-ounce plastic cup in each hand, charges Learoy. Nearing the net he draws back for the ultimate slam dunking, sets, and shoots!

Everything goes slo mo: Bryan thrusts the cups forward; two thick, anacondas of water strike outward; Carlos (shouting the obligatorily drawn out "NOOOOOOOO!!!!") scoots forward in his wheelchair; the snake rivers hit full on, drenching him from head to (please forgive me) toe.

And drenching his remote control unit as well, whose LCD screen flickers an error message, post haste.

The hydraulics controlling the little front tires on Cripple Crip's lowrider wheelchair make it bunny hop up and down. Surprised at first, Cripple Crip recovers, giving Moon and Mad Girl the thumbs up.

"*Ay, chingada! Pinche* water!" Carlos tips the remote over his armrest to shake it out. Half a cup of water streams down, straight onto Moon's laptop! The pouring water creates a remote control unit to laptop liquid firewire connection, fusing them electronically. Carlos's LCD screen happily gleams that it is currently joining the "wireless connection moon-cc-show1." In a gigabyte twinkling the two devices meet, fall in love, and begin networking.

The music gets way, way loud. Dust vibrates from The Forena's steel rafters.

Every houselight in the ceiling blasts on, creating instant daylight inside.

The fans dig it.

With the laptop and remote hooked up and on a wickedly fun honeymoon, Moon and Mad Girl try desperately to get things back under control. Well, mostly Moon, but Mad Girl feeds her info via trace-talk.

Carlos works the remote, still stuck on his plan to launch Cripple Crip to his feet. He only succeeds in making him look more gangster as the chair tricks with lowrider moves. It hops, pancakes, dog legs, slides, and races across the stage with Cripple Crip freestylin' it like he's clowning a bucking, dressed out Impala. For real, dude's gettin' all kinda' jacked up.

Listen up ho'!
I want you to know
I love you I do
This song's your cue
I want you in my stable
So put your cards on my table

The Forena ceiling lights overload and explode, cascading waterfall sparks that disappear just over the crowd's upturned faces.

Mad Girl as Moon calls to Carlos, "I'm doing my best but everything's fighting me!"

Moon keys, trackpads, and clicks to stop the greatness, but nothing works. The lasers stitch mad designs and draw chill characters onto newly spouting multi-colored fog. The gigantic Glock erupts from the floor firing away like the end of the *1812 Overture*. The roller coaster falls to the stage with the Frankenstein electrics racing along its rails, striking its framework with lightning that strobes it into a flittering dinosaur skeleton x-ray. The images and colors on the big screens up above become artistically psychedelic, cornucopic arrays. Cued by misfiring backstage signals, hoochie mamas flood the stage.

Cripple Crip takes it all in stride.

I love you I do
Every word I say is true
Girl with that ass of yours
You won me from the start
So let me roll my 4-wheeler
Down the sidewalk to your hearrrrrrrrrt!

Swept away, unable to control the emotional pull any longer, the crowd surges forward to worship at their deity's feet!

Pho quadruples his efforts to guard the stage, his mighty frame dodging here and there to keep fans from getting to Cripple Crip, knowing he must keep them back to give Moon and Carlos time to expose him.

Raging the stage is that sweet voiced, blond haired, blue eyed, young black girl who started singing *America The Beautiful* with a phat beat at that Cripple Crip MDDO appearance a while back. But now she's red-eye wild and screech-voice strident as she spies Dutch in his seat with a stack of MC Cripple Crip T-shirts on his lap.

"HEY," Blond Blue Black Girl shrieks, "T-SHIRTS!"

Her daddy leads the fray. Like lemmings to the sea other fans join in, rushing Dutch to throw money at him and grab for shirts. Powerless to do little more than stand and let the cash rain down, Dutch throws shirts out to keep his arms from being ripped off. Funny no one cares about the change this time.

Another aggravatedly hostile combination of Moon's keystrokes leads to another backfire: Outside The Forena the 100's of big screen monitors perched atop the 100's of tall stands start broadcasting the concert. Thousands of loiterers who didn't score tickets but stayed to be near the grandiosity perk up.

"Gotta give mad props to that Cripple Crip!" exudes Ice Tray, the large-ish sort of young-ish black guy Dutch transacted business with in the alley earlier. "Tha's cool to pop us his concert for free, 'specially since Dutch didn't show with our tickets!"

"Cripple Crip ees da shit!" says Rudy, the spiky haired, baggy clothed, Hispanic looking teenage boy who had the shoe problems with Dutch. "*Pah! Pendejo* Dutch *es hijo de puta!*" Rudy looks down at the satin red finish of the fly SportsMeUp shoes Dutch sold him. One shoelace is puke green, the other puke orange.

"We gon' kick his ass," Ice Tray says.

"No doubt," Rudy agrees.

Back inside, Moon works hard to shut down the outside monitors, and the lights, and the sound, and the effects, and everything else, but, like Carlos, all she does is keep making it better and better. Now carnie hoochie mamas fly in over the stage, and prisoner hoochie mamas ride the roller coaster, and angel hoochie mamas straddle the giant Glock. Then the fireworks, flash pots, and skyrockets shoot off. Everything melds into a sublime, transcendent madness that scorches the magnificence of its creation into the minds of all who witness its brilliance.

It's the Grande Finale of all Finales; it's New Year's Eve and 4th Of July and Christmas; it's the Super Bowl and The World Cup; Mardi Gras in New Orleans and Carnival in Rio and Oktoberfest in Munich; it's the opening ceremony for the Olympics. In Athens!

Moon should be winning awards for this, no lie.

And Carlos, poor Carlos, the bad luck kid, toggles and triggers, wiggles and tiggles, whisking Cripple Crip hither, thither and yon, trying his best to throw him to his feet. But at every turn the chair-tricks just keep getting phatter and phatter.

This is the invention he *should* get patented---forget the rest!

And Pho works security at the stage protecting the very guy he's grown to despise!

And Dutch keeps tossing out shirts, making money for the guy who screwed his best friend!

And Mad Girl can't keep up with Moon's flying fingers, which makes her feel useless and unneeded, so she hates Cripple Crip for turning her into what she hates the most!

And Janice tries outing CC to *Rolling Stone, The New York Times*, and Scoop Johanson of the *Valley City Gazette* on a cell phone conference call. But all they say is, "Genius publicity stunt inventing this ploy about Cripple Crip being a phony! Photo ops galore, babe! Love your work! *Ciao!*"

And Bryan wamma' jamma's with the show, even though he knows he shouldn't. Can't hold it against him though: it's his job to be honest, and quite honestly the show is greatly greater than great.

And Learoy fights the craving to leap up and bitch slap CC while gettin' shrill up in his grill, but for once she forces herself to rationally think about the future rather than unreasonably blow up in the now. She sits tilted off kilter by it all, quietly trying to see the difference between what's true and what's not, the difference between doing what's needed and what's easy.

It's just all so very totally backwards: The kids have ended up working *against* themselves and *for* Cripple Crip!

Now that's irony!

Furiously experimenting with key combinations, Moon's network stumbles across the main digital clock on the scoreboard way above the stage, the one whose backward countdown has been pushing time forward all night. It patiently tock ticks downward, red numbers unremittingly glinting that only thirty-five seconds remain before reaching zero and show's end. She fights desperately to find some way to win, any way to win...but maybe that's the problem.

Moon wanders the ways in her mind. Breathing empathetically in sync with the clock, she ticks down through timeless knowledge: *Chi, Ka, Fu, Sui, Ku*. No, not the *goddai*, elsewhere runs the path. It's within the violent struggle itself. The scrambling combat, the wild lashing out leaves us lost; the stiff, stubborn, head to head fighting that desires to hurt and injure nets us nothing.

Moon laughs at herself for forgetting how simple life truly is.

All you need is the right balance, and all obstacles can be toppled. The Art of Peace finds the way. Gentleness and love pivot together. They provide the blending needed to adapt to and control the attacking energy. Absorb the momentum, redirect it, topple it. Transcend time and space.

Get back to the basics already.

Standing, Moon bows to Cripple Crip on stage, then to the digital clock on the scoreboard way above.

Time, we always need more time. Can't stop it, but...

She sits, relaxed yet poised, her gentle fingers set softly to the laptop. Slowly she feels her way into the network, finding the clock's strength not by facing it straight on, but by easing in from the side to stand next to it, letting *it* lean against *her* for support. She absorbs the force of time's relentless countdown pushing against her, against them, against the universe.

There it is, the soft touch, then the side-step deflection.

...the scoreboard clock slows down---27, 26, 25---

---almost to a stop---24---and as the clock slows---23---so does the music---22---the show, the sparks, the crowd ---21---until even Moon's own fingers move slow, slower, slowest, until one Tock reaches for an indefinite Tick ---2---

...and doesn't make it, halting all motion, looking like everything is in a suspension of still water, a suspension of time, a suspension of place, and especially a suspension of disbelief...

---everything suspended like---

a vibrant Sunflower basking in dim light
bricks securely set in a tall green wall
kids laughing in The Dark
a boy spinning in a sunset full of orange
a cold alley where hope comforts the lost
statuette puzzle figures alive on a bedroom shelf
a cool glass of spring water on a hot July day
a buzzing bowl where everything is possible

---and everything suspended except---

Carlos and Learoy, stuck in a place where fathomless still pools drown unrevivable dreams.

"Carlos," Learoy says, not having or wanting to shout, "we gotta talk."

He falters with the remote and looks at her, "Yes?"

"In the limo, I said you weren't copping to reality."

A pensive nod.

"I was backwards. I see it now, and it hurts. A lot."

"Kinda busy here," still with the pride, "tell me something I don't already know."

Loudly, "Idiot!" Then a quiet reset. "Quit your pitiful bad luck bullshit and listen to me. You were wrong too."

Not a chance. "About what?"

"About not needing nobody." Compelling wonderment. "Look at all this, right here, and tell me we don't need each other. Now more than ever."

The stilled action stands unavoidable. Pho, Dutch, Moon, Mad Girl, Janice, Bryan, all doing what they must do, what they were born to do: work together at all costs.

"Hey, I knew it all along." Not ready to let it go. "You guys needed the togetherness lesson, not me."

"Not just us guys." Plainly stating the facts. "You made it a big ol' test with that Cripple Crip trick. Do you even know why?"

The pride, finally, eases. Reality and truth linger on the edge, then jump straight in, splashing Carlos fully awake.

"Trust," Learoy says, "it's all about trust. Trust that people will be there for you from one day to the next. Even when they're gone. Do you trust us now?"

His response speaks warmly from his eyes. "How 'bout you?"

She pauses. It comes to her as she speaks, "I always did, I just didn't know the difference. Didn't know how to know it. Didn't know how to...appreciate it."

Learoy and Carlos cast into the still pools of each other's eyes, wondering over the possibilities of reviving drowned dreams.

On each side, ripples on the surface swell to waves of pure seeking. Down below, the flicker of recognition bursts into bright flame, and unlike in the limo earlier, this time they both dive deep, not allowing it to founder. This time their eyes do not look away.

"We're all we've really got."

"Yep. And we've got no where else to go."

"That's cool."

"Yep."

On the scoreboard clock, one second sketches epically to the next. Just one, and not another.

Learoy darts a glance up to the numbers. Her eyes register a decision.

Carlos smiles. "You're gonna do it aren't you?"

Learoy, not unkindly, frowns at him. "Don't see another way. You?"

"Not really. You okay?"

"Yes. One thing: you don't look."

It sinks in. "Everybody and that creep gets to," he can't help but pout, "but me, the guy who's dropped his heart at your feet a thousand times, doesn't? Not fair."

Learoy takes the remote from him and puts it down. She gently gathers his foot between both her hands. "Carlos, this isn't about you. And ain't no way it's about him. This is about G.R.A.S.S., and The Dark, and Samosa Sunflower, and all of us takin' care of each other. Together."

He sighs. "Okay."

"Besides," still holding his foot, she stands. "What'd you say earlier---you wouldn't look if they's the last ones on earth?"

"Silly me," he won't deny it, "I ain't nothin' if I ain't a man of my word."

"I know, Carlos," Learoy smiles at him, "that's why I love you."

Floored. Knocked Down. TKO'd. Tsunamied, Torpedoed, Tornadoed and completely shocked beyond thought, he stammers for words.

Learoy slips softly away toward the stage.

---Moon's fingers fall---

...the scoreboard clock ticks again...

...sounds boom, lights flash, people return to living movement, the show lurches to life...

...Carlos finds his voice...

And anything he might possibly say gets swept away in the cacophonic reawakening.

Time puts everything back into place with all eyes both inside and outside The Forena glued to Cripple Crip, the main event, the star.

Reaching the stage Learoy motions for Pho to clear a space for her.

"You watch closely," she smirks in his ear, "'cause Carlos is gonna wanna hear every last detail. A boost, big man."

Puzzled, Pho easily lifts her then goes back to quelling the mob.

Learoy stands center front stage, her heels on the edge and her back to the crowd.

Some fifteen feet away, enveloped by the outrageous onstage occurrences, Cripple Crip sees her.

Girl, with that ass of yours
You won me from the start
So let me roll my 4-Wheeler
Down the sidewalk to your hearrrrrrrrrt!

He smiles big and blows her their special double kiss.

She smiles even bigger and gives him their special double wink.

Reaching down she crosses her hands at the bottom of her shirt, grasps its bottom hem, and pulls it up over her chest.

With a final relaxed throw Moon takes down all other functioning momentum inside The Forena except for the big screens, a single boom camera, and a spotlight shining down on, you guessed it, Learoy.

Hallelujah! Hallelujah! Hallelujah, Hallelujah!

As one, 37,000+ people take a sharp intake of breath, some in shock, others in surprise, many in appreciation, many more in vast appreciation.

Once again silence reigns. This time the suspension of sound and movement needs little explanation.

It's all about the *Boobage*, baby, and every eye zooms in.

In the band the white jumpsuited, ebony sunglass wearing, goatee bearded, shaved headed, big, fat, iced out, totally mega-cool black guy drops the green tambourine and falls to his knees in supplication.

Under orders to always get the money shot, but this time it's because he can't help himself, the lone boom cameraman focuses in and the Boobage shoots onto the big screens. Heads and eyes dart up, down, up, down, up, down trying to figure out what's better, seeing the *real* big ones on stage or the *really* big ones up above. Decisions, decisions.

The same camera feeds to the 100's of big screen monitors perched atop the 100's of tall stands set outside The Forena. The thousands of people out there stop to gawp, enthralled by the Boobage.

The news van tech guy, pissed about waiting outside while Candice Cotton got to enjoy the show inside, focuses his handheld camera on an outside big screen monitor and uplinks to satellite.

We're going nationwide with what? With the Boobage, baby!

Your neighbor the couch potato halts in mid-chip dip

as the feed breaks into the *I Love Lucy* he's watching. You should run over there in a few to see if he recorded it. Sorry you missed it. Serves you right for sitting here reading a book when you oughta be watching television.

Inside The Forena the mute fixation continues, with tens of thousands of eyes glued to the Boobage.

Everyone except Carlos. Why? Because the one legged wonder twit swore he wouldn't look, gave his word he wouldn't look. Remember? "I'm a man of my word," he said to Learoy, leaving us to say "Needer-needer-needer" to him. And so, because he keeps his word, his stare hangs on Cripple Crip, waiting.

Unlike us more fortunate folks, Carlos gets left out of viewing this divine event. He won't be catching sight of the sculptured rising curves. The natural delights so sweetly swelled are not his to behold. No, he will not snatch a gleeful glimpse of the gloriously glandular, nor will he be enlightened by a neatly nicked narrative of the nipplage, or an avidly avowed adoration of the areola, a chronicling clarification of the copious cuppage, a brashly bold babbling on the brassierage, a meticulous memorial to the massively mammaescious, a precisely penned portrayal of the pom-poms, a chalkboard chalk up of the cha-cha's, a hot homage to the hooters, a detailed description decrying the delightful delectation of the D's!!!

NO!, dearie deariest of dear readers, while all in The Forena gaze upon her, and all outside The Forena worship her, and your neighbor's dip drips from his chip, Carlos becomes the only stoop in existence unable to see the blissful Boobage!

I pity him. No I don't. His loss, not mine.

And so now sadies and judlemen, goys and birls, post-nymphet-but-pre-adultphet-loving Humbertina Humbertonys of all ages, I am proud to vividly, accurately, tastefully, lecherously, whole heartedly present to you the most audacious breasts ever bared in the history of recorded civilization. I've wanted to do this for years---

"HEY, LOOK!"---what's this Carlos yelling about somethi---"HE'S A FAKE! HE'S WALKING!"

THERE! On stage, Cripple Crip is UP out of his chair, walking towards Learoy, caught in the tractor beam of the Boobage!!!

In his moment of triumph Carlos again shouts what he has been dying to shout for God knows how many pages:

"CRIPPLE CRIP'S A FAKE! HE CAN WALK!"

Her job completed, Learoy yanks her shirt down and smooths it over her belly.

---NO! WAIT!!! I DIDN'T SEE THE BOOBAGE! Even more so I desired, needed, craved, incinerated to write about it in stream of consciousness style, with a sort of Woolfian/Joycean architecture (but with a heart). Damn gimp boy's interup---

With the squishy ligament sound of 36,999+ craning necks snapping to new positions, everyone's attention, including the cameraman's (so of course everyone's outside and your neighbor's too) turns from Learoy's---alas---*covered* Boobage to the walking faker.

Regaining his senses Cripple Crip looks down at his legs, looks back up, quick-thinks the only plausible sounding possibility:

"OH MY GOD! IT'S A MIRACLE! IT'S A MIRACLE! I CAN WALK! I---CAN---WAAAAAALK!" He pauses for a sly lookabout. Anybody buying it?

Negative. The crowd is appalled. There are boos.

Mr. Jay Cat, the MDDO President with the mottled pepperoni stick fingers, gets spicy: "Look at him! He's a shyster!"

Clarence, the dapperly dressed blind boy from

G.R.A.S.S., releases the grinning guide dog Max and barks: "Sic him! He's a loser!"

Janitor Ching yellows: "KIRR HIM! HE A BAD BOY!"

A piglet faced stranger from out of town squeals, "He looked taller on TV!!!"

Cripple Crip reads the crowd. "I can walk. And I can run, too!" Which he does, straight backstage.

The crowd hisses, jeers, and gets downright pissy!

The kids converge in front of the stage. With Learoy grinning down they hi-five, give it the bump, hand jive, slap skin, punch it in, hi-low too slow, trace-talk-getdown-lowdown, just feelin' good about---

A balled up shirt bounces off Dutch's head. "Hey! T-shirt man!" a female in the crowd shouts. "Here's your crappy shirt! Gimme my money back!"

In a "Hey me too!" moment, a brittle chorus of "Hey me too!"s rings out. Fifty-four people clump toward Dutch!

"Hey!" A male face shouts. "There's that girl on the crutches who introduced him! I want my ticket money back!"

Another chorus of "Me Too!"s erupts. Ninety-three people clomp toward Janice.

Soon voices by the hundreds join in with "There's the boob girl that ruined the show! Get her!" and "There's that big security guy! Get him too!" and "Hey, these other losers must be their friends! Get 'em all!" (and a few late "Me too!", "Me too!"s).

The crowd rampages!

In a stampeding shower of ticket stubs and T-shirts, with Learoy pulling and Pho lifting, the kids cluster onto the stage to get away. United, they make tracks, cutting the same escape route as Cripple Crip.

Skidding to a stop, Moon lifts her face to the blank scoreboard clock way up above. Solemnly, with an expression of gratitude and utmost respect, she bows slowly. *Domo arigato gozaimashita. Thank you very much for what has happened.*

The clock knowingly glows double zeros, like eyes. The left one winks.

Mad Girl reappears to grab Moon's hand and jerks her away.

Behind them a chanting starts: "Down with handi-rappers! Down with handi-rappers! We want blood! We want blood!"

The rumpus of mobbing, rioting, wailing, carnaging, devastationing follows them. Nothing like a good ol' fashioned state of anarchy to cap off an evening.

The kids bolt through the backstage area, now a storming sea of screaming hoochie mamas, running stagehands, scared security guys, aproned caterers, and all types of folks escaping the melee. On point, the mighty Pho clears obstacles from their path. They make it to the doublewide utility doors and burst through.

Right there sprawls the overly-hyphenated limo. Next to it Cripple Crip sheds his stage clothes fast as he can until he stands only in a white wife beater and black boxers with silver checks.

He looks like any other teen in the world, nothing special. Well, he is in his underwear standing next to a limo, but other than that he's just another face in the crowd.

Seeing the kids, he makes eye contact. He grin-shrugs a semi-contrition before diving into the limo and yelling for the driver to hit it.

Carlos, Dutch, Bryan, and Pho instantly appear at the tires letting out air. The vehicle quickly hisses to its rims.

Carlos makes for Cripple Crip's closed door to dish out a last word.

The wild mobcrowd marches around The Forena. Thousands strong they chant: "Down with handi-rappers! We want blood!"

Sighting the overly-hyphenated limo they chunk a churling attack scream and charge!

Ten feet prior to imminent engagement, the driver door flaps open. A round, pink figure brandishing a pump-action, sawed-off shotgun flashes out. The weapon BLASTS! into the night sky.

With great bumping of those in front, the rabblethrong jerkstops.

Carlos whips around. The kids take up battle positions behind him. On cue, the group strikes their tough pose, posturing for whatever this new trouble stepping from the flash ride presents.

The riotgun wielding stranger single handedly pumps another round for effect. *She* is a very, *very* "sturdy" African-American woman dressed in a Sunday Best pink polyester dress with matching jacket. Peering at the crowd through her dated, silver framed glasses, she adjusts the lacy white doily type hat on her head.

In a gravel voice that's surely scolded naughty children by the legions she says, "Nobody's messin' with nobody here 'cept me!"

The hordemass gets it. *No problem, ma'am!*

She rotates her solid girth to face the kids. Recognizing her supreme authority, they wisely step down; a bulldog nod with a low harrumph rewards their decision. The shotgun is placed on the limo's roof. An ample shadow darkens Cripple Crip's door.

Setting handsome hands to generous hips, her pink sleeved elbows sharply akimbo, she explodes: "FRANCIS REGINOLD ARCHIBALD STANLEY TROUPE!!!" Covering ears with hands (and ear with foot), all present cringe. "YOU GET YO' ASS OUTTA THAT BIG OL' SLIDER THIS INSTANT!"

Learoy and Janice look at each other and mouth, *Francis?*

The rear window timidly glides down and an even more timid Francis says, "Hi mamma..."

"Don't you mamma me!" His mother blasts on, "You a disgrace! You a liar! Gettin' up front those folks on the precious cross of our Lord Savior Jesus! Makin' yo'self out to be what you isn't!"

"But mamma," Francis pleads, his voice definitely losing its ghetto edge, "concert performance runs in our genes! Carrying on our family tradition in the hopes of making you proud of me was my endeavor. I am a rapper now, mamma, that's my life!"

"You a lotta things, namely dead, but you ain't no rapper!" Mamma really lights into him, "Me and Biggie Smalls were the ballaholic OG's back in the day! Dr. Dre's my uncle! Shock G stole the Humpty Hump from me! And who you s'pose gave NWA they A---TI---TUUUUUU---DE?!? You a rapper? Now you just frostin' my glass!"

"Please, mamma," he whine whispers, "not in front of my fans."

"You get your snivel butt outta that boo-ride this instant!" Reaching through the window with a powerful smack hand Mamma grabs hold of his left earlobe and proceeds to yank him out.

"No, mamma no! Not the ear!" he wraps both hands round her thick wrist as she extracts him.

Mamma's deaf to any pleas. "Make *me* miss Bible study meetin' chasin' you down here! Brother Reverend Brown says, 'Oh, Mrs. Troupe, isn't that your son on the television with a bare breasted young woman?'" Still painfully clamped by the ear, Francis drops from the car window to his knees. Mamma goes on, "Embarrass *me*, will you? Make *me* miss scripture recitations and coffee cake, will you? What you got to say for yo'self now, *rappa*'?"

"Oh mamma! This hurts so much!"

Mamma grabs the shotgun from the roof with her free hand and dragturns him to face the dumbfounded congregation. "Now, Francis Reginald, you will apologize to these fine folks for hoodwinking them." She gives his ear a hard shake. "Apologize!"

He tries to speak, but the inconceivably tremendous pain leaves him blinking his eyes and popping his mouth open and closed, like a spastic, bulby-eye goldfish glub-glubbing underwater.

He looks like a total idiot.

The crowd laughs at him. Not just a laugh, but a total, complete, hysterical, finger pointing, rib nudging, slouched over, knee slapping rip-roar so thick with derision it would shatter the Mona Lisa's self-assured smugness.

Mamma drags him off into the darkness. As he hobbles alongside her, she continues the tirade. "I just pray to Heaven your father ain't lookin' down right now! And what will your Auntie Lucy say? And Scoutmaster Smith! You up for your Eagle Scout review tomorrow! You gettin' a mouth full a soap come time we get home---" and on and on and on.

Still rolling in the laughter that will undoubtedly haunt *Francis* to the end of his days, the jolly gathering promenades away, its blood craving satisfied.

Carlos, Pho, Janice, Learoy, Bryan, Moon, Mad Girl, and Dutch look between the departing crowd and the disappearing Mamma and Francis.

"Wow!" Bryan says, overacting a backhanded forehead wipe. "Phew! That was something, huh?"

"Sho' nuff, yo!" Dutch agrees.

Janice as Moon asks, "What now?"

Learoy says, "It's a long way to G.R.A.S.S. Let's get home." She looks at Bryan. "Together?"

Bryan's smile answers the affirmative for them all.

THE LONG WAY HOME

Carlos flips a small bluish toggle on his wheelchair switchbox. A spindly, antenna-like, metal arm pops up from his seatback and plops a worn leather aviator cap with goggles onto his head. Afterwards it retracts and disappears. Putting his foot to the chair's control stick, he pops its knobbed top. It hinges open to reveal an enticingly lit red button.

Captain Carlos throws commands over his shoulder: "Contact! Check. Crew, make ready for take off!"

Behind him on his skateboard, one hand grasping the back of the wheelchair, Pho says, "C'mon Carlos just give it the juice!"

Pho's other hand clutches the overly-hyphenated limo's trunk lid, freshly ripped by him from the limo and flipped to lie metal side down. Dutch, Learoy, Janice, Moon, Bryan, and Mad Girl sit comfortably on the broad, carpeted surface.

"Hit the road, Jack!" Janice calls out.

Carlos slides the control stick forward while pressing the flashing red button. The wheelchair's turbo drive kicks in and it jets ahead, pulling Pho on the skateboard who, in turn, drags the others behind. The trunk lid's scraping on the pavement is really, really loud as they exit The Forena parking lot and hit a deserted, late night Pain Street. Mini-headlights rotate to life under the wheelchair's armrests for Carlos to light the way. Cruising for home, steady as she goes, the trunk lid spews endless rooster tails of sparks in their wake.

Pulled by experience, held together by strength, and running on unity, the contraption is a noisy, bumpy ride. But it's a good ride. Reaching out, Learoy holds Bryan's hand.

We fall away here to hover, watching the makeshift jalopy move away into the night, taking the kids home, these kids who've only ever known each other, who've only ever known the world of G.R.A.S.S. and Valley City. They travel quietly, each thinking, perhaps, that growing up is hard, yet knowing it's even harder when you try doing it alone.

Just a regular bunch of kids being a regular bunch of kids.

And so epically we sketch back up into the sky, no longer like crazy north-north-west handsaw hawks in the daylight. Now, perhaps, we take flight in a slightly more true fashion, like slightly wiser owls gracing the night. Climbing our plumb line straight up we see the glowing man in the moon must have sent the shining sun's chariot careening away hours ago. Safe to also say that sharp edged rainbow vanished with it.

Change. That's what time does for you.

Looking down from up here at the bowlishly nighttime Valley City, some things are not changed. The streetlight dotted crosshairs of Truth and Pain remain tilted, remain painfully out of alignment and a tad off center, a few tocks short of a tick. Yes, it's still a little fucked up. Aren't we all?

But it's cool because, save for that, how else would we recognize the difference between truth and pain, or learn to appreciate either? Wise owls know it merely takes time. And up here above it all, in the realm of suns and moons and rainbows, we can catch a glimpse of what time really is.

Like the sun's chariot, the man in the moon, and the rainbow's edge, it's an illusion.

Mini-LOG

Morning brightness shadowplays along a thick, leafy tree limb growing out over a tall, green wall. Below it, half on the street and half up on the curb, lies a discarded extra-large trunk lid, interior side up.

Off to the right, behind the huge wooden doors set under the black wrought iron G.R.A.S.S. moniker, the clunking sound of the security bar being slid open breaks the silence. One of the doors crawls ajar and Bryan pops out onto the sidewalk, greeting the corner of Truth and Pain with a stretch and a smile. Spotting the trunk lid he runs to it, laughing. He jumps on the edge propped up over the curb trying to make a teeter-totter of it. Doesn't rock enough. Maybe hopping in the middle will make it a trampoline. A little better, but not much.

Pho appears amidst the sound of skateboard wheels grinding pavement. Bryan's face shows an idea is bubbling inside.

"Hey, Pho," he's excited, "try this!" Bending down he grabs the trunk lid. Struggling, he gets it on edge and lets it fall paint side up. He positions it on the curb just right. "Now it's a rad ramp for you Pho! Shred it!"

On his board at the base of the lid ramp, mentally calculating distances and trajectories, Pho's expression says he's dubious. "I don't know Bryan. If I get much air I'll crash into the wall."

Bryan checks it and sees his point. The lid ramp comes off the curb pointing dead on at the tall green wall with only the sidewalk width between them.

"Yo, Pho," Dutch moseys his way from Hope Alley, "do

it, yo. It'll be sick."

"Now I *know* it's a bad idea," Pho responds.

"Why you talkin' that smack, yo?" Dutch is surprised. "When I ever steer you wrong?"

"You never steer nobody wrong," Mad Girl and her belly waddle up behind Dutch from the same direction, "'cause nobody ever listens to your dumb ass, YO."

Carlos, with Moon behind holding his chair handles, emerges from the G.R.A.S.S. gate, chuckling. "Mad Girl," he says, "for once I say you're right, *chola*!"

"I'm always right," Mad Girl counters him. "Go for it Pho! Be a man, not a wimp. And that's right too."

"Yeah, Pho, go for it," Carlos says. "Shoot, I could pull it off in my chair! And I'm a cripple!"

"Pull what off what cripple?" It's Learoy, with Janice no less, showing up behind Mad Girl.

"Yes, yes," Janice joins in, "what, pray tell, is the current topic of discussion?"

Master of ceremonies Bryan presents the issue. "Check it out, Learoy, I made a ramp for Pho out of the trunk lid!"

"And he's bein' a big ol' wuss," Mad Girl labels him.

"I could do it, I just don't wanna smash into the wall," complains Pho.

"Yo, man, I think Mad Girl's right," Dutch backs her up, "don't puss out, yo."

Moon trace-talks on the sole of Carlos' foot. Carlos as Moon says, "Get mad air, mo' Pho!"

"Just come at it from an angle," Carlos reasons. "Pop it up, then twist it down the sidewalk instead of mashin' the wall. Simple."

They goad him: "Yeah Pho, do it!" "C'mon Pho do it!"

"I'll never hear the end of it." Pho rolls his eyes and fakies back fifty feet. With a final reconnaissance of the setup, he calls, "Tell my Ba's I died a hero."

"Sure, sure," Learoy says. "Now go!"

The kids move off to the sides. Bryan counts him down, "Ready! Set! Do it!"

Whoops and yells root him on.

Pho's work foot slaps the pavement for speed. He carves a perfect approach while looking severely badass, getting low on the board. It's gonna be awesome. Ready for flight, he hits the ramp.

The kids all cheer.

Like tinfoil the trunk lid crumbles under his tremendous weight, wrapping itself around the board's nose and plowing it into the curb. His feet stopping suddenly while the rest of him continues at twenty miles per hour sends him heels over head.

He definitely catches air. His immense mass flips over the sidewalk to sickeningly THUD! face first into the G.R.A.S.S. wall. The kids feel the impact in their bellies. Pho cartoon-slides from the wall onto the sidewalk, where he rolls onto his back.

They rush to him. In a frantic burst Janice gets there first, falling to her knees. "Pho!" she yells. "Are you okay?"

The other kids crane over her to see what's up.

No response.

"Should we call a doctor?" Bryan asks.

Janice puts her ear to his chest. "I don't know. Did you see how hard he hit? Pho! Pho!"

Janice's head still to his chest, Pho opens his eyes, winks, then closes them again.

Mad Girl loves it. "Oh, he's dead all right! Lookit him. Doin' the sidewalk stretch like some gangster capped him on a driveby."

Learoy nudges her but can't resist either, "Might as well outline him in chalk. He ain't gonna make it. No way."

Janice freaks. "Pho! You wake up this instant!" She pulls up and beats her small fists on his chest. "Now! Wake up!"

Eyes still closed he smiles big and says, "I knew you still cared."

Janice smacks him again. "Of course I care, you big huge lug! You gigantic jerk!"

"Got ya to say it though," Pho opens his eyes, "didn't I?"

Janice works her way back up to standing. "Just what we need! Another test! Get it straight, dope, I care about you. Don't ever die again!"

Pho pops to his knees and takes one of her hands. "Your wish, my love, is my command. By the way, I brought this for you." He pulls a very crumpled red rose from a pocket and holds it out to her.

She can't stay mad. She accepts the rose and a kiss on her hand. Then she plays at pulling him up to his feet.

Bryan tries yanking the skateboard from the trunk lid's grip. "Looks like my ramp's a goner. Maybe your board too. Sorry Pho."

"A goner, yo," Dutch says, "gone like all my money last night! Yo! Damn that Cripple Crip *Francis* for leadin' us all on, yo."

"Speaking of that," Carlos says, "I gotta say it. I'm sorry. I really messed up putting my friends through all that."

"We all got caught up in it a bit," Learoy says. "Plenty of blame to go round."

"Well all I know," Carlos goes on as they stroll to the G.R.A.S.S. entrance, "is that I'm the only Mexican handi-rapper living in a city that hates black handi-rappers. For once in my life I'm on the A list! I'm calling that record guy. He'll be dyin' to exploit my crippled ass now! My career is set!"

A lowered newspaper truck chugs by. Spray painted on the side is GHETTO PIMP'S HO-N-PAPER DELIVERY SERVICE. A copy of the *Valley City Gazette* sails out to flop at Carlos's front wheels. He looks down and groans.

Pho reads for him. "'Valley City Bans Handi-Rappers of ALL Ethnicities After Riot!!!' Wow. Three exclamation points. Must be serious."

"No! No! No!" Carlos rues. "That sucks!"

"Well," Janice says, "we did have us a time last night, eh what?"

"And we had limo rides!" Bryan smiles.

"And we put on a major concert!" Dutch as Moon says.

"And we got to start a riot!" Mad Girl laughs.

They all bust up. Carlos can't help but join in, just a little.

"Let's get breakfast," Carlos says. "I hear Ching's making French toast! We gotta get in there before it's gone."

Dutch looks at him. "Hey, player, so you learn anything from your play, yo?"

"One thing. I've got to get to my love before anyone else does." He spins to Learoy, his heart completely on his sleeve. "Learoy, last night, when time stopped and you told me you loved me, my heart stopped too. And my tongue. But now I can finally return the words: Learoy, I love you, and my world will only be right when we both surrender to each other in immortal tenderness."

Learoy reacts with hands on hips. "Fool! What you talkin' 'bout? Time stoppin'? Me talkin'? You dreamin' or somethin'?"

Carlos clarifies. "No, remember, at the concert, during the final number, and we had our...our moment together of blissful understanding---"

"All's I can say," Learoy whips him, "is you best oil up

your wheels, Toe Man, so you can roll your cripple butt down the sidewalk AWAY from my heart!"

Everybody laughs again. Carlos stares at her, but he doesn't get mad; he understands that time is on his side.

"Now c'mon," Learoy shouts, "I gotta get my French toast to go! I got a shop to open in five minutes."

They all head through the G.R.A.S.S. gates. Carlos reaches down and pulls the paper up onto his lap. Scanning it again, a smaller story title meets his eyes.

He reads out loud: "'Mysterious Miracle Boob Girl Enthralls Millions on TV!'" There's a screen shot of Learoy on stage with Francis stiffly walking toward her. Her breasts are barred out. "Hey," he shouts at their backs, but when no one turns he decides to keep it to himself for a more apropos moment. "Timing," he says to himself, "is everything."

He starts rolling through the gates, but something down the street halts him for a doubletake. It's a solemn processional heading up Truth Avenue. As they draw closer, Carlos sees what looks like hundreds of stoic men. A small number wear white robes and sag under the weight of bearing full sized crosses on their shoulders. Many more struggle along, hunched over crutches. There is also a contingent of wheelchairs, some mechanized and some not.

Oddly enough, a quite large percentage of the group appears to be non-disabled, middle-aged men carrying cameras and wearing long gray trench coats and hats with brims pulled low over dark sunglasses.

Carlos is hooked. He turns around in the entrance to watch the entourage cross over Pain Street. To his surprise they gather in front of him outside the G.R.A.S.S. gates.

A white robed, dark bearded man with a huge wooden cross over his shoulder addresses Carlos, "Scoos-a, please-a, scoos-a me. My English-a, she's-a not so good-a."

"What up?" Carlos asks.

Encouraged, the man smiles. "We're-a...all of us-a here-a...we're-a here-a to see the Curing Bosoms-a! Peace be unto you-a."

"What!?" Carlos trips hard.

"Yes," a one legged man on crutches repeats Cross Man to help, "the Curing Bosoms of Valley City! Don't you know of her?"

A sincere fellow in a wheelchair chimes in to help. "You know, the Magical Healing Breasts, as seen on TV. The ones that cured the crippled rap singer last night! You look like you could use her assistance yourself, young man."

A panting creeper in a trench coat lifts his camera, "Yeah, we wanna see that girl's boobies. We need to lay hands on them and be cured too!"

The Bad Luck Kid lifts his foot to shoo them away...then rethinks the possibilities. Sharp breath intake; posture steeled erect; Carlos lays his big toe along the side of his nose and ponders a moment. This could be really funny. It's decision time in 3, 2, 1, now.

"You know," he leans forward with a scheming grin, "she may be coming out here in just a little while..."

Chapter the List

TRUTH & PAIN starring the GANGSTERS & RETARDS in... The Mystique-cal Person-a of MC Cripple Crip

by DC Curtis and Bones Kendall

Truth & Pain, LLC is just the authors.
Fans directly support the writers.

(Long live Free/Libre Open Source Software!)

Cover art: Chris Boulter

ISBN: 978-0979893490

TRUTH & PAIN

starring the

GANGSTERS & RETARDS

in...

The Mystique-cal Person-a of MC Cripple Crip

by
DC Curtis & Bones Kendall

www.ingramcontent.com/pod-product-compliance
Lightning Source LLC
LaVergne TN
LVHW050626100826
845148LV00011B/1750

* 9 7 8 0 9 7 9 8 9 3 4 9 0 *